STANLEY PARK
Story

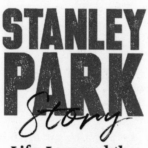

Life, Love and the Merseyside Derby

JEFF GOULDING

First published by Pitch Publishing, 2018

Pitch Publishing
A2 Yeoman Gate
Yeoman Way
Worthing
Sussex
BN13 3QZ
www.pitchpublishing.co.uk
info@pitchpublishing.co.uk

© 2018, Jeff Goulding

A CIP catalogue record is available for this book
from the British Library.

ISBN 978-1-78531-449-0

Typesetting and origination by Pitch Publishing
Printed and bound in India by Replika Press Pvt. Ltd.

Contents

For Angela, my wife, and the Blue in my life, who reminds me that though we follow two different clubs we are one family, sharing one love.

Acknowledgements

In creating this book, I am grateful to many people, whose collective experiences and viewpoints have added a depth and authenticity that I couldn't have achieved on my own. When I set out to write *Stanley Park Story*, I wanted to ensure that the voices of both sides of the Mersey divide were heard.

As a die-hard Liverpudlian, I couldn't have done that without the help and support of many Evertonians. I hope I have done them justice.

So, to Harry and John Colquhoun, Frank and Yvon Wardale, Kevin Dooley and Mick Myers, thank you for your stories and for systematically removing much of the Red-tinted bias from the book. Thanks also to Billy and Joe Goulding, Ian Golder, John Stulberg, Tony Lanigan and Keith Williams, for ensuring I didn't remove too much Red-tinted bias.

I have strived to bring to life long-forgotten details from some of the greatest games, capturing the drama on and off the field. I have drawn on many sources and would like to pay special tribute to several people and groups.

Amgrimur Baldursson and the teams at lfchistory.net, anfieldonline.com, evertonresults.com and toffeeweb.com have compiled amazingly comprehensive records for no other reason than their love of Liverpool and Everton. I salute you all.

I'd also like to acknowledge the support of some great football writers whose encouragement has been critical to my journey as an author. So, thank you to Matt Ladson, Max Munton, Dave Usher, Neil Poole and Steven Scragg. If you hadn't given me a vehicle for my writing and supported me, then I would never have had the confidence to write one book, let alone two.

Finally, I'd like to remember Steve Evans, one of my best friends and a great Liverpudlian. Steve, your legend lives on in these pages.

Foreword

In the spring of 1892, on the banks of the Mersey, a brand-new football club was born. Boardroom strife and a row about the rent had led to Everton Football Club fracturing in two. Out of the debris, Liverpool Football Club was formed and would take up residence on Anfield Road. Everton, Anfield's original occupants, moved out and set up camp at nearby Goodison Park. Only the 45 hectares of parkland, known as Stanley Park, separated these two fierce rivals.

The two protagonists driving the split were accountant George Mahon, the son of Irish immigrants, and John Houlding, a local brewer and politician. They would have had little idea that they were setting in motion a chain of events that would eventually see the football clubs of Liverpool become the most successful in England.

The two clubs have amassed 61 major honours in 126 years of football. No other city comes close. During that time huge social and political upheaval has taken place. The clubs have survived two world wars, economic turmoil and the city they represent has fought its own battles. Through all of that their great rivalry has endured.

Those who support Everton and Liverpool are a people whose DNA can be traced to all four corners of the globe. Liverpool is a truly international city. Its large Irish population brought with it sectarian divisions, but the city has put that aside. The great political struggles down the years have shaped Merseyside into a strongly working-class region, with a socialist outlook.

Merseyside has had its issues with race, but as a people, Scousers reject prejudice and have fought fascism at home and abroad. When the far-right English Defence League attempted a march in the city, they were forced to cower in a lost-luggage room before being driven out of town. Today the only fault lines on Merseyside are football ones.

Stanley Park Story is a collection of facts, personal stories, experiences and a whiff of poetic licence. It charts the recent history of this historic rivalry. It is not an autobiography. The characters and other elements of the story are fictionalised. Any resemblance to actual people, living or dead is entirely coincidental.

It is, though, a tale of one city, two families and three generations of Liverpudlians and Evertonians. We will view the whole story through their eyes.

We join the story in 1962, when Liverpool were promoted to the First Division, after an absence of eight years. The Blues had also spent some time in the second tier from 1951–54, which meant that Scousers had gone 11 years without a league derby. They have enjoyed at least two every year since. This is now the longest continuous football derby in English football.

As a people, Scousers tend to be anti-establishment and anti-cliché. So, in this story, there will be tales of conflict and solidarity but no talk of 'friendly derbies'. Our story is a complex one and the relationship between us waxes and wanes, just like the fortunes of our teams.

The antipathy felt by Blues towards their neighbours after English teams were banned from Europe, in the aftermath of the Heysel Stadium disaster, did not prevent them rallying in support of their Scouse brothers and sisters after the tragedy at Hillsborough, for example.

Like any sibling rivalry, this is a love–hate relationship. We can be brutally critical of each other, but let no outsider come between us. When we need to we can be united and strong in defence of the other, and in the next breath rejoice in our neighbour's misfortune. This is a unique rivalry.

We'll explore all of that, through the lives of Tommy Gardener, a Red, Jimmy Harrington, a Blue, and their families. Tommy will narrate a tale of romance, drama, tragedy and comedy. This is our *Stanley Park Story* of life, love and the Merseyside derby.

Enjoy.

Introduction

Jimmy Harrington was my best mate and my worst enemy. He was a Blue and I am Red. We came together in 1962, and, for a time, we were inseparable. We loved football and we saw it all. League titles, cup finals and European adventures all came our way. We witnessed glory most supporters never see, and we shared in all of it, as comrades.

Sadly, though, like all great friendships, ours was tested, and ultimately broken, for a time. That's part of the story too. It's also part of the history of our two teams. They, too, were once brothers in arms but they've become enemies on occasion. Yet when the chips are down, they find a way back, just like Jimmy and me.

I'm Tommy Gardener. I'm in my 70s now. I've lost Jimmy, but the memories of our friendship and the great games and moments we shared burn brightly in my mind's eye. I want to share all that history with you: the drama on and off the field. More than that, I want you to see the stuff that pictures, film and the record books will never show you.

Photographs and video are a poor substitute for stories, I always think. There's more wrapped up in a moment than mere pixels on a video clip or dots in an image. Film and photography don't capture the conversations, jokes, arguments and laughter.

Friendships that grew up around iconic moments and events, love affairs and break-ups, are the missing pieces of the great jigsaw that lies behind every memento. Every trip across the country to follow our heroes is filled with intrigue. The people who made them, though they may have long since passed on, are as real and complex as any character in a book or a movie.

It's just that sometimes we let them fade from history, and all we're left with is a series of tantalising images, statistics or ghosts on a screen. I can't let that happen to Jimmy and me, or to the great rivalry that is our Merseyside derby.

I have met some incredible people down the years. I have witnessed glory beyond comprehension and, through it all, I have laughed and I have cried. I have hated and I have loved. I've fought battles. I have won and I have lost.

To let all that slip into some dark void, lost forever and reduced to a collection of dusty photographs or grainy moving pictures, is unthinkable to me. So, as I near the end of my journey through life, I have resolved to give flight to my memories, to hand them on to others to enjoy and to pass along when their time comes.

Who knows how long they'll last, what future generations will hear them. That's the magic of storytelling.

There's comfort in thinking that something of us and our lives will always live here, in these words. Call it ego if you like – my wife does. I prefer to think of it as legacy.

I've lived with the idea of writing this book for a while. It became irresistible in the April of 2012 when Liverpool and Everton had both progressed to the semi-finals of the FA Cup and would meet each other at Wembley.

It sparked a flood of thoughts and recollections that I could no longer put off. The roof space of our house became my archive and I began organising the many photographs, match programmes and ticket stubs, each one a treasure trove of recollections and long-lost stories.

I was not alone in my quest. My grandson Robbie would often join me. I appreciated the company and explaining what each of them meant helped me organise my thoughts.

Robbie was eight, and full of questions. He would preface each one with the word 'granddad'. Though I love being his grandfather, it got to the point where I would twitch every time he said it.

Of course, like all kids his age, his curiosity and thirst for knowledge was insatiable, and, luckily for me, he loved hearing my stories about the old days. He was often fascinated by it all and I used his sense of wonder to gauge which tales I'd put into the book and which I would consign to oblivion.

Robbie's dad, my son Joe, was married to Jimmy's daughter, Eve. The little lad was the product of a Red and Blue union. At eight, he was leaning towards Liverpool, but never wanted to upset his mother. So, he'd cheer for Everton when his dad wasn't around. His parents were in on it and found it hilarious. The time to nail his flag to the mast would come, but there was no hurry.

He was round at our house one day; my wife Marie and I often look after him when his mum and dad are at work. He was helping me in the attic when he came across an heir loom that represented something of an origin story, of sorts. It was a photograph of his Granddad Jimmy and me. As I stared at the faded old image in his hand, the whole project came together in my head.

'Granddad, look at this!' Robbie shouted, his voice full of amusement and excitement.

The photo had been taken in a pub near Goodison Park, back in the 60s. I'm still not sure by whom, and I can't recall it being taken at all. We looked like kids, but we must have been in our early 20s. As I gazed at it, thoughts, recollections of sounds and long-lost conversations bombarded me.

'Do you recognise those two fellas, lad?' I asked. From the look in his eyes, I knew he did.

'It's you and "Granddad Two". You look weird,' he laughed.

Happily, I was merely Granddad and Jimmy had been designated as the number two grandfather. He wasn't exactly in love with the idea, but I loved to rub his nose in it.

'We were just a couple of daft kids back then, sunshine,' I told him.

Come to think of it we were probably already fathers ourselves when that photograph was taken. My son Joe and Jimmy's daughter Eve were both born in 1962.

I took the photo from Robbie's hand and stared at it. I must have lingered on it too long because the little one asked if I was alright, and I realised I had a tear in my eye.

'You're worried about him, aren't you Granddad?' he asked.

'Ah he'll be okay. The old sod will outlive all of us,' I said, trying to muster as much fake bluster as I could.

'Granddad!' Robbie's eyes told me I'd said a naughty word. Is 'sod' a bad word now, I thought. Apparently it was, in Robbie's eyes at least. So I apologised, and he laughed. It seemed I was forgiven. Then his face darkened again.

'Will Granddad Two be able to go to Wembley?' It was a question I couldn't answer, and wasn't ready to contemplate. The game was little over a week away.

A few months earlier, I'd have answered that only a death certificate could stop him. Jimmy had spoken constantly of both teams getting through the quarter-finals and meeting at Wembley. We'd all hoped it would be in the final, but we wouldn't turn our noses up at a semi-final. Of course, that's exactly what we got. Despite the fact we wouldn't be competing for the trophy, the idea of a trip to the capital rekindled memories of the 1980s.

But when I became aware of how ill he was, and after I saw him in the hospital, I began to feel that he faced an uphill struggle to make it out of there at all, never mind get to the game. He would prove me wrong in the end. He made it to Wembley alright, but it turned out to be the greatest battle of his life.

The Reds have enjoyed almost total domination in games played between the two sides at Wembley over the years. Everton can boast a draw in the 1984 League Cup Final, a tie they eventually lost in the replay at Maine Road in Manchester.

They had won the Charity Shield in 1985, beating Liverpool 1-0, but that was, well, the Charity Shield. Jimmy was desperate to see his team finally end what he perceived was a Wembley 'hoodoo'.

His cancer diagnosis rocked us all and the verdict that it was inoperable almost broke us completely.

So, I knew full well that the prognosis was grim but didn't feel like being realistic with my grandson. Instead, I chose to paint an impossibly optimistic picture. I was just kicking the can down the road, I suppose, but I wasn't ready for the conversation.

I've no idea if he believed me or not, but he dived back into the box and started rummaging through the photos again. I heaved a sigh of relief and looked back down at the picture in my fingers. My hand was trembling.

I thought it must have been taken in the September of 1962, before the league derby, the first one for more than a decade. It looked like we were in the Willowbank pub near Priory Road.

I remember that day so well. We were both deliriously happy to see our teams back in the First Division. Liverpool had just gained promotion that year and the prospect of many more big clashes lay ahead.

I'm going to tell you all about them. You'll meet some great characters and hear about some remarkable games, travelling from hope to despair and back again. It's an incredible story.

First, though, we need to go all the way back to a time before that old photo was taken, to the January of 1962. That's where our story really begins.

Chapter One

The Cressington Park Incident

I clearly remember meeting Jimmy Harrington. He saved my life that day, and probably my father's too. It was early 1962, January, and the winter frost was still heavy. The day began like any other, dragging tired bones and aching muscles into a freezing-cold coal yard, but it would end with this fella I'd never met before becoming the best mate I've ever had.

I worked on the coal with my dad, Billy. It was horrible work, but I had left school in 1955 without a qualification or a trade to my name. The old man was a driver for a firm called Martindale's, a coal merchant, and he'd always got on okay with his boss. That meant regular work for me.

The pay wasn't great, but, thankfully, I could earn a few bob more through a 'fiddle' we had going. The drivers and their lads would rely on this scheme to top up their pay, feed their kids and pay the rent.

You could never do anything more than get by on the wages we got paid back then. Clothes were handed down from oldest to youngest and often bore the scars of being repeatedly mended.

We relied on fiddles like this to make life worthwhile. In fact, our ability to cheat the system, almost any system, came in very handy as we looked to fund our love of football in the 60s and our trips across Europe throughout the 70s.

Every morning at 7.30 we'd turn up at the yard and start loading the wagon with bags of coal. They were bloody heavy. Kids today would pay good money for the sort of workout we got every day. But in the end, it was no good for my back.

The scam worked like this. We'd ensure that the wagon made it on to the scales carrying the correct load. Then, with the weights and measures fella happy, the truck would roll out of the gates and be on its way. Little would he know we'd be carrying dozens of empty sacks in the cab with us.

Once on the road and far enough from his watchful gaze, me and another lad would jump on the back and start 'cobbing' a little coal from each of the bags and filling up our empties, creating our own secret stash. We'd sell that on to trustworthy customers at a discount and pocket the proceeds for ourselves.

Yes, I know it was wrong, but we never ripped off the ordinary customers. We'd never shortchange our own, the people relying on the coal for their fires in the winter. These were people we knew could barely afford the stuff and we always made sure they got their order in full.

When it came to the rich snobs around Aigburth and Sefton Park, it was a different story, though. Often their coal cellars would be almost full when we arrived, but they'd keep ordering it anyway. 'More money than sense, that lot,' my dad would say.

On the day in question, I arrived at the yard with a terrible hangover. My dad always made sure I was on *his* wagon, an old Bedford. However, there'd usually be a different lad with us depending on who got picked for a day's work.

As I trudged into work, my only wish was that whoever joined us could keep his gob shut and put in a shift. I was in no mood to carry anyone that day. I had no idea that I was about to get way more than I'd bargained for.

I'd been to the match the night before. Liverpool had beaten Chelsea, at home, in the third round of the FA Cup. It had been a classic, at least as far as the press were concerned. For me and every other Red in the ground, it had been a nightmare.

It had started well enough. By half-time, thanks to St John, A'Court and Hunt, Liverpool were 4-1 up and looking worthy of their lead. The second half was a different story, though, and Liverpool went to pieces.

They conceded twice, and the last 15 minutes felt like an eternity in hell. The roar of relief at the end of the game had to be heard to be believed. The cup meant something back then, not like today.

For me, football is about winning. It's about days out in London, or on foreign shores bringing home the silver, and about Liverpool's streets being packed with people and colour, as a team bus laden with trophies winds its way through the throng.

Fourth place in the Premier League might make the club a bit richer, but I always say you can't parade a balance sheet around the streets in an open-top bus. Besides, it's not like supporters see any of the money.

Anyway, I was so happy we'd got through to the next round that at full time I ignored dire warnings from the wife and headed straight for the pub and an inevitable lock-in. It would amount to a declaration of war on the home front, but, as I downed the first pint, I reckoned on that being tomorrow's problem.

As I woke the next day, I quickly realised my monumental error. My head was pounding and my mouth felt as dry as Gandhi's flip-flop. I dragged myself into the bathroom and downed an Aspirin. Downstairs the wireless was blaring loudly in the kitchen. I swore Marie had turned it up on purpose, but in truth my head was so sensitive I could hear my hair growing.

Our Joe was in his high chair; he'd have been seven or eight months old then. Marie's shoulder was as cold as the frost outside. Still, she'd kindly burned me a couple of slices of toast for breakfast. I smeared some jam on them, slipped them into an empty bread bag and tucked them into my coat pocket, which was still slung across the table.

I grabbed it, leaned over and kissed my little lad on the head. I also tried valiantly to kiss the wife, but she just pulled away from me. Realising it was a hopeless cause, I accepted my place in the doghouse and made my way to the bus stop.

Work was tough, especially with a big head like I had. It was probably safer than home that day, though, or so I thought.

The bus ride from the bottom of the road to the yard was a nightmare. I don't smoke anymore, but back then a fag on the top deck was my way of waking up in the morning. Not this time, because as I sat there the motion of the bus and the regular potholes had my stomach in knots. My face was so green a stranger sitting next to me asked if I was ok.

Looking down at the ciggie in my hand, I realised I couldn't face it anymore. I dropped it to the floor and stubbed it out with my foot.

Behind me two lads were discussing the football from the night before. Reaching up, I pulled open the window, sucked in the icy fresh air, placed my aching head against the wet glass and listened.

'I'm telling you now, Shankly will never win the FA Cup, not as long as you've got a hole in your arse,' one, presumably a Blue, was saying to the other.

'Says you. What happened the last time we played your lot in the FA Cup? What was the score then? We're even better now, under Shankly.'

I smiled, despite my hangover, and my mind drifted back to that day seven years earlier, in 1955. Liverpool had been drawn against the Blues, at Goodison Park, in the fourth round of the cup. None of us were relishing the prospect, especially as we were labouring away in the Second Division and Everton were in the big league.

Our third-round tie against Lincoln City did nothing to help matters either. The first leg was a 1-1 draw and we struggled past them in a replay at Anfield.

Still, it was a derby, albeit a cup game, and I remember the sense of anticipation and excitement around the city. I'd left school and was already working on the coal. The stick dished out in the yard in the week running up to the match was fierce. Everton were supremely confident, and who could blame them.

For the Reds, these were the days of Don Welsh, a black and white film compared to the technicolour of Shankly's Liverpool. Shanks was like a movie star to me. When he said something would happen, I had complete faith that it would.

I've since learned that Welsh was every bit the visionary that Shanks was, but, somehow, he just didn't inspire me. Maybe it was my youthful ignorance.

While Welsh rarely got my pulse racing, he certainly had the lads up for that game in 1955. His Liverpool team would shock the Blues and the rest of football.

I remember desperately wanting a ticket, but I was working when they went on sale. So I persuaded my dad to drop me off at the stadium in work's time. He finished the round for me, with some other lad. When I got there, the queue was already halfway around the ground.

I hadn't long been with Marie but even then, she was great. I remember how she brought me a flask of tea to warm me up, and a sarnie to stave off the hunger, as I waited in line in the cold. She'd walked up and down that queue looking for me, too. I felt guilty about my late night, as I recalled that moment.

As I neared the front of the queue rumours began to circulate that they'd sold out. Panic and anger erupted among those in the queue. Thankfully the stories were unfounded, order was restored and I eventually left for home, clutching my ticket. Dad said I looked like I'd just won the pools.

When matchday finally arrived, Goodison was packed to the rafters. The official attendance was 72,000. No one inside the ground believed that for a minute. We could see people sitting on the church rooftop at the corner of the Gwladys Street Stand and there were a few on the roof of the stand itself.

Of course, there was no segregation then and there were as many Reds in the Gwladys Street Stand as there were Blues. I was one of them and the match turned out to be one of the greatest of my life. Goals from Liddell, A'Court and two from Johnny Evans stunned Goodison.

Everton huffed and puffed, but Liverpool were having none of it. There were scenes of delirium all around the old ground every time a ball hit the net, and even the Blues couldn't argue with the result. The talk in the papers was all about how the Christians had slain the lions, such was the shock nature of the result. It was great going into work on the Monday.

Behind me on the bus, the Blue was conceding a little ground to his mate. How could he do anything else?

'Alright, I'll give you that, but that game is ancient history now. It's so long ago Lord frigging Nelson was sailing his galleon down the Mersey at kick-off. Besides, what happened to you in the next round that year?'

It was a good question. Liverpool had crashed out in the fifth round, to Huddersfield Town at Anfield. The Red was on the back foot now and his Blue mate pressed home his advantage.

'You'd have been better letting a First Division side through that day. We'd have sorted Huddersfield out, no bother. You always want your best team representing the city in the cup.'

His mate laughed. 'We did alright last night, didn't we?' he said, referring to the victory over Chelsea.

'You were lucky, weren't you. You nearly threw it away.'

Nobody could argue with that, and thankfully I didn't have to listen to anyone trying to: it was my stop.

Despite my rough start to the day, I was somehow a little early. So I stood and shared a smoke with the lads who were queuing at the gate, hoping for a day's work. The headache was lifting, and my stomach had settled enough for me to consider having a go at the toast in my pocket.

Jimmy was among the crowd of lads hoping to catch the attention of my dad when he arrived. He approached me for a light of his smoke.

'You're Billy's lad, aren't you?' he asked, stamping his feet against the icy ground, attempting to keep his circulation going.

'Yeah, that's right. I'm Tommy. How do you know?' I asked.

'Oh, one of this lot mentioned it when we saw you walking up from the bus stop. Do you think you could put a word in like?'

'Why should I do it for you and not any of these lads?' I asked.

'Desperate for the cash, kid. The wife's expecting like.'

I looked him up and down trying to work out whether he was genuine or not. I decided he was probably telling the truth, but thought I'd string him along a bit longer.

'Red or Blue?' I asked.

'You what?' He looked stunned.

I could see a little panic in his eyes. He had no idea what my colours were. I could almost hear his brain working overtime, desperately trying to compute the correct answer. In the end I saw a now-familiar expression come over his face. It was the one that said, *Fuck it, I'm going to say it and I don't give a shit what you think*. It's a quality of Jimmy's I have always admired.

'Blue,' he said, adding, 'obviously'.

'Ooh, unlucky,' I said with a big smirk on my face.

'Ah eh! You're bleeding joking, aren't you?' He clearly did give a shit. I decided I liked him and burst out laughing.

'Don't worry. I'll not hold it against you. Let's see what my old fella says.'

Jimmy was a decent lad. He could graft, too, but he never shut up. Even when lifting heavy coal sacks on to the wagon, he wouldn't pause for breath. I would catch my dad smiling and knew he liked Jimmy, too.

All that remained was the small job of explaining the fiddle to him. I was sure he would be ok, but my dad was not so trusting. He was probably right to be cautious, to be fair.

He'd had his fingers burned in the past. One of the lads he'd given a day's work to a couple of years earlier turned out to be a nephew of Martindale himself, and he'd been sent in to spy on the lads and make sure there was nothing dodgy going on.

He told me that after he had explained to the kid the way things worked the kid had threatened to go straight to his uncle. It was a terrible mistake. The second his threat left his lips, he was dragged into the coal shed and threatened with all manner of menace by my dad and the other drivers.

They put the fear of God into him and the little snitch pissed his pants. He ran from the yard promising never to say a word to anyone. What followed was a nervy few days, but the little rat had been as good as his word.

The incident had left a lot of the drivers deeply suspicious of anyone they didn't know well. We had no reason to worry about Jimmy, though, and he was up for the scam. With a baby on the way, it had seemed like a bonus gift from the gods.

We finished loading and my dad drove the wagon on to the scales. Charlie, the weights and measures man, approached us. He did a circuit of the wagon, looking underneath and checking the wheel arch, before scribbling away on his clipboard.

He was a drab, miserable-looking fella, Charlie. His hair was plastered to his head with grease, and he wore the same black suit, white shirt and black tie every morning. The National Health Service glasses and the clipboard, permanently welded to his hand, completed the dreary ensemble.

Looking back, I feel a little sympathy for the fella: he always seemed miserable to me. My dad would be less charitable.

'Fucking divvy!' he muttered to himself as he watched Charlie go about his pitiful duties, before calling out of the window, 'Everything alright, Charl'?'

His voice, full of good cheer, belied his earlier contempt. He often wore two faces, my father. Sometimes he wore them in the middle of the same sentence.

Charlie said nothing. He never did. He just waved us on and we rode out of the gates and on to the main road, relieved to finally be on our way. We waited until we were a safe distance from the yard and Jimmy and I jumped out of the cab and climbed on to the bags on the flatbed, clutching armfuls of empty sacks.

We'd barely got ourselves into position, when my dad pulled out and started back down the road. He had seemed irritable that morning, more so than normal, and I had noticed a half-empty bottle of Milk of Magnesia on the dashboard. He hadn't mentioned feeling unwell and I just thought he'd been on the ale the night before, like me.

'Go easy!' I shouted, but he didn't seem to hear me, and just carried on at speed.

'Christ, what's the hurry?' said Jimmy.

'Got out the wrong side of the bed,' I said. 'Let's just start filling these.'

We'd normally tie ourselves to the side of the wagon. It could get bumpy and if you weren't careful you could easily get thrown off the back and into the road. For some reason I didn't bother that morning and it nearly cost me big.

We started skimming coal from the full sacks into our empty sacks. The wagon was bouncing along the road and a few times I had to hold on to Jimmy to stop myself falling off the side.

It was getting dangerous and when we stopped at the lights, I saw my chance to speak to the old man. So I made my way towards the cab. His window was wound down and the engine was idling. I knew he could hear me.

'What's the bleeding rush?' I shouted. He didn't answer, so I repeated it.

'Do you want to get the round finished or what?' he retorted, finally.

He could be a moody bugger my old fella. He'd seen a lot and dealt with more than his share of strife, so I always cut him some slack. We lost my mum when she had me, and he'd basically brought me up by himself. He would be the first to admit he got a lot of help from others, but it hadn't been easy for him. He was just 42 in 1962, but if you saw a picture of him, you'd swear he was a much older man. His tone said there would be no reasoning with him, so we just got on with filling the sacks as he hurtled down the road. The pair of us almost went over the side a few times.

As we neared Cressington Park, in the Aigburth area of the city, the landscape around us changed. The houses there were spectacular. There was none of the bomb damage and craters that were everyday companions where we lived.

This was where the posh people lived lifestyles we could only dream of. The entrance to the park was a tight angle and we'd normally slow down before attempting it, but there was no sign of the engine rolling back this time.

I looked at Jimmy. 'Is he going to drop his speed or what?' I asked. He just stared back at me. The panic in his eyes said it all.

Instead of slowing down, the old wagon seemed to speed up as it took the sharp turn and we lurched violently to our right, as my dad seemed to lose control altogether. I went flying in the air and landed hard on some sacks of coal. The loose rocks dug into my back and I wanted to scream out, but fearful of losing face in front of my new mate, I choked back the scream and got back to my feet.

The wagon still wasn't slowing, though, and we veered again, this time wildly to the left. Then there was an almighty crunch and a horrible scraping sound before I was thrown backwards again.

I'd have been over the side and probably dead or paralysed if Jimmy hadn't lunged at me. He grabbed the collar of my coat and yanked me back. We both landed on top of each other among the coal sacks.

The wagon had come to a stop, its engine spluttering, but somehow still going. I lay there for a second trying to catch my breath and half expecting to see my dad appear at the side, asking if we were okay. After a minute or so had passed and he still didn't appear, I got worried.

'Dad!' I shouted. There was no reply and a little bubble of panic popped in my stomach.

We both leapt to our feet, jumped down off the back and raced round to the cab. Dad was slumped there, his eyes closed and his mouth open. His face was grey. I couldn't tell if he was breathing or not.

'Shite! Go fetch help, now!' I shouted.

Jimmy stood there, like a rabbit frozen in the headlights. I screamed at him, shaking him at the same time.

'He's really sick, Jim! Run up to that house, tell them to call for help, they're bound to have a telephone. Go, now!'

This time it seemed to register and he scarpered off up the path.

My dad was in the hospital for two weeks after that. Thankfully we didn't lose him that day, though that was his first coronary. Jimmy had saved me from certain injury, maybe even worse. By running and getting help, he probably helped save my dad, too.

I was forever indebted to him. There was no big emotional stuff or anything like that. That's not the way we were. There were no hugs or tears. It was all sort of unspoken, really. He knew how grateful I was, and I knew he knew. Our journey had started.

Chapter Two

The Return of the Derby

By the autumn of 1962, Jimmy's life had changed for ever. His wife Elaine had given birth to Eve in the July and, just as it would be for the rest of his life, Eve's impact on him was profound. This is also how he saw the return of the derby, after such a long absence.

The new football season got underway in the August and a slew of sleepless nights did little to dampen the excitement he felt about what lay ahead. Liverpool had gained promotion from the Second Division, which offered the tantalising prospect of the first league match between Reds and Blues for 11 years.

As soon as the fixture list was printed, it was the first game everyone in the city looked for. Everton owed Liverpool big for their demolition of the Blues in the FA Cup seven years earlier. There'd been a succession of Floodlit Challenge Cups and of course the Liverpool Senior Cup had provided some relief, but the chance to have a go at the Reds in a proper league game was almost too good to be true.

Jimmy and Elaine lived with her father Robert in a council house in the Sparrow Hall area of Liverpool, not too far from Goodison Park. Elaine's mother had died a few years earlier and she and her dad had shared the house ever since.

The two men got on well, which wasn't quite a miracle but was no mean feat, given that the living arrangements weren't exactly spacious and coupled with the fact that Bob was a Red and a member of the Orange Lodge.

Jimmy had been brought up Roman Catholic, thanks to his mother, Sarah. For some families in Liverpool, such complex tribal allegiances could be difficult to navigate. However, Jimmy maintains that it was never that big a deal for them.

That's probably because, by the end of the 1960s, sectarianism in Liverpool was beginning to weaken. Both sides had fought side by side in the Second World War, and many returning soldiers had little time for such squabbles while there was a city to rebuild.

Liverpool, a major port, had been ravaged by the Blitz, but improvements in housing after the war had a positive impact. Overcrowding in areas like Scotland Road, which was predominantly Catholic, and Everton, inhabited mainly by Protestants, would become less of a problem, as families moved out to new residential areas in Kirkby and Speke, among others.

The power religion held over those communities would wane and mixed marriages were commonplace. That's not to say the tension disappeared altogether, though. There was still the occasional scuffle, particularly around marching season.

It was nothing compared to the old days, though; the older generation in the city had seen the worst of it.

Jimmy's nan, Catherine, would tell of how, when she had been a young girl barely ten years old, she had been caught up in a sectarian riot. One Sunday in the summer of 1909 she had joined a march from St Joseph's Church near Grosvenor Street.

The parade's path was blocked by lines of protestors from the Protestant community, who saw it as a provocation. According to her they were shouting obscenities and hurling objects. She would later acknowledge that the air had been thick with expletives, hurled from both sides of the divide.

The situation became desperate but the police, having granted permission for the march in the first place, were determined it would go ahead. They waded in to clear the obstruction, and the resultant battle led to heads being cracked like conkers.

'I'd never seen so much blood before that day,' she had said, recalling how men and women had fallen to the ground in the scuffles. If it had been intended to restore order, the police charge did the exact opposite. Catherine recalled how, to use her own words, 'the whole place went up in flames after that'.

Her stories of people fighting with swords and hundreds of arrests sounded far-fetched, but she spoke with a conviction that was hard to doubt. During a trip to the library, Jimmy discovered that she had been telling the truth.

The trouble was so severe that up to 30 schools had been closed and some homes were burned out. Both traditions suffered because of the trouble, which led to five days of rioting. It would lead to a de facto segregation of the two communities, and a government report would later label Liverpool the 'Belfast of England'.

The horrors of 1909 represented a peak in terms of the city's sectarian violence. By the time Jimmy met Elaine at an Orange Lodge dance in 1955, Liverpool was a very different place to the one his nan grew up in.

He'd walked in there with a mate he knew from work. Jimmy was a 'can lad' for a firm of painters and decorators, a job he described as being nothing more than a 'glorified skivvy'. The daily abuse dished out by the tradesmen made his life a living hell.

They never broke him, though. If anything, the experience toughened him up. If he could come through that school of hard knocks unscathed, there was little in the world that would faze him.

It probably explains why he thought nothing of walking into a lodge dance as a Catholic boy, and why he never batted an eyelid when asking his future wife for a dance.

If Jimmy feared anyone in those days, it was his mam. She was a woman with a fierce reputation and was known to be as handy with her fists as any streetwise kid who fancied himself as the cock of the neighbourhood. She often mixed corporal punishment with industrial language, before topping it off with the sign of the cross. Jimmy had learned to make himself scarce, whenever he heard her utter the phrase 'God forgive me', as it was usually a pretext to receiving the back of her hand.

Despite being a regular at mass, her denomination didn't prevent her from marrying a Protestant called George Harrington. George would later convert to Catholicism, not for Sarah but after suffering a mild stroke. While recovering in hospital, he claimed he had seen a vision of 'our lady' standing over his hospital bed and that it had changed him.

It probably had more to do with the bottles of ale smuggled in by his brothers, or was a product of his condition, rather than divine intervention, but it was powerful enough to propel him into church every Sunday for the rest of his life.

In his younger days, George's relationship with God and his earthly servants was less than congenial. Jimmy recalled the day when his dad had frogmarched a priest out of the house. The man had made the mistake of telling Jimmy that he'd go to hell if he didn't start turning up to mass. Truth was, that for Jimmy, God, the Devil and the afterlife just didn't matter that much. If anything, his upbringing had taught him that Catholic and Protestant were nothing more than labels and that they were never more powerful than mam or dad, or brother or sister.

So, when he saw his future wife across a crowded room, sipping orange cordial, and decked out in Protestant regalia, her religious upbringing would have been the last thing on his mind. He married Elaine in the spring of 1961 and the photographs still hanging on his living room wall prove that both sides of the family just got on with it.

In any case, as the 60s began to blossom, another old religion was starting to reassert itself in Liverpool: football. Anfield and Goodison, situated at either side of Stanley Park, resembled places of worship and had far healthier congregations than the cathedrals at either end of Hope Street.

When it came to the battle for footballing supremacy, Red and Blue were far more than just labels, of course. But no matter how cruel the tribal insults became, if you were an Evertonian, a Liverpudlian could just as easily have been your brother, father or neighbour.

So Liverpool in the 1960s was, as it had always been, a giant melting pot of different tribes and cultures. You could be a Catholic or a Protestant, a Blue or a Red, but that didn't necessarily stop you becoming family.

In 1961 just two things divided Anfield and Goodison. They were Stanley Park and the football league. Everton were in the First Division; Liverpool were fighting to get out of the Second. By the summer of 1962 only the park separated them, and it has been that way ever since.

Jimmy woke up on 22 September 1962 with a spring in his step. It was Saturday, which meant no work and a trip to Goodison for the game. But this was no ordinary football match: this was the derby, and the first one in more than 11 years.

His stomach was in knots and he felt like a kid on Christmas morning. The game had consumed him for weeks, but the last five days in work had been unbearable. The nervous anxiety had been overwhelming and he couldn't wait for the referee's whistle and the end of the phoney war.

He felt confident, but the Reds had been annoyingly mouthy in work. Like their manager, Shankly, they had ideas way above their station. Everton were flying in the league and trailed top spot by just two points, yet Harry Catterick had been reserved. He didn't go in for the sort of bravado in which his counterpart regularly indulged.

The Blues' boss knew the game inside out and prided himself on a scientific approach to football. He didn't go in for hyperbole and rhetoric, but Jimmy did. He'd told more than one Liverpudlian that week that they were going to get their arses kicked and he was secretly looking forward to Monday morning, when he was going to enjoy rubbing their noses in it.

Jimmy had arranged to meet me in the Willowbank before the game for a pint. My dad had been off work since his heart attack and as Jimmy had a licence to drive the wagon he was the obvious choice to take on the round. It meant regular work for him from that day on.

We made sure Dad still got a cut from the fiddle money. He was grateful for that and when he eventually got back behind the wheel, he made sure Jimmy was kept on.

Jimmy became quite close to our family, but he'd still enjoy making my life a misery after the game if Everton won. He'd only have me to torture this time, though, as my dad had gone back into hospital. We'd agreed to have one pint after the match and be at the hospital in time for visiting.

So, with confidence soaring, Jimmy went downstairs and sat himself down at the kitchen table. A note, next to the teapot which was still warm, said that Elaine had taken Eve to the shops. She'd see him after the game.

He poured himself a cuppa and sat back to read the *Echo* derby special, which sat neatly folded on the table. Beneath the headline, which screamed 'DERBY DAY IS HERE AGAIN', was a picture of the Everton team, resplendent in their blue kit. Above it, a cartoon Kopite, complete with rattle, danced with a Toffee Lady, her head furnished with a scarf and a dress billowing around her legs.

Looking at that team, Jimmy felt there was just no way they could lose. Liverpool had suffered more defeats than victories up to this point. He scanned the faces of Bingham, Vernon, Labone, Young and West. They looked tough and resolute.

'Who've they got?' he said out loud to the empty kitchen.

Jimmy was convinced that the Everton boss, Harry Catterick, had snatched Liverpool's only decent player. Everton had signed Johnny Morrisey from under Shankly's nose. The rest of them were no match for the Blues, he thought.

Morrisey had been at Liverpool since 1957, but he had only made 17 starts in five years because of the form of Alan A'Court. Everton seized their opportunity in 1962 and signed the player just weeks before the derby. Shanks had no idea. The board had done the deal without telling him.

Jimmy finished his tea and decided to throw a couple of rounds of bread under the grill, before turning on the wireless. The sun was out and it looked a great day for a game of football.

The radio crackled into life, halfway through a great song, Elvis's 'She's Not You'. Jimmy cursed his luck at missing the start of the song. Music, of course, was the other big thing in the city back then. The Beatles hadn't conquered the world yet, but they'd release a record soon and were already dominating the local music scene.

As the song faded out it gave way to the news. Not surprisingly, the impending battle at Goodison Park featured heavily. The headline was that Ian St John wouldn't be playing and would be replaced by Kevin Lewis.

Jimmy beamed. He couldn't stand the Scottish forward. Liverpool had paid £37,500 for him and they'd been robbed as far as he was concerned.

Kopites loved him, though, and after he'd scored a hat-trick in the Liverpool Senior Cup Final against Everton, he'd seared his name into derby folklore. The Blues had edged the tie 4-3, but we had found a new hero.

Jimmy polished off his toast and left the house a half hour later. His mood was soaring, and, as he marched down the road, a song bounced around inside his head. 'We hate Shankly and we hate St John, but most of all we hate Big Ron, and we'll hang the Kopites one by one, on the banks of the Royal Blue Mersey.'

By midday the Willowbank was already full, and the air was thick with ciggie smoke and the smell of beer. A crowd of kids were sat on the pavement outside the door, waiting for their dads who were inside. These were the days when Scousers went to the game in suits, even ties. The old guard wore flat caps, but the heads of the younger generation were adorned with no more than Brylcreem.

You could tell Reds and Blues apart if they were wearing a stripy scarf; otherwise it was impossible, until the banter started. Jimmy spotted me fighting my way through a crowd in front of the bar, clutching two pints and trying desperately not to spill them. I had a rolled-up cigarette perched on my lower lip and was concentrating deeply as I dodged elbows and wayward cigarettes.

Jimmy eyed me struggling and made a beeline for me, rescuing one of the pints from my grasp.

'Alright, la',' he said.

I took a drag on my ciggie and blew smoke at the ceiling, before answering.

'Yeah, you?' I said.

'I'll be even better at full time,' he replied.

It had started already, and I felt a rush of excitement.

'I see you're as cocky as your captain today.' I was smirking when I said it.

'What do you mean?' He had no idea what I was on about.

Jimmy had missed Roy Vernon's column in the *Liverpool Echo* in which he had boasted about how Liverpool's attacking line would 'perish' in the face of the Everton defence. To be fair, both teams had been at it, and Ron Yeats, our towering centre-half had been crowing about how there was nothing Everton striker Alex Young could do to surprise him.

'You lot have got a nerve talking about being cocky, haven't yer? The way Shankly goes on, you'd think your lot had already won the bleeding lot.'

It was true. Bill Shankly had set about tackling Liverpool's inferiority complex, by telling anyone who'd listen how great his players were. It had worked on some, but not on Evertonians, who'd been dining on First Division football since 1954. They'd also won the coveted FA Cup twice, something Liverpool had failed to do, despite a few attempts.

'I haven't heard him making any brave predictions this week, have you?' I said.

Shankly had realised that the team he had led to promotion were underachieving. He probably hoped they'd choose the derby as the game in which they would finally ignite their season.

'Not surprised, are you?' said Jimmy. 'He's probably shitting hisself.'

I laughed and asked if he was coming with me to see me dad after the game.

'Yeah. I'll see you back in here, we'll have a quick one and jump the bus into town. That okay?' he replied.

I said it was and we continued the football-related back and forth until it was time to wander up Priory Road to the ground. The air was filled with the excited chatter and laughter of Reds and Blues, walking side by side into battle.

We got to the turnstiles by half past one. The crowd was huge and was already snaking its way around the stadium. We were both in the Gwladys Street end. Segregation was unthinkable and completely unnecessary back then.

As we reached the front of the line, a fella in front of Jimmy was handing the steward on the turnstile a coin. He pocketed it, before allowing the bloke to lift his kid over. That sort of stuff was going on at every game and reported attendances were always taken with a pinch of salt.

Inside the ground, conditions could be uncomfortable even during a run-of-the-mill league fixture. In the derby, there was barely a hair's breadth between us.

As kick-off approached, supporters were beginning to sway from side to side. In the days of standing on the terraces, the crowd would take on a life of its own. It would resemble a flock of birds, swooping and soaring in formation, their movements in perfect synchrony.

Songs would start in the same way. A small group would get one going and then everyone would join in. They'd be pitch-perfect and never miss a beat. Anfield and Goodison were like the world's greatest orchestras, with never a need for a conductor.

You'd never end the game in the same place as you started it, having been buffeted and shoved around, like flotsam on a great sea of people. The packed conditions would breed camaraderie and great humour. The atmosphere generated in those days was incredible.

Behind us a group of Blues began singing 'We Shall Not Be Moved'. They sang it in tune, not like today. It was a song, after all, not a chant. In response and immediately to Jimmy's right, a group of Liverpool fans chanted 'Liverpool, Liverpool!' Then came an inaudible shout followed by laughter.

'What did he say?' I asked.

Jimmy was killing himself laughing at this point. 'This fella just shouted, "Some bastard has pissed in me pocket!" Then he goes, "My butties were in there."'

I laughed too, before quickly checking my own pockets. Luckily, they were dry, for now.

That may sound barbaric to the modern football supporter. It was. However, once you were in the middle of the crowd, there was no way you were seeing a toilet until you got back to the pub. Supporters would while away the hours before games drinking pints of beer, before queuing in the street outside the ground for up to an hour or more. It was therefore easy to understand how they'd end up relieving themselves where they stood.

Kick-off was minutes away and the tension was palpable. The sound of drums and flutes rang out, as both teams spilled from the tunnel to the sound of 'Johnny Todd'.

'Fucking *Z Cars*?' I shouted.

Everton had started running out to that tune at Goodison Park during the 1962/63 season. Jimmy had no idea why they had chosen that one as their anthem. It had been the theme to the TV show *Z Cars*, a hard-hitting crime drama, filmed in Kirkby, Liverpool. He loved it nonetheless and would say how it made the hairs on the back of his neck stand on end.

All four sides of the ground roared and the noise was ear-splitting. God knows what the players and match officials made of it. Surely they wouldn't have been able to hear themselves think, let alone the sound of each other's voices.

Nobody in the terraces heard the referee's whistle, but the game was underway and a sudden surge from behind launched us forward towards the goal. Jimmy ended up behind the net. I was several rows back. We had been separated. That would be it for the rest of the match, and we wouldn't see each other until we met in the pub afterwards.

Everton raced at the Liverpool defence and the Reds seemed to wilt. Suddenly Jimmy Furnell, the Liverpool goalie, fumbled the ball and Roy Vernon immediately pounced on it and slotted it home. Pandemonium erupted all around me.

There was barely a minute on the clock and Everton were in front. The whole stand seemed to shake as the Blues celebrated. None of us were aware that the referee had blown his whistle for a foul on Furnell. Joy turned to fury and some fella shouted angrily, 'Nothing fucking wrong with that, ref! Nothing at all.'

Behind him a Red shouted, 'It was a foul; keeper had the ball.'

'Bloody fix, more like it.' Came the reply.

Then Everton had another goal, prodded home by Dennis Stevens this time, chalked off for offside. Evertonians were fuming. Liverpool were rocking, and I feared the worst. A Blue standing in front of me turned and said,

'These have got no chance, lad. Not a cat's chance in hell.'

'We'll bloody murder them,' said another.

I wasn't wearing any colours. They had no idea I was a Red. 'We'll see lads,' I said. They smirked and looked away, as they realised I was a Liverpudlian.

Just six minutes later, their words were starting to sound prophetic. It had been a breathless opening, a real spectacle. Liverpool's defence were all over the place and a breakthrough seemed inevitable. Then it came. Gerry Byrne handled the ball in the penalty area and a huge roar went up.

A crowd of players surrounded the referee and it seemed to take an age for him to signal a penalty. In truth he'd pointed straight to the spot, but I didn't see it.

Scenes of delirium greeted the decision. I was disconsolate. This could be embarrassing. Jimmy told me later that he thought some of the Liverpool supporters near him looked like they would lynch Byrne, if they could have got their hands on him.

'Who's taking it?' shouted someone to my left. 'Vernon of course,' came the reply.

Vernon was a goal machine for Everton. Tottenham's Jimmy Greaves would be the First Division's top marksman that season, but Roy Vernon's goals would play a big part in bringing the title to

Goodison in May. I had no doubt he'd score. As the Reds lined up on the edge of the 18-yard box, the Everton skipper calmly charged towards the ball and smashed it to Furnell's left. The keeper made a half-hearted attempt to paw at it, but it was hit with such power he had no chance.

It was 1-0 and one-way traffic so far. I had gone quiet, along with many Reds, who were nervously chewing their nails.

'This is what it's like playing a real First Division side!' the fella in front of me taunted, his voice filled with mischief.

'Game's not over yet is it?' I said.

'Might as well be,' he retorted, and laughter filled the air.

I would have my revenge, though. Just over five minutes later the game was level again and it had been the man standing in for Ian St John who bagged the equaliser.

A'Court had made a blistering run down the left-wing and careered towards the Blues' defence before swinging in a looping cross. George Thomson should have dealt with it easily. Instead, Callaghan nipped in and stole the ball from him before delivering a chip from the byline to the waiting Lewis, who knocked it in gleefully.

I screamed at the top of my voice. Others swung their scarves in the air. Our first goal in a league derby for more than a decade, and it tasted sweet.

A Blue shouted, 'Hello, they've woke up have they? It's the first real chance they've had.'

'Yeah, and we scored it,' I replied. I was in my element.

Jimmy maintained he was never worried and with the half-time whistle signalling a temporary respite in the battle, the only thing exercising his mind was how he was going to relieve his bladder. The place was so packed, the chances of making the toilet were non-existent.

He could see that the bloke in front of him had a newspaper under his arm. He tapped him on the shoulder and nodded at the paper.

'You finished with that, la?' he asked.

Seeing the look of desperation in Jimmy's eyes, the guy nodded and handed the paper to him. Jimmy shouted a warning to those around him, and a circle formed as he relieved himself through the rolled-up copy of the *Daily Mirror*.

In 1962, there was no nipping down to the concourse for a pie and a pint or checking your phone for the latest scores. The facilities were antiquated and basic. Nobody questioned it. We didn't know any different.

As the game resumed, there was no sign the atmosphere would burn itself out. In games like that, you'd start to tire after a while. The constant toing and froing took its toll and with all the shouting, your throat would be raw by full time, and your mouth parched.

Somehow, the Blues' supporters would overcome their fatigue and laryngitis in the 62nd minute. The ball was looping around in Liverpool's penalty area and a series of tackles and lunges went in to try and clear it, most notably from our keeper, Jimmy Furnell.

He missed the ball and the player completely, and none other than Johnny Morrissey latched on to the chance and struck the ball home. The Blues were back in front.

A roar, so loud it would have rattled the windows of the terraced houses around the ground, split my ears. Our lads looked dejected. Of all the players to grab the second, it had to be Morrissey, a former Liverpool player stolen from under Shankly's nose.

To Jimmy it was nothing short of poetic and he screamed his lungs out. He knew he'd pay for it later, but he couldn't care less. He was no doubt thinking of me, and the stick he was going to give me.

Everton tried to put the game to bed but somehow failed to make their dominance pay. As the game approached its conclusion, the gung-ho atmosphere was replaced with a sense of nervous tension. Blues were biting their lips apprehensively as the clock ticked down.

They were seconds from victory. Then, for them, disaster struck.

Again, Alan A'Court picked up the ball in the Everton half, on Liverpool's left flank. He had acres of space in front of him and the Blues seemed to be dropping off him. He launched another looping cross into the box which was headed down by Kevin Lewis. Then, through a scramble of legs, Roger Hunt poked the ball into the net.

The Reds were beside themselves with joy. We danced and punched the air. All we'd achieved was a draw, but you'd have thought we'd won the FA Cup.

For Jimmy, it was bitterly disappointing. Everton were going for the title and this was a point dropped. He cursed his team's luck as the referee sounded the final whistle.

The gates opened and the crowd spilled out into the night. The fresh air was a welcome relief from the stuffy, crammed conditions inside, but the sense of despair wouldn't leave Jimmy as he strode down the road towards the pub.

He must have expected me to be in celebratory mood and seemed genuinely surprised to find me as disappointed as he was. He asked if I was kidding, but I wasn't.

'Fancied us to win that,' I was saying as I stood at the bar holding a crisp pound note in the air, hoping to attract the barmaid's attention.

'You're kidding, aren't you? We absolutely battered you,' Jimmy said, incredulous.

'Well I wouldn't say that. If it wasn't for the referee, Hunt's goal would have won the game for us,' I argued. I wasn't winding him up, either. I meant it.

'How many of those have you had?' said Jimmy, nodding towards my pint glass. 'We should have been 3-0 up before you got your first goal. The referee saved your lot from an absolute hiding.'

I laughed. 'Neither of them was a goal for me. The first was an obvious foul and the second a mile offside. As for your penalty, there's no way Byrne meant to handle that ball; definitely accidental.'

'You lot have been in the Second Division so long you've forgotten the rules of the game,' he said. I can still remember the look on his face, and it still makes me laugh to this day.

'Maybe,' I countered, with a twinkle in my eye, 'but you still haven't beaten us in the league for over ten years.'

I felt like the cat who'd got the cream and it clearly infuriated him, probably because I was right. Everton had not held bragging rights in the league since 1951.

That game had been a cracker, too. It had been a 2-0 win for the Blues at Anfield, with Jimmy McLaughlin McIntosh getting both goals. He was a big, strong and pacey Scottish striker who spent three years with Everton, scoring 19 times in 58 appearances.

Neither side had been anything to write home about back then. Both were scrapping it out in mid-table. Liverpool had won the Goodison derby 3-1, so the victory across the park had been so sweet for the Blues.

Jimmy hadn't been at that game but he remembered the stories about how 'Mac' had stunned a home crowd of almost 50,000 with two goals. Both were stunning headers within two minutes of each other.

Everton had been all over Liverpool, and their defence had completely nullified the likes of Liddell. It was their attack that did all the damage, though. The local press described Everton's strikers as 'fast and devastating'.

In the second half, Liverpool had been attacking the Kop and Jimmy's school-mates had told him the noise had been terrific. Nevertheless, Liverpool got no joy from the Blues' back line.

Later in the game, McIntosh had been knocked out, after crashing into a stone wall behind the goal at the Anfield Road end. He would enter derby-day folklore by jumping up and immediately carrying on with the match. These days, he'd have been in the hospital before the final whistle.

'Is that all you've got? You were totally outclassed today. Ok you got your point, well done, but that's all you'll get this year.'

He was right, but more about that later.

Deciding I was too tired to argue, I finished my pint and suggested we jump on the next bus to see my dad. Jimmy agreed and drained the last dregs from his glass.

'We'll finish this later,' he warned.

I laughed. 'I'm looking forward to it,' I said with a wink.

It was dark outside and the post-game crowds had already died down. They'd been replaced by gangs of teenagers, all 'dolled up' and ready for a night in the clubs on Mathew Street. A group of them were stood chatting eagerly and laughing at the bus stop as we approached.

Jimmy grinned as he watched their faces, animated in conversation and full of excitement. They were puffing on their cigarettes, pretending to look like movie stars. Their features lit up as they giggled at jokes he couldn't make out, and their eyes sparkled as they were caught in the lights from the passing traffic.

He reflected on how this was a different world to the one he had been born into. It was like the snows of a seemingly never-ending winter had finally thawed and the first flowers of spring were in bloom.

It was the 60s and the post-war austerity his parents had endured was fading fast. He realised he was still a young man and, as far as he was concerned, he was living in the centre of the entire universe. It felt good to be alive in a city that would soon live in the consciousness of every teenager on the planet. Then he thought of Eve and the life she would go on to live, and he smiled to himself – she was going to have a fucking ball, he thought.

Chapter Three

A Last Look at the Old World

My dad was sat up in bed and holding court with the other men in the ward when we arrived. He looked like he was enjoying himself, and there was no sign of the illness that had dogged his life since January. He noticed us marching up the ward towards his bed and his face lit up.

'Here's my lad, Tommy, and his mate,' he declared proudly. 'They've been to the match.'

'What was the score lads?' shouted another patient.

'Come on fellas! Don't you know?' I said.

'Sister wouldn't let us have the radio on,' said Billy; then in hushed tones, 'Right battle-axe I can tell you.' Casual misogyny was the order of the day back then and the rest of the patients laughed.

'Two each,' Jimmy said. 'We were robbed.'

'Fair result, lad?' said my dad, ignoring Jimmy and looking directly at me. He was smirking, and it really wound Jimmy up.

'Jimmy doesn't think so.' I answered sarcastically.

'Really? I'm shocked!' he winked and beckoned for us both to come closer.

'Come and sit down, lads. Tell me all about it.' Billy cleared some papers off a chair next to the bed and instructed Jimmy to get another one from an empty bed across the way.

We each began recounting details of the game. I can still see his face now, watching us, smiling, as we argued over every moment. He was enjoying himself. In truth, so were we.

'Sounds like some game, lads. I'm sorry now I couldn't go. It's great to have the derby back isn't it, eh?' he said, when we had finally run out of steam.

That was at least something we could all agree on.

'No game like it, if you ask me,' he went on. 'Maybe a cup final, but even then, if you lose to another team you can take it, eventually. Losing to this lot, though ...' he gestured to Jimmy, 'You've got to live with them, work with them. You know what I mean.'

'It's the same for us you know Bill,' Jimmy laughed.

'No, you're right. That's what I'm saying,' he winked.

'So, Dad, have they said anything about when you're getting out yet? I was trying to change the subject.

'Shouldn't be long now, lad. I feel fine. I could have played today, if they'd let me out.'

We laughed, more out of politeness than anything else.

'Have you told your mate about you being born on derby day?' he said, neatly switching the conversation away from his current circumstances.

Jimmy looked surprised. 'You've never mentioned that. Besides, weren't you born on Christmas Day?' he said.

'He was, and they played a derby on Christmas Day in 1940. I was there,' my dad answered.

'Get away!' He pronounced it 'Gerraway!'

My face must have darkened, because Jimmy suddenly looked like he regretted taking the bait.

'Never felt like talking about it, Dad. You know, because of me mam and that,' I mumbled.

We'd lost Mum shortly after I was born. I never knew her. All I had to go on were old pictures, coupled with the stories people told me. I'd created a pretty decent image of her in my mind, but it was undoubtedly idealised.

'Can't believe they played games during the war at all to be honest with you,' said Jimmy. He was hooked and despite my obvious discomfort, he couldn't help himself.

It was true. Football had carried on, after a fashion, throughout the war years. It hadn't been easy, with many players drafted and the Blitz. The official football league was suspended, so games weren't recorded. What players there were, were organised into local divisions. Liverpool and Everton played each other many times, but the most remarkable encounter came on Christmas Day 1940. That was the day I was born.

That year had been one of the darkest of the war, as Hitler and the Luftwaffe launched their Blitzkrieg on English towns and cities. Liverpool, being a hugely significant port, suffered the heaviest bombardment of any English city outside London.

The city centre, Bootle and Wallasey sustained catastrophic damage and 4,000 people lost their lives between August 1940 and May 1941. Dad told Jimmy how a bomb had hit an air raid shelter in Durning Road, killing 166 people. Churchill would later describe it as the single worst incident of the war.

The Germans kept up the bombardment right up to 22 December. My dad remembered how Mum, Edith, had come home on the 21st, from a cleaning job she had on Upper Parliament St. She had been utterly terrified, telling him how she'd heard the sirens and had gone to the front door of the house she was in to watch for the planes.

It sounds a ridiculous thing to do now, and he had also thought so back then. He had shouted at her for being so foolish, but she had told him a strange curiosity had come over her and she was transfixed by the sight of tracer bullets making their way to their targets in the sky. The gentleman who owned the house had pulled her back inside, and into the air raid shelter with his family. If he hadn't she'd have probably remained there, rooted to the spot, a helpless witness to catastrophe.

Only after she had emerged from underground and saw the smoke and flames on the distant horizon did she realise how perilous her situation was. She was heavily pregnant and Dad could have lost both her and the baby in the raids, a fact he was quick to remind her of.

It seems incredible to think that anyone would think of organising a football match against the backdrop of such carnage. Yet that's exactly what had happened.

The Reds and Blues had been part of the North Regional League and faced each other six times in the 1940/41 season. Liverpool had been beaten four times and another of the games was a draw. In total the Blues put 15 goals past Liverpool that season, with the Reds recording nine. The fixture that took place on Christmas Day would prove to be their only win. It was a remarkable game, given the context. However, it held huge significance for Dad, and the rest of the family, too.

Mum still had a few weeks to go before her due date, but Dad had been insistent he wouldn't go to the game, just in case. Going to a match on 25 December wasn't unusual back then and the tradition continued long after the war, with the last Christmas Day programme taking place in 1959.

Mum would hear none of it. Something that was pretty typical of her by all accounts. She had wanted him out of the house, so she could prepare a meal for them, she said. In truth she probably wanted to have a little time to herself.

In the end he had reluctantly agreed to go and headed off to Anfield on his own. It was a decision he would carry with him to his grave.

Despite the constant fear of being bombed, amazingly, about 5,000 people huddled together inside Anfield. Dad was in among them, freezing on a half-empty Kop. He would watch his side run out 3-1 winners. Given Everton's dominance, it must have felt like a Christmas miracle.

I could see Jimmy was watching Dad intently, as he recounted the story. My father had the expression of a man lost in another time, another world. He was directing his words at us, but his eyes, perhaps his mind, were elsewhere.

'We never did well against Everton back then. I suppose George Kay, Liverpool's manager, found it hard to put a decent team together. Mind you, he did manage to unearth two future stars, Billy Liddell and Bob Paisley.'

I was looking down at my feet. I'd heard the story many times, and I knew how it was going to end. I wanted to be anywhere else but there at that moment. Still, I knew Dad needed to get it off his chest again.

He'd go back to those days, in his head, many times, as he worked through the grief and the guilt. I'd come to realise that this was a good thing. After all, burying it would surely be far worse. My job, no matter how uncomfortable it got, was to sit quietly and listen.

'It wasn't a great game to be honest,' he went on. 'Not much happened until the last 20 minutes. The players just seemed to be going through the motions. Then Len Carney blasted a shot into the back of the net. He hit it so hard, the keeper had no chance whatsoever.

'That warmed us up a little and then almost straight from the kick-off Nivvy raced on to an Eddie Spicer cross and hit the second.'

'Nivvy?' said Jimmy.

'He was a great player, lad,' said Dad. 'He was a South African. His proper name was Berry Nieuwenhuys.' Dad stumbled as he struggled with the pronunciation.

'As you can probably tell, nobody could say his name properly, so we all just called him 'Nivvy', like,' he laughed, remembering.

'Anyway, at this point I couldn't believe the scoreline. It looked like we were going to win one for a change. Then your lot grabbed one back and were all a bit pig-sick.' He gestured to Jimmy and smirked.

'We needn't have been too bothered, though, because Carney put the game beyond doubt with about five minutes to go.'

'I know that name,' said Jimmy. 'My dad's mentioned him, I'm sure. Wasn't he in your title-winning side after the war. Was it 1947?'

'That's right, lad.'

Jimmy was enthralled, despite this being a tale of Red conquest. Dad continued.

'He was getting on by then, though, Jim. Must have been in his early thirties in '47. Clever fella, too. Used to be a schoolteacher. A headmaster I think they said. He also saw active service in the war and won medals for bravery. A really good sort, you know. Anyway, you can imagine I was in a great mood when the game ended, and I made my way home.'

My dad's good mood would be short-lived. His whole world was about to change forever.

There was so much grief in the years between 1939 and 1945. No family escaped the grim shadow of loss. Dad was always quick to acknowledge that we were just one of the countless families who suffered. Still, that would not have helped him deal with what he found on his return from the game.

He had raced from the ground, eager to get home early and spend as much time with Edith as he could. This would be their last Christmas alone, before the baby came. Of course, that would make all those to follow even more special and exciting, but he knew their relationship would change forever as a result.

As he turned into the street where they lived he was met by a crowd of neighbours who were milling around on his front doorstep. He would later recall a sense of foreboding, even then.

It may have been a joyous sign, neighbours gathering to greet a new birth. But he knew. Maybe he had registered the troubled looks on their faces; maybe it was a sixth sense. Whatever it was, he raced to the front door and barged past the crowd assembled there.

There were attempts to restrain him, but he was too strong and suddenly found himself in the living room. In front of him was Betty Lambert from down the street. He'll remember her face forever. It was tear-stained, a harbinger of the misery to come.

'Oh, Billy, I'm so sorry,' she cried.

'Where is she? Where's Edith?' he had shouted.

Behind her was a curtain that separated the living room, where they did everything, including prepare meals, from the sleeping area.

Betty was holding a little bundle of rags and her face was etched with pity. Billy saw a tiny hand poking out from the top of the blanket, but his mind was racing, and he didn't comprehend that he was staring at his son's fingers, reaching out and exploring the air outside his cocoon.

'She's lying down, resting, Bill. It wasn't an easy labour and she lost a lot of blood.' She noticed his face turn even paler, adding, 'Oh don't worry. We've cleaned her up all nice like. You can go in.'

Mum had realised she'd gone into early labour and managed to stagger to Betty's house a few doors down to summon help.

Betty Lambert was the local midwife. She never had any qualifications, but it was like that back then. Most streets had a midwife, and sometimes someone who would help 'lay out' the dead. Betty would later tell me that she'd realised all was not right the minute she set eyes on Mum.

Apparently, my dad was as white as a sheet, and he just walked past Betty as if she wasn't there, muttering, 'I need to see her.'

Mum was drowsy, and Dad remembered that she looked terribly pale. Her lips were dry and cracked and he helped her to a sip of water from a cup on the bedside table.

'Is he alright, Bill?' she asked, her voice no more than a whisper.

Dad's thoughts were bouncing around in his head and he struggled to get hold of them and force them into some form of coherent order.

'What? Who?' he stammered.

Somehow his wife managed a smile, and he would tell me that in that moment her whole face lit up the room.

'Our son, of course,' she said, before closing her eyes. Her brow creased and her mouth contorted as she dealt with a spasm of pain.

Then Dad realised what she meant, his mind suddenly connecting with the memory of that bundle of cloth Mrs Lambert had been holding. Then in his mind, he was screaming, *He! A son. I've got a son!*

'He's perfect, of course. Just like his mum.' His voice was soothing, and he stroked her forehead.

Edith smiled again. 'Flatterer.' Again, she whispered the word and he almost didn't catch it. Then she closed her eyes and drifted off into a sleep from which she would never wake.

They would get her to the infirmary, eventually. However, there was nothing the doctors could do. He was sure they had done what they could, but she was just too weak. She eventually succumbed to an infection and died a week later.

The whole episode almost broke Dad, emotionally and financially. These were the days before the National Health Service, and, if it hadn't been for a collection by neighbours and the help of the church, he may have gone under.

He didn't, of course, and Dad managed to give me a decent life. It had been a struggle, but he wasn't alone. It was a collective effort, and everyone just rallied around – friends, neighbours and family. It was like that in those days.

The story was finished. Jimmy's mouth was agape, and Dad had paused, his eyes glistening with the threat of tears. Then he seemed to awaken from his recollections and refocus, before sighing and managing a faint smile.

'So,' he said, 'that's how this one came into the world. On derby day in the middle of the bloody Blitz. Hard to believe, looking at him now, that he was once just a tiny scrap of a lad in a bundle of rags, curled up in my arms.' He winked at the two of us and laughed, noticing how much I was cringing with embarrassment.

Jimmy's face had drained of colour and he swallowed hard before saying, 'Bill, I erm, I had no idea. I'm so sorry like.'

'Ah that was all a long time ago now, son. In any case, I'm sure his mum will be smiling down on us from heaven. Especially when she sees what a good job I've done knocking this fella into shape, eh?'

Jimmy laughed.

'You two don't know you're born. It's a different world now and there's so many opportunities for you and your children.'

We both nodded. There was no denying it, and I couldn't imagine going back to those days, when so many struggled day by day for mere survival. Then Dad said this:

'Me, well I don't know how long I've got before I meet up with Edith like, but let's hope I see the Reds win the cup at least once before I go, eh?'

'Fucking hell, Bill! I doubt even our Eve will get to see that,' said Jimmy, and with that the tension was gone.

We all laughed. I gave Jimmy a playful punch on the arm, more out of gratitude for easing the heavy cloud that had descended on the conversation than anything else. Dad pretended to swat him with his newspaper.

Fortunately, the old fella would get his wish and would die a happy man, in 1966, after seeing Shankly's boys lift the cup for the first time a year earlier. I'll always be glad he got that far.

Chapter Four

1963: The Beatles, the Atom Bomb and Goodison is Invincible

In 1963, a new world was dawning. The year may have started with a long, dark winter, but for Jimmy, it would end with the glorious sunshine of Everton's league title win. This was a year of momentous events, with the assassination of American President John F. Kennedy taking place later that November. As far as Jimmy was concerned, though, you could call time on 1963 on 11 May; nothing that came after would matter.

His pride surged as he watched his heroes being crowned champions of England after going an entire season without losing at home. If he'd had a cigar, he'd have happily lit it up. One supporter had taken one to the game and he handed it to Everton hero Tony Kay at full time. Photographs would later show him puffing away on the touchline.

It was well deserved, too. This was undeniably the greatest Blues team since the days of Dixie Dean, and they had just secured their first league title since the war. Jimmy would crow that, with their six championships and two FA cups, Everton were the pride of Merseyside, no matter how much Shankly huffed and puffed.

The Reds finished eighth. All we had to crow about was the fact that we'd avoided defeat in both derbies. That would cut little ice in the playgrounds and workplaces throughout the city, and Evertonians could look forward to a whole summer of lauding it over us Kopites.

Jimmy Greaves's 37 goals had powered Spurs to second spot and had helped them win the UEFA Cup Winners' Cup. However, Everton's consistency at home plus Roy Vernon's 24-goal haul kept the Blues in front.

The noise inside the ground had been so loud that the *Echo* suggested it would 'disturb the pigeons at the Pier Head'. Evertonians across the city found themselves wrapped in the simple and joyful escapism of football, shielded from the uncertainties of an increasingly volatile world.

Beyond the confines of Goodison Park and away from the banks of the Mersey, trouble was brewing in Vietnam, and the Cuban missile crisis had reminded everyone that war and destruction were never far away.

The so-called 'Polaris Sales Agreement', which placed US nuclear missiles on British soil, placed a giant bullseye on the Faslane Naval Base. This all meant that the population went to bed each night not knowing what the world would look like when they woke up.

The Beatles had reached number one in the albums chart and were about to conquer the world. Their invasion of America wasn't far away and they would carry Liverpool on to the world stage with them. The city's nightlife was the envy of the country and Jimmy felt right in the middle of it all. So, as he watched the victory parade, his heart soared. Was there a better place to be on planet Earth? He doubted it.

The Blues finished six points clear at the top of the table. If it hadn't been for a ferocious winter, which meant that no football would be played at Goodison between December 1962 and February 1963, Jimmy was convinced the Blues would be even further in front.

The eventual thaw had allowed a few away games in the FA Cup to go ahead in January, but the first league encounter to come after the snows had receded was a 3-1 reverse away to Leicester City, followed by a dull goalless draw to Wolves on 23 February. They would soon find their groove, though, and after an exit from the cup, at the hands of West Ham, their march to the title was unstoppable.

It was all looking so positive for the Blues, on and off the pitch. The following year, in the April of 1964, they would announce in a match programme that they were investing around £110,000 on improving their training ground at Bellfield in the West Derby area of the city. More followed in the years ahead, and Catterick would return silverware to the trophy room throughout the decade. Everton would become known as the 'School of Science'; its pupils studied their routines daily at Bellfield.

If he could, Jimmy would have gladly gone back in time, grabbed the younger, cockier version of himself by the collar, and lectured him on the need to drink it all in and savour every drop. Success in football is never a given, nor is it permanent.

For me, things felt very different. There was no despondency, just a sense that the Reds were in the middle of some sort of genesis. I'd have never admitted it, but Everton were a much better side than us at that point. Sure, Shankly's men could match Catterick's in a one-off match, but we had a slight inferiority complex.

Liverpool were holding their own after promotion from the Second Division and an eighth-place finish felt about right. Hope of glory was kept alive by a great run in the cup.

We had beaten Wrexham, Burnley and Arsenal on the road to the sixth round and our reward was a home tie against Ron Greenwood's West Ham. The semi-final felt so close we could almost taste it.

Anfield was boiling by kick-off. The Kop swayed as supporters strained for a view of the action. They chanted rhythmically, 'Liverpool, Liverpool', as their red heroes fought tirelessly to break down a Hammers' rearguard, martialled by Bobby Moore.

I was in the middle of it all that day. I remember clearly, as Roger Hunt latched on to a Jimmy Melia ball, the crowd surged forward and I found myself pinned against a bar. I kept my head up, though, and saw him slot the ball past the on-rushing West Ham keeper. The place exploded and somehow I managed to wriggle free from the barrier.

All around me there was scenes of utter chaos. I almost had the shirt ripped from my back at one point. Supporters stumbling and falling in celebration would reach for anything as they steadied themselves. Then, as the pandemonium subsided, the singing would start. Supporting the Reds from this unbelievable vantage point was relentless and exhausting. I loved it.

My wristwatch told me there were just eight minutes left. In my mind I can still see St John clinging to the netting, as West Ham's defence lay collapsed in the 18-yard box. He had chased the ball into the net. But he needn't have bothered; it had made it there under its own steam.

We'd done it again. For the sixth time in our history, we'd made it to the semi-finals of the cup. If the season was going to end in glory, we would need to navigate our way past Leicester City in Sheffield. After that, anything was possible.

I made the trip to Hillsborough to see the game. The cup run had given everyone connected with the club real optimism. I remember heading off to the game in a mate's car. It was an old banger, but it got us there alright. The image of a folded-up *Liverpool Echo* on the dashboard sticks in my head. Its front page declared, 'On, On to Wembley'. Sadly, though, it wasn't to be.

This would be a game that would rankle with us all summer. Shanks would describe it as a 'travesty of a result'. Ian St John would refuse to give Leicester any credit after the game, and newspaper reports put the Reds' possession at 98 per cent.

At full time I was furious. I couldn't believe we hadn't won it. I'd have been disappointed with a draw, but to lose was unbelievable. My anger was with the referee, the football gods, anyone but Shankly and his men.

We knew Shankly was building a team and there was an incredible affinity and affection for the man. He spoke the language of the people, and when he said Liverpool would be successful Reds' supporters believed him. So, we were patient.

Football was a very different beast back then. I often think he'd have been under pressure in today's game. What a loss to the Reds and football if we'd have moved him on too early in those formative seasons. Maybe there's a lesson there for today's supporter.

So, when the final whistle sounded and the hopes and dreams of another season were laid to rest, instead of booing, my mate Albert and I ran around to the players' entrance to wave off the team.

It had seemed the most natural thing in the world to do. I would later tell my son, Joe, how we had wanted to show how we appreciated the lads' efforts. We would take any defeat, as long as the team gave their all. You always got that with Shankly's Reds.

Ian St John may have been spitting fury and venom at his opponents after the final whistle, but it didn't stop him recognising the tremendous support the team had received on their way home. He would tell the newspapers,

'I wonder if any other team would have had a send-off such as that at such a stage of the cup competition; I doubt it very much.

'Not only that, but at almost every stage of the journey cars laden with supporters passed us with horns blaring, colours flying and thumbs from all the occupants.'

I had been a passenger in one of those cars, trundling along the motorway in hot pursuit of my heroes and shaking a defiant fist at them every chance I got. Alongside me, and driving, was Albert. I'd met him at work and would forge a great friendship with him in the coming years.

I'd left Martindale's at the back end of 1962 and got a job on the production lines at Ford's in Halewood. Dad hadn't been happy, but the pay was better and the work easier. As well as meeting my new friend, I was also introduced to trade unionism and politics. In 1963 that became the other great passion in my life.

In truth I had already started to have questions about how power was exercised over people like me and my family. Don't misunderstand me, I had no doubt that things were getting better. My dad had lectured me often enough about conditions pre-war, and life without the welfare state and the National Health Service.

Prime Minister Harold Macmillan had told everyone that they'd 'never had it so good'. Maybe, but as far as I could see, there were still too many people who were doing far better than those who did most of the work.

For me, such questions were thrown into stark relief near the end of my time on the coal. I'd turned up to work one morning, my back aching after a tough week of lifting, and immediately got into a row with that officious bureaucrat, Charlie.

All I wanted to do was get out on the road and make my rounds. The way I saw it, the quicker I got started, the sooner I'd be home. But this fella was taking his time inspecting the wagon, making sure the boss wasn't being ripped off.

'Anyone would think he was saving his own money,' Jimmy had muttered. 'He's just a working man like you and me. A few bob more and he turns into fucking Hitler.'

I laughed, but there was a truth in that. Martindale wouldn't have even known this fella's name, and yet here was this clipboard-warrior keeping the lads in line for him.

Life was improving for people like me, but as far as I was concerned so it bloody should. I didn't see why I should feel grateful. To me, what I had was no more than I earned through solid graft. In truth I wasn't being paid enough for my labours.

The Charlies of this world were there to make sure people like me never got ideas above our station. They were doing the bosses' work for them, I thought. I was angry back then. I still am.

When I met Albert Jones, it was like I had found a long-lost mate. We connected straight away. He would later go on to be an organiser of a group called Big Flame. They were active in both the Liverpool and Dagenham plants in the early 1970s.

Conveniently for me, though, his football was also Red. In addition, he owned a battered old car, which would drive us to many a game throughout the 60s. Those away days became an unrivalled political education.

It meant that Jimmy and I were now on separate paths, though, and that created a problem of its own. That's when the drift began to set in.

Chapter Five

Lies, Handbags and Purple Hearts

It was tough being an Evertonian in the autumn of 1964, and as Jimmy stood on the Kop ahead of the Merseyside derby he was wishing he could be anywhere else in the world. The Reds were reigning champions and we weren't about to let anyone forget it.

I had been completely unprepared for the 1964 title win. We had complete faith in Shankly of course. He'd delivered promotion from the Second Division and we all loved him. None of us expected us to win the First Division just two years later, though.

It was like a fairy tale. For the first time since 1947, Liverpool were a force again.

In typical style, Shanks promised even more glory the following season. Talk of conquering Europe made it into a *Liverpool Echo* 'Championship Special', and we lapped it all up. Of course, the great man also had his eyes firmly set on the FA Cup, which the club had never won.

Our arrogance and cockiness were already getting on Jimmy's nerves, before the derby kicked off on 19 September 1964. However, it was the treatment Kopites dished out to the young girl dressed as 'Mother Noblett,' a symbol of Everton Football Club, that really got under his skin.

Just as it is today, it was a tradition before Everton's games for the Toffee Lady to walk around the ground throwing sweets into the crowd. Back then it used to happen at Anfield, too, before the derby. I'm not sure if this was the last time it happened, but it probably was.

As the crowd were going through their usual pre-match warm-up routine, which back then meant reprising songs from the 'hit parade', 'Mother Noblett' wandered in front of the Kop, dispensing Everton Mints. The reception she received was, to say the least, uncharitable.

Mother Noblett was a real character who owned a sweet shop near Goodison in the late 19th century. She found herself in competition with 'Old Ma Bushell' who sold Everton Toffees from a place called The Toffee House.

After the boardroom split that led to the creation of Everton and the move from Anfield to Goodison Park, she came up with an idea that would cement her as the one and only Toffee Lady. She created black and white-striped sweets called Everton Mints. They became an instant hit and were gobbled up by Evertonians, who subsequently became known as the Toffees.

However, her young namesake wasn't doing so well at Anfield in 1965. As torrents of abuse, orange peel and rolled-up wads of paper rained down on her, Jimmy was fuming. 'Gobshites!' He shouted. 'She's only a kid, you fucking divvies!'

An older Red stood next to him agreed. 'It's not on. They wouldn't have it if it was their daughter, would they?'

'Should be ashamed of themselves,' said Jimmy. The disgust in his voice was palpable and it was too much for a younger Kopite, stood a few rows back.

'Fuck off! It's only a bit of fun like. She's not hurt is she,' he shouted, to loud approval from those around him. Jimmy thought twice about arguing. What was the point. Then someone shouted something that made his blood boil.

'She's probably handing out the purple hearts.' There was roars of laughter all around him and Jimmy felt like punching someone.

The shout was a reference to a supposed expose in the *Sunday People* that alleged that the Everton championship team of 1963 had been on drugs. The so-called journalist in question was Michael Gibbert, the same fella who had cost Tony Kay his career. Gibbert exposed the fact Kay had bet against his own team, Sheffield Wednesday, in 1962.

He had placed a bet of £50 that his team would lose at odds of 2/1. Despite that, he had been named man of the match during the game. The idea that he had been half-hearted, or worse still, thrown the game, seemed ridiculous. Nevertheless, the punishment was severe. Kay saw jail time and a lifetime global ban.

As with accusations of drug taking in the Everton squad, the stories had seen former team-mates receiving pots of money in return for their revelations. The headlines about purple hearts had originated from former Blues' goalkeeper Albert Dunlop who, it was said, was paid handsomely for his 'insights'.

I later came to understand that Dunlop was a sad figure. A Scouser who had represented his club but who had struggled with alcohol issues throughout his life. He was said to be unpopular with team-mates, and there was certainly no love lost between him and Tony Kay in the years that followed.

Jimmy thought the stories were rubbish. They were great ammunition for Kopites, who were revelling in their new-found status as the 'pride of Merseyside'. Visits to Anfield, and, to be fair, other away grounds, would see Everton greeted with purple, heart-shaped balloons. It went on for a while, before people got bored with it and moved on to something else.

The ground was packed out, as you'd expect for the derby, with over 52,000 crammed into Anfield. As Reds, we were in confident mood. With hindsight, we probably should have seen what was coming.

Our start to the season had been lacklustre, having lost four, drawn two and won only two matches from our opening eight league games. We had absolutely battered some team from Finland in the European Cup, but that had surprised nobody.

It had been our first ever game in the competition. They were called Knattspyrnufélag Reykjavíkur, and the first leg away from home had ended 5-0 to Liverpool. We'd go on to win the tie 11-1 on aggregate, but it was no mask for our inconsistent league form.

As kick-off approached the atmosphere was building and the volume of noise inside the stadium reached crescendo. It was getting stuffy in the middle of the Kop and Jimmy loosened the collar on his shirt and was regretting wearing his jacket to the match.

From the tiny tunnel at the front of the Main Stand, a ball was launched on to the pitch, signalling the arrival of the two teams. A huge roar went up. Then as the teams entered the field of play, marching side by side on to the turf, a deafening din of 'Everton, Everton' met by 'Liverpool, Liverpool' filled the skies around the ground.

Everton won the toss and bravely decided to turn Liverpool around, forcing them to defend the Anfield Road end in the first half. Andy Rankin, the Blues' keeper, was afforded generous applause as he ran from the halfway line towards the massive seething and swaying throng. However, when he failed to recognise the gesture by clapping back, he was roundly booed.

The atmosphere bubbled, just as it always did on these occasions. Little did we realise it was about to ascend to new heights. It took just 60 seconds for Everton to silence the Liverpool faithful and send their own dedicated followers into raptures.

The Reds had launched an early attack, straight from the kick-off, but the Blues' defence intercepted it quickly. The resultant clearance found Johnny Morrissey on the left. He lobbed it into the middle, and 'Big Ron' Yeats made a complete mess of his attempted clearance. All he succeeded in doing was prodding the ball to Derek Temple, who smashed it past Tommy Lawrence into the top left-hand corner of the net.

Pockets of celebration broke out all around the ground, and Jimmy noticed a few Blues around him celebrating, while Kopites cursed and fumed. The champions were rocking and there was still 89 minutes to play.

The pace of the game was frenetic. Jimmy found himself moving from ecstasy to sheer panic in a matter of seconds, as a Roger Hunt header crashed off the bar. It was a breathless start and the players couldn't possibly keep it up.

Thankfully, from the point of view of Jimmy's heart, injuries to Gordon Wallace for Liverpool and Jimmy Gabriel for Everton led to a temporary cessation of hostilities. Gabriel looked to be knocked out, as the Everton trainer could be seen administering smelling salts, assisted by Reds' physio, Bob Paisley.

He immediately came around and got to his feet. There was no stretcher, no visit to hospital for an X-ray. Just a whiff of some potion in a bottle and off he went. The Blue half roared their approval.

Chances galore followed, for both sides, but Everton's defence was rock solid. Slowly confidence was growing among the Evertonians in the crowd. For their part, the Reds seemed increasingly frustrated with their own players.

They almost launched a full-scale revolt when, on 35 minutes, an error by Willie Stevenson let Freddie Pickering in on goal. Ron Yeats seemed to be back-pedalling, and Pickering took his shot. Jimmy thought it was going wide, and, by the looks of it, so did Tommy Lawrence. He let it roll tamely past him into the net.

Cue more scenes of crazy jubilation, matched only by the furious cursing from the Red half. However, it was nothing compared to what happened when Colin Harvey bagged Everton's third goal, with half-time only minutes away. Jimmy's head felt like it was going to explode, and he couldn't wait to shove the earlier words of every gloating Liverpool supporter right back down their throats.

To him, this felt like just desserts for their poor sportsmanship before the game. It probably was, in fairness. The abuse that poor girl had suffered didn't sit right with me either. I don't think there was any real harm intended, but still, she was just a kid.

On the pitch, Everton had caught Liverpool cold. We had struggled all season to recapture the form that propelled us to the title in May. Our strikers were firing blanks and we were clearly missing Alf Arrowsmith. Everton looked hungrier and quicker to every ball.

It was a fact that wasn't lost on Jimmy, and it would make Morrissey's fourth in the 64th minute almost poetic as far as he was concerned. As we know, Morrissey was taken from Liverpool without Shankly's approval. Pinched from under his nose. That fourth goal must have had the Scot fuming with rage.

Anfield on a warm autumn Saturday may not have been his usual idea of heaven on earth, but as far as Jimmy and every Blue inside the ground that day was concerned, it might as well have been. Liverpool had been routed, and Everton's football was sumptuous.

If the Reds' players hadn't quite lost their heads, then their supporters had. With about 20 minutes to go, Peter Thompson and Dennis Stevens got themselves into a bit of a scrap. As the referee stopped play, some lad in the Kemlyn Road Stand ran on to the pitch and aimed a punch at Stevens.

Jimmy thought it was hilarious and even Kopites joined in the laughter, as the fool was unceremoniously bundled off the pitch and out of the ground. Shankly's Reds had lost the game and some in the stands had lost their dignity.

In the end, full time came as a blessed relief. Jimmy was upset that Everton hadn't made it five, but he was happy to 'settle' for the four. As far as I was concerned, it was going to be a terrible few months, until the next derby. Little did I know I wouldn't find much joy in that game, either.

Liverpool may have been champions, but it took us a while to get over that defeat on our own turf. Work on Monday morning was horrific. It was going to be that way until Liverpool got a chance to redeem themselves. They would, of course, but not against Everton. Instead, redemption would come at Wembley, in May 1965.

I'd been at Anfield with my new mate, Albert. We'd also been in the Kop, but near the back of the old stand. We'd agreed to meet Jimmy in the Flat Iron pub at full time. I didn't fancy it for obvious reasons, but I'd never hear the end of it if didn't take my medicine.

Besides, I'd have to take it sooner or later, so best to get it out of the way as soon as possible.

In truth I wasn't too bothered about anything Jimmy could dish out, football-wise. Of much greater concern to me was how him and Albert would get on. They'd met each other before, and there was obvious needle between them.

Albert was the quiet, serious type; a thinker. Whereas Jimmy's only real interest was having a laugh and football. He epitomised the carefree, almost arrogant Scouser of the 1960s, in love with life, football and music.

I'd caught him rolling his eyes and muttering under his breath a few times, when Albert and I had started discussing anything other than the game. I hadn't quite realised how much we were irritating him, though.

Jimmy was already at the bar, when we arrived, grinning like the cat who got the cream and dutifully getting the ale in. He said nothing at first. He just smiled as he handed us our pints. I knew what he was doing. He was prolonging the agony.

'Go 'ed,' I said. 'Get it over with.' Despite the fact I felt pig-sick, I was smiling. We'd been here before and we would be here again. It would hurt for a while, but I could take it.

'What?' he replied, feigning innocence.

I laughed. There was a natural order to these things, and sometimes the best thing was to just let it play out. I'd do the same to him if the shoe was on the other foot.

Albert just supped his beer quietly, refusing to join in. He didn't do banter or jokes, preferring to discuss tactics and team selection. Despite that, he was a good mate and we had grown close, mainly out of a mutual interest in politics. We were also working together at Ford's back then. Despite my misgivings, I decided to take the bait that Jimmy was dangling. 'You know what I mean. You're just dragging it out. Come on, give us your best,' I said, steeling myself for the inevitable onslaught.

'No, mate. It's not in my nature, as you know, to take the piss,' said Jimmy, keeping up the pretence.

'Fuck off!' I laughed, almost choking on my beer.

'No need for that language, Thomas,' he replied. 'I just expected a little more fight from the champions. That's all I'm going to say. Obviously last season was just a flash in the pan.' He took a swig of his beer, smirking.

What he wanted was an argument, to see he'd wound me up. I wasn't going to give him the pleasure, at least not now. So, I just laughed. Out the corner of my eye, I caught Albert rolling his eyes and tutting, though.

Jimmy clearly spotted it too and looked annoyed. He'd have taken that from me, I think. But he didn't know Albert that well, and vice versa to be fair, and the dismissive gesture clearly got under his skin.

Albert, who hadn't realised he'd been caught, handed me his pint and left for the toilet.

'What the fuck's the matter with Khrushchev there? Can't he take a joke like?' Jimmy's irritation was obvious, and the reference to the former Soviet leader was a dig at Albert's political allegiances.

'Ah, take no notice of him,' I said. 'He's a serious fella that's all. He doesn't mean any harm.'

'He's a Commie, isn't he?'

I laughed. 'What's a Commie, Jim?' I didn't think he'd know and I was right.

'You know, a Russian like.' He was looking annoyed and a little bit flustered now. To my delight, he'd allowed me to move the conversation away from football.

'He's from Speke, Jim. Not Moscow,' I said, before emptying my glass. 'Same again?'

'Yes. Bitter please. Look, a man's politics are his own as far as I am concerned. If you want to go goose-stepping up to Anfield every other Saturday with Chairman Mao over there, that's your business, but can he at least crack a fucking smile occasionally?'

'Chairman Mao is Chinese, Jim. Besides there's nothing wrong with standing up for workers and wanting a bit of equality, is there?'

I waved my money at the barmaid and ordered another round.

'Well I can understand you moaning about inequality, Tommy lad, seeing as how you've just had your arses kicked by your betters today.'

I tried to look like I wasn't bothered, but I had forgotten to tell my face. Jimmy saw my agony and smirked.

He was right about us receiving an arse-kicking, at least in terms of the scoreline. Having said that, I couldn't help thinking the result flattered Everton a little.

Liverpool, I thought, had created enough chances to at least grab a draw but our strikers were so wasteful. Whereas almost everything Everton touched turned to goals.

I guess that's what Ronnie Moran meant, when at full time he had barked at a reporter, '4-0! That was the easiest derby I've ever played in.' He was stretching credibility with that one to be honest, and I suppose he was just hurting like the rest of us. It was far from easy, but a more clinical Liverpool might have made the scoreline a little more respectable.

I thought about bringing that up, but realised I'd be leaving myself wide open to abuse and decided against it. Instead, I just shrugged.

Then a group of Blues in the corner of the bar started singing a song aimed at Ian St John. It had been a staple ever since The Saint grabbed a hat-trick in the Liverpool Senior Cup Final, just after the Reds had signed him. The Blues still won the game, but they'd ear-marked St John for special treatment from that point on. It went to the tune of 'John Brown's Body', and it went like this:

'St John's body lies a-mouldering in the grave,
St John's body lies a-mouldering in the grave,
St John's body lies a-mouldering in the grave,
and Alex Young goes marching on.'

All the Reds in the bar started shouting and hurling good-natured insults. It was loud and raucous, but there was no hint of aggression, or threat of violence.

Albert was making his way back from the toilets, just as all the fun was kicking off. He looked over at the Evertonians enjoying themselves and the look on his face suggested he'd just spotted a dog turd on his shoe. That was enough for Jimmy and he lunged at him.

Even considering his annoyance with Albert's earlier behaviour, it was an overreaction. I guessed this had been coming for a while. Fortunately, I managed to get in between them, before any real damage was done.

Then the landlord appeared at the bar, next to us. 'Problem, fellas?' he said.

'He's the one with the fucking problem,' screamed Jimmy, pointing at Albert. The pub fell silent and a few of the lads who had been singing stood up, sensing a fight was on the cards.

'Calm yourselves down, or you'll have to find somewhere else to drink. Do you hear me?' said the landlord.

'Just a misunderstanding,' I replied.

'No need for that,' said Albert, who was clearly rattled. He looked flustered, and a little embarrassed. He wasn't a fighter, clearly. He couldn't wait to get away.

'Tom, I'll see you on Monday.' He walked out, pushing past Jimmy as he went. As soon as he'd gone, so too had the tension.

We both reached for our pints on the bar and looked sheepishly at the landlord. 'Sorry, boss,' we said, in unison.

'It's alright now,' I said, hoping that would be enough to avoid being barred. 'Sorry for the bother like. Can I get you a drink?' Even if he'd asked for a short, it would have been a small price to pay to avoid being tossed out on our arses.

This fella looked capable too. He was built like a brick shithouse, as we used to say back then.

Instead, he just shook his head. 'Just behave yourselves,' he said. With that he disappeared into the back room again.

'What's the matter with you?' I scolded Jimmy. I couldn't see why he had reacted the way he did. 'You won 4-0. You should be happy. Why are you looking for a fight?'

Jimmy's jaw dropped. He was clearly furious with me. 'Might have known you'd take his side,' he said.

'Come on, Jim. It's not school, lad. There's no sides. You just took off for no reason.'

'Is that right?' he said. 'Well maybe I've had enough of people like him looking down their noses at people like me.'

He took a swig of his beer and slammed it on the bar. It was still half full. 'And I've had enough of that too. I'm going home.'

'Jim, come on, don't be like that,' I pleaded.

It was no use, and with that he left me standing there with two and a half pints to drink in a room full of delirious Blues. Lovely.

So, as I watched him walk out the door, my jaw agape, all I could do was finish off our beers and brood on what was a terrible day. The endless serenade from the Toffees in the corner didn't help either:

'We are the Scousers
The cock of the north
We all hate United
And City of course
We only drink whiskey
And bottles of Brown
The Everton Boys are in town.'

I didn't see Jimmy again until the spring of 1965. Just in time for us to lose another derby.

Chapter Six

The Blues at the Double and the Reds Run to Wembley

The year 1965 was a momentous one in English history. In many ways it marked the end of one epoch and the start of another. The crusty and prudish old world was being swept away and a more liberal and futuristic world was being ushered in. The death of Churchill and the election of Harold Wilson's Labour seemed to symbolise all of that.

In music the Beatles ruled, but the Stones would emerge in 1965, too. While Mick Jagger couldn't get any 'satisfaction', Mary Whitehouse was striking a blow for the Stone Age and waging a war against the sexual revolution on our TV screens. Not that most of us could afford a television.

In the world of football, the chastening defeat at Goodison had helped to convince me that we wouldn't be retaining our title. I could handle that to be honest. After all, Liverpool hadn't done that since the early 1920s. Teams very rarely won back-to-back titles in them days.

My dream was to win the 'Holy Grail', the FA Cup. The fact we had never won that competition was like a running sore for Liverpool supporters. Everton had of course won it twice, and just as we would have done, they lauded it over us at every opportunity.

Even winning the title wouldn't be enough to stop them. 'Come back when you've won the cup,' they would say, dismissing our achievements with a single killer phrase. We had no answer. The FA Cup was the pinnacle.

Every kid dreamed of playing at Wembley and winning the FA Cup. Every player's biggest wish would be to score the winning goal in a cup final. It was almost bigger than winning the title, and certainly more coveted than the European Cup.

During the 1964/65 season, Liverpool made a heroic run to the semi-final of Europe's premier competition. After a spine-tingling night at Anfield, when the mighty Red Army had ordered the Milanese, in song, to 'Go back to Italy', Liverpool would be denied a place in the final after some dubious refereeing decisions in Milan.

Tommy Smith was feeling murderous and Shanks was fuming, but my eyes were on the greatest prize of all, the FA Cup. It's completely changed now of course and all Reds now place 'Old Big Ears' – the European Cup – at the top of their must-have list. Not then. That competition was only ten years old and the FA Cup was written into English football's DNA.

The defeat at Goodison in September had ended a remarkable sequence of five games without defeat for Liverpool on Everton soil. The game at Anfield was a chance to put that right and end months of torment at work at the hands of the Blues.

I'd avoided Jimmy's merciless barbs, as we weren't speaking. Sadly, for me, though, there was never any shortage of people ready to remind me of the defeat.

I went into the game at Anfield, in the April of 1965, on something of a high. The FA Cup Final was just over two weeks away and of course we had an epic semi-final in the European Cup to look forward to as well.

Our domestic cup run had been fantastic. There were so many great stories along the way. I'll never forget Ron Yeats inexplicably picking up the ball in his own penalty area and conceding a penalty, in the game against West Brom at the Hawthorns.

Apparently, he had later claimed he had heard the referee blow his whistle, but it had been someone in the crowd. Fortunately, the resultant pen was missed. Liverpool won the game 2-1 and would face Stockport in the fourth round.

The first game was at Anfield and ended in a 1-1 draw. Liverpool were now making hard work of it, a reputation we've never quite shaken off. The tie against Stockport stands out for non-football reasons.

Albert and I had become closer, after Jimmy had launched his toys out the pram back in September. We'd planned to go to the replay at Edgeley Park together with a mate of his, Pat. I can't remember his surname, but Pat worked as a painter and decorator and his van and ladders would come in very handy.

He'd sorted himself a ticket for the match, but Albert and I had no luck at all. We ended up getting into the match by scaling the perimeter wall, with his set of ladders. It must have been a hilarious sight to the dozens of Reds milling around by the turnstiles.

Once we were in, Pat would drag the ladder down, throw it back in his van and drive off to park up. He then calmly walked through the turnstile clutching his ticket as if nothing had happened. We would have a right laugh about that when we met up on the inside.

This sort of stuff has been commonplace for decades. It still goes on today, despite the emergence of modern stadia and automatic ticket barriers. It's harder now, but supporters of all clubs engage in the practice. The dilapidated state of many of the country's grounds throughout the 60s, 70s and 80s made it easier.

Of course, Liverpool progressed with a routine 2-0 win, thanks to two goals from Roger Hunt. He struck five minutes before half-time and grabbed the other five minutes before full time. The Reds were in the fifth round and we were starting to sense something magical was afoot.

The next round brought an away tie against Bolton Wanderers. We eased past them alright, with a 1-0 win at Burnden Park. That then set up a sixth-round tussle with Leicester City at Filbert Street. That game was a nightmare. Leicester turned up and decided to put 11 men behind the ball.

Despite their lack of adventure, they almost won the game when Tommy Lawrence rushed out of his goal to clear a long ball and got stuck in no man's land. Leicester could have killed us stone dead right there and then but squandered their chance. The game ended 0-0, which felt like a victory after that near miss.

We'd bring them back to Anfield and, thanks to the great Roger Hunt, we managed to progress 1-0. Suddenly the semi-final was looming, and the excitement was really starting to build.

I didn't get to the semi-final, which took place at Villa Park. The Reds went through with a 2-0 win.

The result sounds comfortable enough, but both of Liverpool's goals had come late in the game.

Peter Thompson got the first just after the hour. Then there was late drama when the Reds won a penalty. Gordon Milne should have taken it but his bottle went. His replacement surprised every Red in the ground: it was Willie Stevenson who stepped up.

He had been having a decent game but had little or no track record from the spot. He crashed it into the roof of the net. It looked good, but he would later admit he had intended to hit it low to his right. It didn't matter in the end. The Reds were in the final. The 'Holy Grail' was in sight.

By contrast Everton's season was almost devoid of drama. They had gone out of the cup in the fourth round, to Liverpool's eventual cup-final opponents, Leeds United. Liverpool represented the city's only hope of silverware and it felt great.

After holding Leeds to a 1-1 draw at Elland Road, the Blues had crashed out 2-1 at Goodison, in the replay. By the time they came to Anfield, maintaining their local pride was all they had left.

In the run-up to that game, I had the unenviable task of going around to Jimmy's house. I had heard through Marie, who had been told by Elaine, that he'd lost his job at the coal yard. Apparently, he'd got into a fight with some fella and they had given him his cards on the spot.

With my dad frequently off sick, there was no one to defend him from the management. Being well connected in the union, I was in a good position to sort him out with a start at Ford's. Despite us not talking for months, I knew it was the right thing to do.

Still, I was nervous as I approached his house. I had no idea what sort of mood he would be in, or if he would even speak to me at all.

Elaine answered the door and ushered me in with a smile on her face. Clearly, Marie had tipped her off that I was coming round. She shouted Jimmy, who was upstairs, and then continued to clear away dishes in the kitchen. Eve was playing with her dolls on the couch in the living room.

'You want some tea,' Elaine shouted over her shoulder, as she scrubbed plates in the sink. 'There's plenty left in the oven.' We call an evening meal 'tea' in Liverpool.

I was starving but decided to lie. 'No thanks. Already eaten, love.' I shouted. 'Could murder a brew like.'

I heard her laugh and she said something indecipherable over the sound of tap water filling the kettle. Then came the sound of footsteps on the floorboards upstairs and Jimmy appeared at the top of the landing.

He looked genuinely surprised to see me and, to my relief, there was no sign of anger in his face. That was a real plus. So far, so good, I thought.

'Alright, kid. What's up?' he said as he walked down the stairs. His voice was a little more quiet than usual. He clearly felt unsure of the situation, too.

That immediately relaxed me. We had a level playing field. Elaine emerged from the kitchen and the three of us stood awkwardly in the hall for a moment. It was Jimmy's wife who broke the tension.

'Kettle's on, Jim,' she said. 'Why don't you two go in the living room and talk. I'll give Eve her bath.' With that she swept the baby up into her arms and disappeared.

We both sat on the couch. The room was sparse. No telly in the corner like there would be today, just a radio on the sideboard in front of the window. A clock ticked loudly on the mantlepiece.

'How's things?' I asked. Pointless small talk seemed a good place to start.

'Bloody rubbish,' he replied and took a tin of tobacco out of his pocket.

The living room door swung open and in walked Elaine with two mugs of tea. She set them down on a small table in the middle of the room.

'I'll leave you two to it,' she said, and left.

'I heard about you getting the sack,' I told him. My voice gathered strength as I realised this wasn't going to be as difficult as I had imagined. 'To be honest, Jim, that's why I am here.'

He took a sip of his tea and looked up at me. 'Oh yeah?' he asked, setting the mug down and making a start on a rolled-up cigarette.

I took a deep breath and told him that a space had opened on the line. The job was his, if he wanted it. The only issue was he would have to join the union.

Jimmy didn't look happy about that. However, back then the place was a closed shop and if you weren't in the union, you couldn't work.

'Why do I have to pay subs to some union just for the privilege of working in a factory?' he asked.

I could feel my temper starting to rise. This kind of argument used to really wind me up. To be fair it still does.

Fellas like Jimmy were usually quite happy to accept the pay and conditions won by their union membership, but woe betide anyone who suggested they pay their dues on time, or worse still ask them to join a strike in pursuit of a pay rise. They'd usually rather someone else made that sacrifice on their behalf.

Jimmy could see the look on my face and chose to back down. He smiled and said, 'As long as I don't have to go to any meetings.' There was a twinkle in his eye and I knew this was just his way of maintaining face.

It wasn't much but I took it. I was in no mood for another row.

'Very generous of you,' I said, and laughed.

'That's my nature,' he said, and smirked before adding, 'Thanks, kid. I really appreciate it.'

That was it. No drama, no recriminations or hassle of any kind. We were right back to normal. It was like nothing had happened. Jimmy started work at the plant shortly after that. It was an act of kindness on my part that didn't end well for me, but we'll talk about that later.

We finished our tea, Elaine came back with some biscuits, Jimmy smoked his cigarette and we chatted for about an hour about the footy, of course. I said I thought we could beat Leeds in the final. Unsurprisingly, he didn't. We laughed some more, I said my goodbyes and then I was off.

I suppose Liverpool's focus had shifted significantly by the April of 1965. That sounds like an excuse for another miserable derby defeat, I know. However, these were the days of no substitutions and it was standard practice for the team sheet to be the same, week in and week out.

Competing in a 42-game season and managing two cup runs was no easy task with just 11 players. Today's huge squads and rotation would have been unrecognisable in 1965.

Still, despite any fatigue the players may have been feeling, Liverpool put up a decent fight. It just wasn't enough to stop Everton claiming the bragging rights for another season.

Once again, I was at the game with Jimmy. Albert couldn't make it; I think he had a wedding to go to or something like that. We were both in the Anfield Road end this time.

This was a rearranged game after the original fixture had been postponed back in the January. The resultant fixture congestion would see Liverpool play three games in seven days, with the derby the last of them on a Monday night. Not that any of us would have accepted tiredness as an excuse for what happened.

It wasn't.

Liverpool just weren't at it and Everton wanted it more. It was a bitter blow as it came on the back of back-to-back 3-0 defeats to Spurs and West Brom. It also annoyed me no end that the first side to beat us in our new all-red kit was the team from across Stanley Park who played in blue – Everton.

We'd wear that kit in the final, but before that game we'd get a timely reminder that we couldn't take anything for granted. Liverpool looked dead and buried by half-time. Goals from Derek Temple and Johnny Morrissey had put Everton 2-0 within half an hour.

Jimmy was delirious and I almost felt like going home in the interval. Not because I couldn't take getting beat, but because I couldn't take his gloating.

In the second half, Everton took their foot off the pedal and Liverpool upped their game. They'd given themselves a mountain to climb. When Willie Stevenson converted a penalty with 15 minutes to go, I still didn't fancy us to get anything.

There were the usual derby handbags, and at one point the referee had to intervene to stop Ian St John from lamping someone, but it was all too little too late. The Saint almost levelled with five minutes to go, but Gordon West pulled off an unbelievable save to deny him. In truth, it would have been hard on Everton if that had gone in.

So, the Blues had salvaged some honour from a season best forgotten for them. For Liverpool, attentions turned to Wembley. It wasn't easy, but the prospect of finally getting our hands on the cup would ease the pain of that Blue double; not that Jimmy didn't take full advantage on the way home.

Neither of us had any idea that our city and its two clubs were about to witness unparalleled joy: for once, for the next couple of years, there would be more than enough glory to keep all of us happy.

Chapter Seven

Shanks, The Saint and the Holy Grail

1

Sunday 2 May 1965 is a day that will live with me until the moment I take my final breath. Sure, the day before was quite special, too. That was the day my football club ended its decades-long wait for the FA Cup and the celebrations had lasted into the early hours.

However, I had needed to make do with watching the game on a neighbour's television, which of course couldn't compare to being there. On the Sunday, the morning after that historic triumph, we finally got to see the FA Cup in person.

Football is about participation, and if you are not actually playing in the game then your proximity to it is all important. To be separated from the action has always been painful to me. For some reason I have come to feel that if I am at the game I can exert some control over events. Watching on telly or listening on the radio leaves me feeling powerless and the nerves can be hard to live with.

I've been told often enough that this is complete rubbish, that whether I am at the game or not has no bearing on the outcome. I suppose that's true, maybe. It's just that I've been to too many games where I've felt the power of the people around me, seen the impact the players of the noise we make, to completely give up on the idea that the team really is better off with me at the ground.

So the agony of not getting a ticket for Wembley had been intense. They were, as you can imagine, very highly sought after. As my dad was fond of saying, they were as 'rare as rocking horse shit'.

The club's task was the equivalent of Jesus feeding the five thousand, with no more than a loaf of bread and a few fish. They dealt with it by running a lottery to determine who got a ticket. I didn't.

We had considered going down to London, but Dad wasn't well enough. In the end, a neighbour, I remember her as Mrs Thompson, opened her doors to the neighbourhood. She was one of the few in our road who had a TV. By the time kick-off arrived her parlour was rammed.

As often happens when you assemble a group of Scousers to observe an event, it didn't take long for a party to break out. Soon, sandwiches were being buttered, cakes appeared from nowhere and were piled on top of a pasting table, which had been hastily covered with a tablecloth. Nestled underneath were crates of beer in brown bottles, brought by neighbours.

The team's picture was taped to the downstairs windows. I think we'd cut that out of a *Liverpool Echo* and there was bunting draped around the walls. The kids had cut mini FA cups out of card and we pinned those in the windows upstairs, along with the letters, L, F and C.

A few of the older fellas, my dad included, had worn rosettes. I was wearing my 'Beatle suit', complete with black tie, and I had half a tub of Brylcreem on my head. I really thought I looked the part like.

Just when it seemed we couldn't squeeze any more people in front of that TV, in came the kids. They had been playing footy in the street outside and, typically, barged to the front of the crowd, sitting themselves down on the floor in front of the television just as the game was about to get underway.

I can picture the scene in that crowded living room even now. The grown-ups were perched on every piece of couch they could find. When the couches were full, they sat on dining chairs, deckchairs or lined the wall. On the floor, and bathed in the light of the TV, were the kids, including our Joe.

A few couldn't get in the room, and lurked in the doorway, craning their necks to catch sight of the action. Nobody wanted to get up to go the toilet, because they knew their space would be gone when they came back.

The national anthem came on and we watched intently as Shankly and Revie led the teams out. The look of pride on the great man's face echoed my own and brought a tear to my eye. The Reds looked determined and professional but I felt Leeds looked cocky. One of them was juggling the ball as he strode out on to the pitch and playing head tennis with it. That really got on my nerves.

The tiny, by modern standards, black and white screen was like a window on a stunning vista, which included vast swathes of supporters. It seemed they were crammed into every inch of the old stadium, with barely an inch between them, save for the giant stone steps that formed descending corridors between each section of the terraces.

The Leeds fans had flags and some of them were wearing paper hats; some were homemade and some which they had clearly bought were adorned with images of their heroes. They weren't a patch on the Reds, though, who seemed to completely outnumber their opponents. Despite the monochrome images, I could clearly make out the Liverpool supporters because of their stripy scarves and the occasional banner they hoisted above their heads. What a stunning backdrop to a battle to be fought by heroes, whose time for victory had finally arrived.

The tension was building with every tick of the clock and at times it threatened to become too much. By the time the referee was ready to signal the commencement of hostilities, I was at bursting point.

The pressure building up in my chest and in my head was becoming uncomfortable. My stomach was in knots and I'm sure my face must have been beetroot red.

I knew that, somehow, I needed to release the tension before my heart gave out, so I leapt from my seat and shouted, 'Come on Liverpool!' It was like I had completely forgotten that I wasn't at the game.

There was an almost involuntary nature to it. It worked a treat as far as I was concerned. Suddenly, I felt so much better and I could start to enjoy the occasion again. I guess everybody must have been feeling the same way, because none of the adults laughed at me or looked at me strangely; instead they just joined in, until it became a deafening chorus.

On the floor the kids couldn't believe their eyes. They started laughing, clearly delighted at seeing the adults lose it. The expressions on their faces were of pure joy. I get emotional now just recalling that moment.

Then someone shouted, 'It's about to start.' Quickly, we settled ourselves down. The nerves were gone now. The referee blew his whistle and we were off and running.

A few of us had begun the day politely drinking tea from Mrs Thompson's best china, but that wouldn't last. As soon as Gerry Byrne went down injured she was straight under that pasting table, cracking open bottles and handing them out like ammunition in a gunfight. It seemed the tension was getting to her, too.

Byrne eventually got up off the turf and played on. He looked sore, but none of us had any idea that he had suffered a broken collarbone. In truth, neither did Shankly, until full time. It would all add to the legend surrounding our first cup win and would make Byrne's assist for the eventual winner even more remarkable.

From that moment on, the game felt like a war of attrition to me. I must have chewed through every fingernail. There were chances at both ends and the tackling was tough at times. This was too great sides going toe-to-toe, with no quarter given and none sought.

When the referee blew for full time, signalling another 30 minutes of agony, we were all as exhausted as the players on the pitch. The breakthrough hadn't come.

All the ale had gone by now, and nobody was willing to go out for more, At least, not until the cup had been won. We'd have to endure extra time without alcohol. It didn't matter, though, because at the end of it everyone in that room felt drunk with joy.

The consensus was that we would do it. We felt that Liverpool under Shankly were like a machine. They were simply fitter and hungrier than Leeds. Our theory was borne out by the way they lifted themselves after Leeds had levelled, Roger Hunt's 93rd minute goal being cancelled out by Billy Bremner.

Hunt had opened the gates of heaven only for Bremner to slam them shut in our faces. The players could easily have collapsed at that point, but they refused to submit. At home, we felt the same way. Liverpool couldn't lose this. They just couldn't. So instead of despairing we all continued to scream at the television.

Somehow, the players summoned the belief to go again, and just nine minutes after Bremner's heartbreaker, the Reds were back in front through Ian St John. Pandemonium ensued in the Liverpool end. It wasn't that much different in Mrs Lambert's living room.

I remember, as if it were yesterday, Ian Callaghan getting to the byline and whipping in a cross, which The Saint nodded home. Amazingly, it was Byrne who had set the move in motion.

We almost knocked the couch over in our celebrations. The kids were dancing and laughing, and I was waltzing around the room with Marie. Out of the corner of my eye, I caught sight of my dad. He was sat quietly on a dining room chair in the corner.

He looked like a man whose life's dreams had been realised. Then he saw me looking at him, smiled and nodded to me before wiping a tear from the corner of his eye.

Later that night we were stood in the back garden, smoking and swigging warm beer from a bottle. I still don't know where the extra ale came from to this day. We were reflecting on the season and an incredible day, when he turned to me in all seriousness and said,

'Son, you know I haven't been well these last few years. It's been tough going but I've hung on, fought it as best I could.' He had lowered his voice and I could barely hear him over the raucous sounds and music coming from inside.

'I know, Dad. You're cut from stone. It'll take more than a few heart problems to see you off,' I said, not realising this was going to be a serious talk.

'Listen to me,' he said forcefully. 'Never mind that stuff. I've had a good life, lad. I've seen you grow up and make a family of your own. I've got a lovely little grandson, too. To be honest that should be enough for any man …'

'Dad,' I interrupted him, sensing this was going somewhere I didn't want to be. He ignored me and pressed on anyway.

'Today though, son, seeing the Reds lift the cup at last, I can't find the words, lad. It means so much. I'm telling you, if the good Lord takes me tonight, I'm ready. I'll go willingly, and I'll be the richest man in heaven.' He was crying, and it was almost too much for me to take.

I did what I've always done in these situations. I made a joke of it. My father was reaching out. He wanted to discuss his mortality; maybe he had things he wanted to say but I just cut him off.

I did it because I couldn't handle the emotion, or how real the conversation was becoming. I wanted to retreat into the superficial and the mundane. I regret that to this day. I didn't get many deep moments with my dad, and I avoided all the chances I got to explore who he really was.

I wish I had listened more, encouraged him to go on and hugged him. Yes, I wish I had held him and told him how much he meant to me, how loved he was. Instead I said,

'Frig off you daft bugger. You're going nowhere. Now drink your beer and shut up.' I said it with a smile, but I will always regret those words.

My dad laughed and wiped away his tears with the sleeve of his jacket. He chugged back the beer and said, 'Take no notice to me, son. It's the beer talking.'

Behind us we heard a commotion in the kitchen. It was cheering, jeering and laughter in equal measure. Then the back door swung open and Jimmy spilled out into the yard. He'd clearly been drinking and had a huge grin on his face.

'Alright lads,' he half said, half belched. His breath reeked of ale and whiskey and he had a rolled-up cigarette perched impossibly on his bottom lip. With that, the tender moment between my father and I was gone forever.

I looked at Jimmy in disbelief. 'Well you're the last person I expected to see tonight,' I said.

Jimmy was swaying quite a bit and he eventually found the wall with his back and propped himself up.

'He's decided to become a Red after today, I'll bet you,' said my dad.

'No fucking chance, Bill. I promise you that will never happen,' Jimmy slurred.

'Fair enough, Jim. Well in that case let me get you another beer. You can join us in a toast to worthy winners.' I still couldn't believe he had turned up. I'd have bet money on him giving me a wide berth for a few days.

'Why do you think I'm here, Tommy? You know I'm a Blue, right? Well I am. If you cut me in half now, it would be like a stick of Blackpool rock. You'd see Everton right the way through me.'

My dad and I agreed. He went on.

'But never say I'm a bad sport, right?' We promised we wouldn't. 'Your lot won fair and square today, and that's good for the city, isn't it?' He slid slowly down the wall and was crouching near the ground.

'Get him a chair from inside,' my dad said, and I immediately went to fetch one.

When I returned with an old worn-out deckchair, the pair of them were talking about the homecoming. We each took one of Jimmy's arms, lifted him up and then sat him back down in the chair. It wasn't the most sensible thing to do, but I placed a fresh bottle of booze in his hand.

Jimmy had committed himself to coming to the homecoming with us, to welcome the team home at Lime Street. Neither my dad nor I believed for one second that he would turn up, though. He had promised he would, but at the same time he smelled like he had drunk enough to float a battleship.

The party wound up at about three in the morning, when we joined the last stragglers and left for home. Our Joe was fast asleep, despite the noise. I carried him along the road to our house. Luckily Marie had remained sober and was able to supervise me as we wandered along.

I placed him in his little bed and joined Marie. We talked for a while, before I drifted off into a deliriously happy sleep in which I dreamed about the Reds dancing on the Wembley turf.

2

My dad, Jimmy and I had been camped at St George's Plateau from early in the morning. We'd watched the crowd file on to the cobbles in front of the war memorial and eventually fill up every available space. Finally, when there was no more room, they climbed up the steps and clambered on to statues. Some sat on top of the lions and others clung to lampposts.

We'd made a pact to get up early and go into town together. Jimmy had gone on about how Liverpool's triumph was good for the city. The fact there were three FA cups residing on the banks of the Mersey was a source of civic pride, he said.

In the end I had believed he was being genuine. Nevertheless, I thought he would be too hungover to follow through. To his eternal credit, he was waiting for us when we called at his house. He looked fresh and raring to go, too. I have no idea how he did it. My dad and I were dog-rough.

When we arrived, there were already thousands of people milling about. The front of Lime Street station was completely different back then. Where there are steps leading up to the main station concourse now, there used to be a tunnel. The players would disembark and be herded on to an open-top bus, ready for the parade. Then they'd emerge, turning left on to Lime Street, directly in front of where we stood.

We foolishly believed we could reserve a space for Marie, who was joining us later with Joe. In truth, she had no chance of finding us in that crowd. I later found out she had been watching from the top of the steps in between the giant stone colonnades of St George's Hall, just a few hundred feet or so from where we were.

We'd decided to go to St George's Plateau rather than the Town Hall because I had wanted to see them as they came out of the station. I wanted to be among the first to clap eyes on that lovely piece of silver.

I had reasoned that we could then walk, or run alongside the bus, to the Town Hall. That would prove impossible. I was going to get one shot at seeing the team, so I was determined to savour every moment.

My excitement was growing as the time for the parade approached. The police had placed a human cordon, the thinnest of blue lines, in front of the giant throng, creating a space in front of the station, to allow space for the buses. They were struggling to hold back the crowd, which had developed a momentum of its own. It was like the Kop only three times as large.

Somehow, we had moved close to the front, just a couple of rows back. I strained to look back over my shoulder and could see people climbing on the statues. One of the stone figures had a traffic cone placed on its head and a scarf hanging from its outstretched arm. There were police all around watching this happen, but none intervened.

There was no hint of trouble. It was a celebration and something special for the city.

Then we started to sing. It felt like thousands joined in with chants of 'we want the team, we want the team,' then 'Shankly, Shankly' and of course 'We won the cup, we won the cup, EE-AYE-ADDIO, we won the cup.' It was joyous, raucous and very emotional.

Then an almighty roar went up, as it seemed like the parade was starting. We realised it was a false start as the press bus, full of photographers, eased its way out of the tunnel. It moved left, slowly, and made its way along Lime Street towards the ABC Cinema.

The crowd surged and jostled, and the police leaned back, holding hands and trying to stem the tide. Amazingly nobody broke ranks.

Then came the team bus. I remember it vividly. Plastered to the windows was a series of simple white cards bearing the words, 'LIVERPOOL FC CUP WINNERS 1965'. A banner reading the same was stuck to the front, across the top of the grill and above the two shiny headlights.

On the top deck, on the side facing us, we could see Roger Hunt, Ian Callaghan and Tommy Smith. Behind Smith someone held the cup aloft. I couldn't make him out but I could see the trophy. A mighty deafening roar filled the air and the players beamed. Their expressions said they'd never seen anything like it. They hadn't.

Behind Callaghan was Ron Yeats. He was saluting us. Then I saw The Saint, who was just taking it all in. Behind him was Shankly himself, imperious and charismatic. These were his people. He had led his troops into battle and returned victorious with the spoils of war, just as he had promised he would.

Remembering these scenes makes me recall one of the great anthems of that era. It says everything about the esteem in which we held the manager and his players. It has been added to down the years. Tales of modern conquest now swell its verses, creating one of the more complicated and haunting stanzas in the Kop songbook. It went like this,

> 'Here's a song about a football team
> The greatest team you've ever seen
> A team that play total Football
> They've won the league, Europe and all.
>
> A Liverbird upon my chest
> We are the men, of Shankly's best
> A team that plays the Liverpool way
> And wins the championship in May.'

The legend of the 1965 team still echoes down the decades, and this verse has since been added, along with many more,

'Now back in 1965
When great Bill Shankly was alive
We're playing Leeds, the score's 1-1
When it fell to the head of Ian St John

A Liverbird upon my chest
We are the men, of Shankly's best
A team that plays the Liverpool way
And wins the championship in May.'

I turned to my right and my dad was crying. It caused a giant pang of emotion to bubble up from deep inside and I choked back my own tears. To my left Jimmy was clapping enthusiastically. He was a Blue through and through, but this was a team from his city, bringing pride to its people and he was happy to pay his respects.

Then the bus slipped by. It was followed by two others. I guess they were full of club officials and the players' wives and girlfriends. They slowly wove their way into the distance, affording us the briefest of glimpses of our legends and then they were off to soak up the adulation in the streets of the city centre.

All that was left was the small task of getting home. The crowds had jammed up the roads and there was no chance of getting a bus ride back. We couldn't afford a cab back then, so we made our way back on foot.

As we did, we chatted excitedly about football and living in the greatest city on earth. We had everything: two of the best teams in England, the Beatles and the FA Cup. Little did we know things were about to get a whole lot better.

Chapter Eight

Muhammad Ali, Eddie Cavanagh and the FA Cup

On 14 May 1966, Jimmy stood at the edge of the Wembley pitch. His chest was bursting with pride as his heroes ran past holding the FA Cup aloft. One year earlier, Liverpool had done the same thing. This was Everton's third cup.

The Reds' defence had fallen at the first hurdle, with a 2-1 defeat to Chelsea. I was stood just a few rows behind Jimmy, clapping dutifully, as the Blues paraded the cup on their lap of honour. The story of that day still makes me laugh. It amazes me to think that I wasn't there in 1965 to cheer on my own side, but I was a year later to see Everton win it.

It was a day that began with a chance communion with a sporting legend and an icon, arguably the greatest there has ever been. It would end with the Blues clutching an equally legendary and iconic trophy, arguably the greatest in world football.

In the middle of it all was a hilarious solo pitch invasion that would bestow legendary status on the interloper, amid claims that he was the 'first hooligan'. The man in question was Eddie Cavanagh and, while 'hooligan' seems a harsh description for such a joyous moment of unbridled passion, he was clearly some character.

Our claim to fame was that we were there when Eddie made his solo flight into the history books. We would dine out on the story for years to come. However, his was just one moment among a host of dramatic and comedic episodes that occurred that day.

It had been a difficult season for the Blues. Everton had failed to land a single blow on Liverpool in the derby, losing 5-0 at Anfield and only managing a goalless draw at Goodison. They'd also had to put up with us winning the league title that season.

The cup had provided a welcome respite. In reaching the final, they'd negotiated some difficult opposition, particularly in the later rounds. They had also put on something of a defensive masterclass.

Everton reached Wembley without conceding a single goal. In the first three rounds they'd scored a total of nine times, dispatching Sunderland, Bedford Town and Coventry City. Then they met the two Manchester clubs, City in the quarter-final and United in the semi-final.

It took two replays for them to put City to the sword, with an eventual 2-0 win. Next up were United on a muddy pitch at Burnden Park in Bolton.

Man United were a decent side even then. Scousers didn't hate them the way we do these days, and I don't think they hated us either. It would be a few years before the ugly side of the rivalry would kick in.

United won the FA Cup in 1963 and the league championship in 1965. They'd do it again a year after Everton, in 1967. They had the likes of George Best and Denis Law, and of course Bobby Charlton and Nobby Stiles. The latter would dance as England won the World Cup in the summer. For their supporters, United could be frustrating to watch, though, and Jimmy hadn't been too worried about them before kick-off.

His mood had been helped by news that George Best was out injured. His confidence turned out to be well placed and Everton made it a miserable season for United by knocking them out of the cup with a 1-0 victory, thanks to a goal from Colin Harvey. Matt Busby's men had already gone out of Europe and would look on enviously as Liverpool ran away with the league title.

Jimmy had not missed a game, home or away all season and was certain to get a ticket for the final. He was keen for me to go with him, pointing out that he had come to the homecoming with us the previous May. I didn't take much persuading to be honest.

As far as I was concerned, it was a day out at the cup final, which was a big deal back then. Besides, we were all Scousers together in them days, and it was bound to be a great laugh.

There was just one problem, though. Tickets were strictly rationed and I had no chance of getting one. Mind you, I wasn't alone: about half the lads on our coach didn't have one either. It didn't stop any of us travelling, though.

So, on the Friday before the final, we all made our way into town, straight after work. Jimmy and I were both on the lines at Ford's by then. He had settled right in and was thriving there. He would go for a foreman's job the following year, and he got it.

The coach was leaving at midnight from Lime Street and would take about ten hours to get to Wembley. This was before motorways came into their own. We had the M1 from 1959 but the journey from Liverpool to the capital in 1966 was largely via country lanes.

We'd been on the ale a good few hours before we boarded the coach and were carrying plenty of bottles on with us too. It made for a raucous and hilarious trip. I remember we must have gone through the full catalogue of Beatles songs, which I was fine with. Not so much with the Everton songs. Still, I took it all on the chin, even this one:

> 'Oh, we hate Shankly
> And we hate St John
> But most of all we hate Big Ron
> And we'll hang the Kopites one by one
> On the banks of the Royal Blue Mersey
> So, to hell with Liverpool and Rangers too
> We'll throw them all in the Mersey
> And we'll fight, fight, fight
> With all our might
> For the lads in the Royal Blue Jersey.'

The whole coach was belting it out and all I could do was grin as I stared out of the window. The ale helped, but only a little.

We arrived in London around mid-morning. The sun was shining and there were Blues everywhere. The predominant dress code was black suits, white shirts and even ties for some of the lads. Many had blue and white-striped scarves and rosettes pinned to their chests.

As soon as we arrived we planned to head straight for a boozer, despite it being mid-morning. An intriguing rumour had swept through supporters, though, and it made us change our plans. People were saying that Muhammad Ali had been seen jogging in Hyde Park.

Ali was in London ahead of his second fight against Henry Cooper. He won them both. Ali was more than a fighter. He was a global icon and a huge celebrity. He was more than just his fists. He was cocky, arrogant and often poetically witty.

Maybe Scousers saw a little of themselves in the man who would cast off his given name of Cassius Clay and define himself on his own terms. This was something every Scouser could get on board with.

So, we put the pub on hold and all of us legged it to Hyde Park as fast as we could. Sure enough, we found him. He was running and shadow boxing in his grey flannel tracksuit, hood up over his head. A small crowd had gathered around him.

There were photographers all about too, who snapped him and the onlookers repeatedly. Photos appeared in the newspapers and many have emerged online years later. I knew it happened because I was there, but others later claimed it to be a myth.

Ali was like a king, a movie star and there was this aura about him. It was like being in the presence of some other-worldly figure. We must have had an impact on him as he would later dedicate one of his trademark couplets to our city,

'You ain't no fool, if you from Liverpool.'

Later, we heard chatter that he'd been seen on Wembley Way. Apparently, he'd ditched his training gear and was dressed up like a million dollars, strutting around like he owned the place. A few lads were moaning about the fact that he had a ticket, while loads of genuine Blues didn't.

Many of us would have to find creative ways of getting in to see the game. I had grown a little braver after my exploits at Stockport, but there wasn't a snowball in hell's chance of me climbing the drainpipes to get in through the open windows above, like many supporters did.

Many succeeded, too. Stories abound of supporters emerging in the Everton dressing room, much to the amusement of the players, and in various cupboards and storage spaces. I even heard of one lad who got in early and hid in a rubbish bin, before being found and ejected.

I chose a more direct and far less imaginative route: that of attempting to leapfrog the turnstiles. It took me three tries before I eventually got in.

The first two attempts saw me grabbed by the same steward and immediately thrown out. One of them made me laugh when, in a broad cockney accent, he said, 'Listen, Ringo, no ticket no football. If I clap eyes on you again, I'll get a copper to deal with you. Do you hear me?'

No doubt, he thought he was insulting me with the Beatles reference, but with my mop-top in full bloom, I took it as a compliment. It was a case of third time lucky in the end. I was in and this time I managed to outrun another steward, before eventually meeting up with Jimmy before kick-off.

The official attendance was 100,000. Given the herculean efforts of some to see the game, it was surely much higher than that. I suspect the same thing was going on at the opposition end, too. Nobody wanted to miss their team in the final.

The FA Cup was the pinnacle of English football. It maintained its allure throughout the 70s and 80s, too, before succumbing to the voracious appetites of the money men. I remember it was also a regal occasion attended by real royalty, like John Lennon and Paul McCartney.

Both were at the match that day, to see Everton lift the cup.

The stadium was packed to the rafters, as you'd expect. It was also a sea of blue. Everton's opponents that day were Sheffield Wednesday who played in blue and white stripes. They'd wear white that day, while Everton were in their usual royal blue tops with white shorts.

Most Everton fans inside the stadium were wearing blue and white-striped plastic hats, which had been on sale throughout the city in the run-up to the final. You could also buy them on Wembley Way. The sense of anticipation, even for me, a Red, was intense. Yes, I'd have preferred to be watching Liverpool instead of Everton, but this was my first cup final in the flesh and I couldn't help but feel excited.

We suffered through a rendition of 'Abide with Me' and then the national anthem. The pomp and ceremony were all well and good but we were all just desperate to get the football underway.

The team selection had caused Blues some concern. They'd been expecting Fred Pickering to come back into the team after a spell out with injury. Instead, Harry Catterick had put his faith in a youngster called Mike Trebilcock.

The club had paid something like £20,000 for him to Plymouth Argyle, and his inclusion didn't exactly fill the Blues with confidence. It would turn out to be a masterstroke and at the end they would be singing the young lad's praises.

Things couldn't have got off to a worse start for Everton, though, with Wednesday going a goal up inside five minutes. I remember them huffing and puffing their way through the opening 45 minutes, but not getting anywhere near Wednesday.

To be fair it was the same for the team from Yorkshire, too, who never looked like adding a second. As the referee blew for half-time, Jimmy just shrugged, looked at me and said,

'We haven't even turned up yet, lad. We'll have these in the second half.'

His words seemed almost prophetic when Alex Young put the ball in the back of the net after the restart. However, the referee had disallowed it and fury erupted among the watching Blues. Their anger would reach fever pitch when on 57 minutes disaster struck. Everton went 2-0 behind.

As the ball hit the back of the net I could see the look of sheer despondency on faces all around me. I foolishly decided to offer a few consoling words.

'Never mind' Jim. Sometimes it's not your day. You've had a terrific run to the final,' I said, and I meant it, too. I had no desire to see them lose and I genuinely felt for him. Besides, the journey home was bound to be a nightmare after a defeat.

'Fuck off, you.' He muttered. 'You're loving this.'

I could sense his desperation and didn't push back. I think he realised I was being genuine, because he then said quietly, 'It's not over yet, Tom.'

I doubt that even he believed that but I nodded anyway. Amazingly, though, he was absolutely spot on. In the space of five crazy second-half minutes, Everton were level. Their hero in that epic fightback? Mike Trebilcock. The youngster had blasted in two goals to drag his team right back into the game.

The scenes in the Everton end of the stadium were almost riotous, with people falling over each other, fists pumping and plastic hats in the air. You'd have thought the game was won already.

Somehow, I managed to stay on my feet but Jimmy had disappeared under a pile of bodies. The noise was thunderous. Then, from behind me this fella ran past us, leapt over the tiny perimeter wall, dodged the stewards and was on to the pitch in search of a player to hug.

Even now I can see him clearly in my mind's eye. He's running towards his heroes, arms raised in wild celebration. He was wearing a dark suit but he would soon lose his jacket. A copper was chasing him and amazingly the slightly overweight and balding Scouser was leaving him for dust.

Desperately trying to catch him, the policeman flung out an arm and just about managed to grab a fistful of jacket. It seemed for a second as if the game was up. Instead the man we would later come to know as Eddie Cavanagh simply turned on the afterburners. As improbable as that sounds given his physique, he pulled away from his pursuer and the copper simply landed in a heap on the turf.

A huge roar went up around the stadium as supporters revelled in this brazen act of defiance and sheer abandon. Eddie was away, in his shirt and braces. I can imagine that Lennon and McCartney would have been highly amused, even if the other royals weren't.

In the end, Eddie, the living embodiment of every Blue in the stadium, had his dash for glory brought to an abrupt end. While one officer lay crumpled on the ground a second managed to bring him down with a tackle more reminiscent of rugby than football.

Suddenly Eddie was surrounded, dragged to his feet and hauled off the pitch and, we thought, out of the stadium altogether. It was a classic moment, an expression of pure joy and sheer defiance. Its ending may have been inevitable, but Eddie had lifted spirits every bit as much as Trebilcock's equaliser had.

Some so-called respectable commentators may frown on such an act. I prefer to think of it as a passionate supporter who simply couldn't help himself. He had fallen victim to a spontaneous moment of delirium. No harm was done, and Eddie's story is now part of cup-final legend.

From that point on there was an air of inevitability about the game. There was only ever going to be one winner, after Trebilcock grabbed the equaliser. Everton were clearly in the ascendency and Sheffield looked out for the count. To lose their lead after being two up was an enormous psychological blow.

The Blues took full advantage and immediately went on the attack, bombarding Wednesday's goal. With every attack the noise from the Blues inside the stadium rose. I'd love to know what the decibel count was; it must have terrified the life out of the men from Sheffield.

The third arrived in the 74th minute, not that I had any idea how long was left. My recollection was always that the game ended shortly after. I've only recently come to realise that there was a full 16 minutes to go. There was plenty of time for an equaliser, but Everton had broken their opponent's spirit.

I can remember the winner clearly. The ball broke off one of their defenders and Derek Temple was on it in a flash. There was only the keeper to beat and Temple unleashed a powerful shot that seemed to go straight through him.

Temple's celebration was a little understated, as if he hadn't appreciated the magnitude of the goal. Maybe he thought that this crazy game still had one final twist left in it and didn't want to count his chickens.

Whatever his reasons, there was no such restraint in the Everton end. A chorus of 'we've won the cup, we've won the cup, EE-AYE-ADDIO, we've won the cup' broke out. I couldn't bring myself to join in, but I did feel the same rush my mates did. This was an incredible fightback.

The Blues hung on to their lead and the cup was won. At full time, Jimmy fought his way to the edge of the pitch. There were plenty of police and stewards there to prevent another invasion, but Jimmy had no intentions of doing that anyway. He just wanted to get close to his heroes and the cup.

As the Wednesday supporters headed out of the ground, we remained for a while, taking in the trophy presentation and witnessing the jubilant parade, before making our way back to the coach.

We chatted enthusiastically as we went. I remember we were fixated on the prospect of another derby in the forthcoming Charity Shield. It would be played at Goodison Park and the opportunity to host one of English football's showpiece events in our home town was a mouth-watering prospect.

We had no idea at that point, just how much of a spectacle that game would turn out to be. Neither could we foresee the calamity that awaited us in the car park.

Our driver hadn't been from Liverpool and he didn't like football, a fact he wasted no time in telling us on the way down to Wembley. He was also a bit of a busybody and had threatened to throw us off the bus when some of the songs we sang 'outraged public decency'.

This was ironic, given the fact that, while we were watching the game, he had lost the keys to the coach and his wallet while attempting to get decidedly indecent with a young girl who had knocked on the window as he dozed in his cab.

He'd been an easy mark and instead of having his 'wicked way' with her, he was held up at knife point. She had been immediately joined by an accomplice the second he opened his doors. The pair made off with his wallet and his takings for the day, slashing his tyres as they went.

The bus was therefore out of action and we needed another way to get home. We had no choice but to separate and negotiate whatever spare places we could on any coach that would take us. Most of us would travel back sitting in aisles or as the third person on a seat originally intended for two.

Some of the lads talked of swapping ciggies or beer, in return for a few hours in a seat, but I had no such luck and had to lie in the aisle for most of the journey back to Liverpool. By the time I got home, I could barely walk straight.

It was a sobering end to a great day out at a footballing carnival. I doubt it dampened the spirits of the Blues, but it certainly did mine. We wouldn't meet up again until the following day, on Everton's homecoming parade.

Chapter Nine

Homecomings, Trophies and Painful Goodbyes

The Everton team would return to the city by train. They'd disembark at Allerton station, around ten miles from the city centre. There they would board a parade bus, provided by Liverpool Corporation, which would ferry them along the streets of the city to St George's Plateau. The reception they got was every bit as remarkable as the one afforded Liverpool the year before.

After that experience, in which the city council had invited the team to a civic reception at the Town Hall, the municipal authorities had learned lessons. The space in front of the Town Hall on Castle Street is a natural bottleneck and the resultant crush had led to several hundred injuries.

It had therefore been decided to move the reception to the more open vistas of St George's Plateau, which could accommodate more people and the crowd could spread out. It turned out that the change in venue made little difference, and pandemonium would ensue on Lime Street. In truth, the police and emergency services had been simply overwhelmed by the scale of the welcome.

As we made our way to Lime Street once more, I joked with Jimmy that if one of us won it in 1967, the city of Liverpool should get to keep it. Such was our confidence in the quality of football being played on Merseyside we genuinely believed this would happen. The furthest thing from our minds was the prospect of danger and crushing.

The newspapers would say 100,000 people had lined the route into town. I have no doubt they were right. Just as it had been the year before for Liverpool's homecoming, the streets were gridlocked as the bus weaved its way slowly into the city centre.

We must have waited three or four hours for it to arrive. The crowds were huge. Official estimates said another 150,000 people had been on the Plateau. I'd say it was at least that number, maybe more. Again, people had climbed on to anything to gain a good view of the team and the cup.

There were so many perched on one bus shelter that it collapsed under their weight. I learned later that a few hundred people suffered injuries, just as they had in 1965, when Shankly's men lifted the cup before a huge throng in front of the Town Hall. Thankfully none of them were serious.

When the bus eventually arrived, it came in from left to right alongside St George's Plateau and crawled towards William Brown Street. I was sat on top of one of the stone lions and Jimmy was halfway up a lamppost, waving like a madman.

He had lost his blue and white hat long ago. At the front of the bus we could see the players were holding the bright silver trophy aloft. A huge roar went up and the noise was incredible, as a huge chorus of 'We shall not be moved' filled the skies above the city centre.

Despite the vast crowds, the players somehow managed to alight the bus and make their way through the hordes and into the great hall. I'm not sure how they did it, because I'm certain they would have been mobbed as soon as they stepped off the bus. Whatever happened, they eventually emerged on top of the steps to even more rapturous applause and cheers.

I remember seeing the Lord Mayor, his gold chains hanging around his neck and sparkling in the sunshine, pouring a giant bottle of champagne into the FA Cup. I can still see Brian Labone inviting Trebilcock to drink from it. He did his very best, as I recall.

This was a magnificent occasion for the city. It was Everton this year. It had been us the year before. We all just felt like we were living in the most special place on the planet, never mind the country. If it hadn't been for an obviously bent referee in Milan, the Reds might have added a European Cup, too.

The Blues could have added another FA Cup, but for a Jeff Astle goal in the third minute of extra time to win it for West Bromwich Albion in the 1968 final.

That defeat left tens of thousands of Evertonians to make the excruciatingly long journey home.

This was a period of extraordinary dominance by the two teams from Merseyside. In the entire history of Liverpool and Everton, there had never been another period in which both had enjoyed such success in parallel.

In the four years since the Reds had achieved promotion, restoring the derby to our great city, the two clubs had won three league titles and two FA cups between them. Everton would add a fourth title at the end of the decade.

Of course, when it came to civic pride it wasn't just the football. We felt invincible as a people. The world was in awe of our sportsmen, entertained by our actors and comedians and danced and sang along with our musicians. Liverpool was undoubtedly the cultural centre of the universe.

Future generations would see both teams monopolise trophies in the 1980s, but by then the fortunes of the city itself were very different. Liverpool would go from being the nation's cultural darling to its troublesome enclave, with aspirations for independence and desire for revolution. However, in the sixties we embodied confidence in ourselves and an unrivalled lust for life.

The Liverpool of 1966 might as well have been on another planet compared to its post-industrial successor. Football in the 60s was one of many escapes from the hardships of life. In the 80s it became the only one.

In the May of 1966 we felt like we had it all. Just a few months later, in the August, we would be in no doubt that we were living in very special times. At Goodison Park we witnessed what was undoubtedly the most remarkable Charity Shield in history.

Liverpool would win it 1-0, thanks to Roger Hunt, but the result was an irrelevance. The game would prove a sideshow to an even bigger spectacle and I'm proud to say I was there, along with over 63,000 others, to witness sights and sounds that would surely never be seen again in English football.

Those of us who were lucky enough to attend would watch in awe, as players from both clubs paraded the World Cup, FA Cup and league championship trophy around the pitch before kick-off. Our players had helped England win the famous Jules Rimet trophy and the FA had either offered to let the clubs showcase it before the game or someone at either Liverpool or Everton had persuaded them to release the footballing equivalent of the crown jewels.

Jimmy and I were in the Gwladys Street end that day with arms across each other's shoulders. It was an emotional occasion for many reasons. Of course, there was immense pride in our city, and great anticipation about the game. It was good to be sharing that with Jimmy. For me, though, there was someone else that I would dearly have loved to have had with us more than anyone else: my father. He had passed away a month earlier, leaving a gaping hole in my life.

Before he went he had given me a gold locket. I'd never seen it before. The chain had long since been broken, but he'd kept the heart-shaped pendant. It was highly polished, and I could tell it had been a treasured possession of his.

As the players ran around the pitch, holding aloft the spoils of their many victories, there were roars of approval and applause all around me. I stayed silent. The accolades continued, seemingly for ages, but I just clutched the locket in my fist.

Inside it was a picture of my mother and father on their wedding day. It looked a lovely image to me. It made their relationship seem real. As I gazed at it, their life together became more than just a collection of half-baked stories and quips.

Dad never talked about his marriage to Mum much. I had guessed it was too painful. The best I got were things like, 'Your mother used to say...' or 'Your mum would be spinning in her grave, if she heard you say that.' She was a phantom to me, a legend, but nothing tangible I could pin down.

I would never have told him any of that, of course; it would have hurt him. But how could I feel any different about someone I had never met, someone whose voice I had never heard or whose warm embrace I had never felt.

Seeing that image, though, I don't know why, but it just had a huge impact on me. Maybe it was seeing them together, smiling and happy. Perhaps that connected her to my dad and by extension to me. Whatever it was, it was powerful and I have kept that locket close to me ever since.

So, as the revelry continued unabated for what seemed like an age, all I could do was talk to my parents in my head. It seemed insane but some part of me wanted to tell them about how great this was.

This was their city. Their generation protected it, worked their arses off to build it, and it was them who kept it going through some of the darkest days in its history. In the case of my dad, people like him would put it back together after it had been destroyed in the war. So in my mind I kept saying, *Look, Dad, look, Mum, look at what we have become. All that sweat, all that toil and the pain; it was all for this. Thank you.*

I really believed all of that. I still do. The 60s might have been the age of the baby boomer. Yes, youth might have taken charge, shaking away some of the cobwebs that had come to paralyse the old order.

There had indeed been a social revolution and all the old ideas were starting to be unpicked. It's true that it was my generation who did all of that, but we were only there to do it because of the sacrifices of our mothers, fathers and grandparents.

Those people had endured the bloodbath that was World War II, survived the Blitz and sent fascism packing. Then, weary from their efforts and nursing the wounds of battle, both mental and physical, they had come home and rebuilt a new society. One in which we were free to dream of a better life for us and our own kids.

We owed them everything.

I missed my dad like crazy. I missed his voice. The one in my head. The one that would scold me when I was about to make a stupid mistake or the one that would tell me to keep going when it seemed life was getting too much. I had spent so many years asking, 'what would my dad do' that the idea of a life without him was, well, impossible to fathom.

Most of all I felt alone. That may sound daft, and it probably is. After all, I had Marie and young Joe. I had Jimmy and Albert and the lads at work. My son was my flesh and blood and in time I would become the voice in his head, his connection to history.

That's it, I guess. Your parents are that connection to life, the unconditional constant that gives your life meaning and explains why you're here in the first place. More than that, they are a safety net.

By that I mean whenever stuff isn't going well, or relationships are breaking down, even as an adult, you always feel there is a home, people you can return to. They're an umbilical cord to the safety of your childhood.

I never knew my mother of course, and that meant I only ever had the one voice in my head, and one haven. I'm not a religious man, never have been. So, I never had that sense she was looking down on me or anything like that. To me she was gone. I had been robbed of her and all I had were second-hand images.

Dad was everything to me. He could be a pain in the arse and there were times when I wanted to throttle him. I guess all kids, even the grown-up ones, feel like that from time to time. But I needed him and had never confronted the idea of losing him, not really.

I knew, in my heart of hearts, that nobody lives forever, but I just chose not to think about it. When he went, it was like that cord had been cruelly cut. My safety net pulled from under me and I came crashing down to earth, hard. The pain was immense.

I wished he could have been next to Jimmy and me at Goodison, on that Saturday afternoon in August, to see his team and his city become the envy of football. I wish he could have been with us in the pub afterwards as we discussed our eventual domination of the world, telling us not to be daft buggers.

But all things come to an end eventually. Even the great loves in your life. In the days and weeks that followed, I would recall that night on the eve of the 1965 homecoming parade and what my dad had been trying to tell me.

He'd seen all he needed to see. I think he was saying that he was ready to go, if only I'd let him get it out. It's of some comfort to me that he would go with no regrets, and that he got to see our beloved Reds lift the cup before he went.

In many ways that iconic and singular moment at Goodison Park would prove the high point for the derby in the 1960s. It was a coming together of forces it seemed; the social, political and cultural stars seemed to align over Merseyside, propelling the city of Liverpool on to the world stage. The trophies were just part of it but by no means the whole story.

They flickered for a while, and burned brightly once more the following year, 1967. Liverpool and Everton were drawn against each other in the fifth round of the FA Cup. It was a tie that once again pitted the country's two biggest teams against each other.

After the famine of the 1950s, 1966/67 would become a high point of the feast with the Reds and the Blues facing off four times in a single season. As the city prepared for another epic struggle, Liverpool were top of the league. Everton were ninth.

This was the greatest show in town as far as we were concerned: Shankly against Catterick, league champions against FA Cup winners, the Reds against the Blues. At stake was Merseyside supremacy. Once more the future moods of an entire population of people hinged on the outcome of 90 minutes of football. The whole city wanted to be at Goodison to see their heroes fight for glory.

There was just one problem, that of space and the availability of tickets. In its heyday Goodison could cram in over 70,000 supporters. It would be uncomfortable and perhaps even dangerous, but official attendances show that it regularly happened.

However, even that wouldn't be enough to satisfy the hunger on the banks of the Mersey to see this game. The *Liverpool Echo* would write off the rest of the competition, declaring this to be Merseyside's own cup final.

In all the years I've been following my team, through so many big trophy runs, I can scarcely recall a pre-match atmosphere like this one. You couldn't escape the game anywhere: at school, work or home. Everywhere you went, whether it was the pub or down the shops, all the talk was about the FA Cup derby.

This meant the two clubs and the city had a problem on their hands: how could they possibly satisfy the appetite of the people. They would come up with what was, at the time, an innovative and creative solution. Gigantic screens were erected at Anfield, where the game would be relayed live for the first time ever in the FA Cup.

This was no satellite link-up; the technology on offer was closed circuit television. Still we lapped it up. As the match got underway, I would be at Anfield and Jimmy would be at Goodison, watching the same game. It was incredible, almost incomprehensible to us.

However, even more remarkable is the fact that, as I pen these words, this remains the largest attendance at a derby match in the history of the fixture. Almost 110,000 people would watch, 66,000 at Goodison and around 44,000 at Anfield, as Alan Ball scored the only goal of the game, taking Everton through to the next round.

Unfortunately, that would prove to be the high point of the season, and perhaps the decade. It was an era in which I had found a great mate, seen Merseyside's two teams rise like cream to the top of a milk bottle, watch my city explode on to the world stage and say goodbye to the greatest man I ever knew. A bitter-sweet era, indeed.

The near parity between Liverpool and Everton that characterised the 1960s was over, too. The next decade would see the Red half ruthlessly hoard all of football's treasures and move its juggernaut on to the European stage.

Chapter Ten

Revolution Blues

By 1970, the common refrain in the footballing world, and from Evertonians everywhere, was that Liverpool were a fading force in the game. Their title wins in the 1960s would presage a drought that would last seven long years.

Shankly would have to build a second great side and he would throw everything he had into the project. We would all have to wait patiently until 1973 before we could enjoy the fruits of his labours.

Luckily for us, after the famine came a glorious feast that few of us could have dreamed of, even in our wildest of fantasies. Looking back, it is easy to think of it as our just rewards. Perhaps it was compensation for the misery of the previous seven years. In truth, it was a combination of applied football knowledge, sheer bloody hard work and an environment in which managers got time to build a team.

We gave Shanks that time. Nobody, the club or the fans, put him under pressure. He would have done that himself. It just didn't enter our heads to have a go at him. To us, the great man was simply irreplaceable.

Such patience is inconceivable in today's game. Managers get sacked after one season without success these days. In fact, some get sacked even when they've won a trophy.

The modern football fan should reflect on the fact that if such a culture had existed in my day, Liverpool would have been deprived of one of the greatest managers of all time. We might even have sacked Paisley after he ended his first season in charge without a trophy.

What a loss that would have been. Especially given the fact he won 20 honours in nine years at the club, cementing himself as the greatest English manager of all time.

For their part, Everton supporters continued to have faith in Harry Catterick's 'School of Science'. It seemed entirely justified, too. In the opening games of the season they had raced into an eight-point lead at the top of the table.

However, they did suffer the odd wobble that year. By the time Liverpool made the trip to Goodison Park in the December of 1969, their lead had shrunk to just three points.

Defeat to Liverpool and a victory for second-placed Leeds United would see it reduced to just one point. First place and what had seemed like a triumphant march to the title was in jeopardy. That meant Everton would go into the game under a great deal of needless pressure. Their supporters would have felt it, too.

Not that we thought we could possibly take advantage; Liverpool hadn't won a league game at Goodison Park in the entirety of Shankly's reign up to that point. It was like a festering sore to him and us.

All that would change, though, on 6 December 1969, with the Reds running out 3-0 winners. Shankly's sense of personal satisfaction was writ large in newspaper columns the following day.

'I've waited ten years for this result,' he would say. So too had all of us. It would prove to be Everton's only defeat at home in the league all season. In all they lost just five times on their way to the title, in 42 games.

The first half of that game was like trench warfare, with the midfields dominating. It was all very scrappy with a few tasty tackles flying in and bookings here and there. Then the game exploded in the second half. First Emlyn Hughes put Liverpool in front. Then came a moment of hilarity for the Reds inside the ground.

Bobby Graham, who was having a great game, whipped the ball out to the left and Hughes prodded it on to Peter Thompson. Gordon West, in the Everton goal, made a hash of his attempt to deal with the cross and Sandy Brown, the Everton full-back, headed it into his own net.

We were jumping around, clapping and laughing hysterically at the same time. The Blues standing nearby looked like they would have strung their goalkeeper and defender up from the crossbar if they could get hold of either one of them.

Everton had a go and a young Joe Royle looked lively upfront, but Big Ron Yeats had the measure of him. Then, with about 15 minutes to go, Bobby Graham grabbed our third and put the game to bed. It was a great day. We had finally beaten them on their home turf. It would prove a hollow victory in the end, though.

By the end of the season Liverpool had slumped to fifth in the table and Everton had finished the campaign in first place, nine points clear of Leeds in second. They'd also returned the 'favour' in the derby at Anfield, winning 2-0 in front of a dismayed Kop, thanks to goals from Alan Whittle and Joe Royle.

That had been a miserable day all round. Almost 55,000 watched in horror as Everton exacted their revenge. The win meant they were three points clear of Leeds United, although they'd played one game more. Still, we all knew they were in the home stretch now with just five games to go, and we couldn't see them throwing the league away at this late stage.

Their rivalry with Leeds that season had reignited memories of the so-called 'battle of Goodison', which took place in November 1964. Everton were the reigning champions but struggling in mid-table. Leeds were newly promoted and sitting in fourth place.

On the face of it there was little at stake, but you'd have never have guessed given the ferocity of the tackles on the pitch and the atmosphere off it. Back then Goodison was a terrible place for opposition teams to visit, such was the hostile nature of the crowd.

At both ends of the pitch great semi-circular barriers had been constructed behind each goal. It was to protect visiting goalkeepers from being hit by objects from the terraces. All sorts of missiles would be hurled at opponents, even darts.

Leeds were no shrinking violets either and on 7 November 1964 they were seemingly in no mood to be intimidated. Clearly, the reputations of the Everton supporters and Goodison had gone before them, because United came looking for a fight. That's exactly what they would get.

To be fair, the reputations of both sets of supporters were exaggerated by the national print press, and the 'dirty Leeds' tag, along with portrayals of thuggish behaviour on the terraces, wouldn't have helped with the atmosphere before the game.

It seems that the hostile atmosphere created by Evertonians and their sheer passion for their team fed the media narrative, which in turn wound up Don Revie's men. It was a sort of perfect storm of newspaper hype and footballing fervour that made a pitched battle on and off the turf almost inevitable.

The game started at a furious pace and tackles were flying in left, right and centre. Both sides were at it, but when Johnny Giles left stud marks on Sandy Brown's chest, the Everton player was having none of it. He launched a fist at the Leeds United player and was immediately sent off. This was after only four minutes had elapsed.

Leeds took advantage of the extra man and after a quarter of an hour were in front. Suddenly there was a Blues' fan on the pitch trying to punch Billy Bremner. It was chaos and already starting to boil over. If Johnny Morrissey, who himself was a hard lad, hadn't restrained the supporter, God knows what would have happened.

I remember Jimmy, who was at the game, telling me it was a 'mad house'. Every time Leeds went near the touchline they were bombarded with a volley of missiles from the home end.

He said the game had completely descended into farce when, five minutes before half-time, Derek Temple had been fouled by Wille Bell right on the touchline in front of the baying Everton supporters. The referee himself and the Leeds physio were pelted, and the game was halted for ten minutes.

Jimmy said that the ambulance fella had refused to take a stretcher to Bell, who was also apparently hurt. I've since read accounts that he told the Leeds United trainer, 'Willie Bell can fetch his own fucking stretcher.'

The poor guy probably didn't fancy getting pelted with coins for his troubles. Who can blame him. For the first time in English football history, the referee led both teams off the pitch. In the dressing rooms their managers pleaded with their charges to calm down. In the terraces nobody left the ground.

If the game had been called off, there would surely have been mayhem. Luckily that didn't happen.

Once the players deemed themselves ready to resume, an announcement in the stadium warned fans that any repeat of violence would lead to the game being abandoned. It had no effect whatsoever, and Jimmy always maintained the atmosphere and the battle on the pitch became even more intense in the second half.

Leeds hung on and won the game 1-0. That meant they, and the referee, faced the difficult challenge of escaping the ground in one piece. Somehow, they made it out safely and their bus flew out of Liverpool, bearing a few scars it has to be said. For the referee, it wasn't so easy.

He had to be held back, while mounted police did their best to clear the streets around Goodison of furious supporters. Jimmy said he'd made his way straight home, because the atmosphere was almost riotous. He was a married man, he said, and he didn't fancy the aggro.

So, given the history between the two sides, pipping the team from Yorkshire to the title in 1970 would have been extra sweet to Jimmy and all Blues. The celebrations would go on long into the night. In Leeds it would have no doubt left a very sour taste.

The 1969/70 season would prove to be the high point of the Catterick era. The Everton squad, packed with club legends such as Joe Royle, Howard Kendall, Colin Harvey, Brian Labone and Alan Ball, would be at the top of the table or thereabouts for virtually the entire season. On their day they were unplayable.

Still it had been none other than their nearest rivals, Leeds United, who would give them their biggest scare early in the January of 1970. The Yorkshiremen beat Everton 2-1 at Elland Road and the Blues then lost their next game to Sheffield United. They won the subsequent home match but followed that up with another away defeat to Southampton. It was a mid-season slump that threatened to derail their title challenge and it gave Leeds the top spot for a brief period.

However, Catterick pulled his team together. From that moment on the Blues would remain unbeaten until the end of the season, winning ten and drawing four of their remaining 14 games.

It would prove to be the last act and a final defiant hoorah for a team and a city, at least for a few more years. All around us, it seemed the joyous, swashbuckling attitude felt by most Liverpudlians, Red or Blue, was starting to unravel.

Just ten days after Everton were crowned champions of England, Paul McCartney announced he was leaving the Beatles. The band would split later that year, after a court case brought by McCartney in London. Just as in football, the youthful and optimistic exuberance of the 1960s was being put on hold.

In terms of the wider society, we'd all been through a period of rapid change, during which many of us harboured thoughts of eventually sweeping aside the old world, permanently. Living in a place like Liverpool had that effect on people. We thought there was nothing we couldn't do, no foe too big to topple.

I suppose it wasn't just us, though, and the mood at large was perfectly encapsulated in Dylan's poetic polemic against the establishment, 'The Times They are A-Changin''. Dylan had penned that song in 1964 and four years later, in 1968, it seemed his prophecy was coming to fruition.

In the United States, civil rights demonstrations had led to riots and ever greater demands for equality from black Americans. Martin Luther King had been assassinated, an act that resulted in outrage across the globe. Of course, another black activist, Malcolm X, had also been murdered in 1965.

The anger led to partial changes and an end to segregation, even if the walls of bigotry and racism remained intact in other areas of American life. What mattered was that the genie of equality and social justice was out of the bottle.

Everywhere you looked, it seemed that people were in revolt. Whether it was riots in Paris, anti-Vietnam War protests across the globe or Czech activists demanding freedom from Stalinist Russia, the world was in flux, and it was the biggest issues that had moved people on to the streets.

Not all these movements were progressive, though. The world was a polarised place, full of inequality and huge contradictions. On the one hand there was the hope of the peace movement and the European revolutions, and on the other there was the hopelessness of Biafra: starvation in one part of the globe, disgracefully coexisting with vast wealth in other parts of the world. It enraged a generation. But not everywhere, and sadly not everyone.

In Britain the rising anti-establishment sentiment and spirit of peace and love was juxtaposed with the vile rhetoric of Enoch Powell and his 'rivers of blood' prophecy. All these social fissures could easily have led to a lasting social and political revolution. Instead, though, we just seemed to settle into a depressing war of attrition.

For me, the 'struggle' became less interested in the huge challenges faced by all people on the planet, and more about the depressing mundanity of factory life. It seemed to me like waging trench warfare, against a much more powerful and far more united enemy.

When you enter into such an arrangement with the established order, there's only one way it's going to pan out: a long, painful stalemate, disillusionment and the eventual unravelling of everything you have fought for and won.

So, just as the Beatles' creative zeal and youthful optimism gave way to simmering resentment and an acrimonious split, the spirit of the sixties also gave way to a decade of miserable workplace struggle.

On the national stage it would eventually usher in a government with a grudge against organised workers in general and Liverpool in particular. That was the government of Margaret Thatcher, of course. Much more about her later.

On the football field, though, Liverpool could not be toppled, and, although one of our sporting teams would suffer a period of regression – the seventies were a miserable time for the Blues – the other would rise to European prominence, just as Shanks had promised. It was just a shame he didn't stick around to lead the charge.

Football would remain a potent escape from the drudgery of working life throughout a decade of strife. Commentators talk about the seventies like they are some sort of Dark Ages. That's too simplistic in my view. Yes, there was hardship and workplace discord, but there was also progress of a kind.

I remember the seventies for long summers and bitterly cold winters, street parties and glorious homecomings. The streets were filled with children, playing football and tennis. *Top of the Pops* and *Match of the Day* came into their own and we had our first holidays during that decade. It might have been Towyn, Wales, and not the Algarve, but these were great times.

The so-called 'winter of discontent' of the late seventies, which paved the way for the Thatcher era, owed it roots to that earlier discontent and militancy whose seeds had been sown at the end of the 1960s. I was part of those early beginnings and, in the summer of 1969, became involved with a political group operating inside the Dagenham and Speke plants of the Ford Motor Company.

We called ourselves the 'Big Flame' and hoped we'd spark the inferno of revolution, first in the motor industry and then the world. Obviously we never managed that, but my participation in the group did light a fire under my friendship with Jimmy that would threaten to burn all ties between us.

It would mean Jimmy would have to soak up the glory of the 1970 title win without me. As far as I was concerned he had committed an unforgivable act of betrayal. In his eyes, I'd completely lost my mind.

We'll come to the whys and wherefores of all that in good time, but first let's go back to the football for a little while longer. Everton's championship of 1970 meant that they would qualify for the European Cup the following season.

Liverpool would enter the Fairs Cup, which, as far as I was concerned, was basically a money-spinning exercise dreamed up by a football pools' mogul from Switzerland and his mates. In those days there was no lottery and dreams of getting rich hinged on picking the correct number of score draws from the weekend's fixtures.

The Fairs Cup had very odd entry criteria and I still don't fully understand it now. It was essentially a competition between European cities who regularly held trade fairs. League position didn't seem to count for much and there was this bizarre – to my mind – one city, one team rule.

That would deprive Everton of a place in the competition at one point. The tournament would eventually be taken over by UEFA and was renamed the UEFA Cup, with different rules attached.

The Reds got as far as the semi-finals in 1971, before being knocked out by none other than Leeds United. We had initially progressed by beating Hungarian side Ferencváros, Romanians Dynamo Bucharest, Hibernian of Scotland and German giants Bayern Munich.

I wasn't that bothered about the competition at the start of the season but when we reached the semis against an English rival, there was added spice to it. I desperately wanted us to get to the final and experience an away game on the continent.

It wasn't to be, though. Don Revie's Leeds would grab a 1-0 victory at Anfield, thanks to a goal from Billy Bremner. A frustrating 0-0 draw at Elland Road ended our European adventure two weeks later, on 28 April 1971. I was livid. A competition I couldn't give two hoots about a few months earlier had ruined my season.

Everton would advance to the quarter-finals of the European Cup before succumbing to Greek champions Panathinaikos on away goals. The Greeks had got a 1-1 draw at Goodison and held Everton to a goalless stalemate in the return leg in Athens.

It was the start of a miserable week for the Blues, as they would crash out of the FA Cup after a semi-final clash with Liverpool at Old Trafford, just three days later. Before that, though, Jimmy would enjoy a spectacular and eventful away day in the German town of Mönchengladbach. I would probably have gone along for the ride, but events intervened.

By the autumn of 1971, Jimmy and I hadn't spoken to each other for months. It looked for all the world like there was no way back for us at all. The whole thing came to a head during a dispute at work back in the January. We'd walked off the line in what became known as the 'parity strike'. We were fighting to be on the same terms as workers in the Midlands plant.

The strike lasted until the end of March and no wages meant these were difficult times for Marie and me. The strike committee organised help, but it was a real struggle. Nevertheless, we were a determined lot.

Towards the end of the dispute the company offered a settlement, and union leaders Jack Jones and Hugh Scanlon recommended acceptance and an end to the strike. The rest of the plants in the UK accepted it and went back to work, but not us at Halewood.

Albert and I continued to agitate, along with others, for a continued push for a better deal. They couldn't sell any cars without the gearboxes we made; we still had the upper hand, we argued.

We stayed out for a while longer, but eventually in the absence of backing from the leadership the lads voted to go back. However, before that a few had already begun to scab. To my absolute horror, one of them was Jimmy.

It was late in the March and we were standing around a metal bin at the entrance to the plant. It was filled with kindling and burning brightly. It was spring, but nobody had told the weather. We were warming our hands by the flames.

Picket duty had been monotonous work. The strike had been solid, with nobody attempting to cross into work, not even the foreman. All that was about to change.

On the morning in question, at about 8.30, we'd had little to do but turn away a few trucks delivering parts and we were waiting for the next shift of pickets to arrive. I had just lit up a ciggie and couldn't wait to get home to my bed when I noticed a car coming towards us down the road into the factory.

I recognised it straight away. It was Jimmy's Mark III Cortina. He'd been doing alright since he got the foreman's job.

As it drew closer I noticed he wasn't alone. He had a passenger next to him and I could make out people in the back seat. The car was heading straight for the gate.

It wasn't going that fast and I stepped out in front of it. He was a good 20–30 yards away. I stood tall, so he could see exactly who it was and held up my hand. In it I was holding a placard, which demanded a 35-hour week and £15 wage increase across the board.

Instead of slowing down the car sped up a little and honked its horn. I was furious at this act of defiance.

For a moment I held my nerve, despite Albert and the rest of the pickets screaming at me to get out of the way. This is Jimmy, my mate, I thought. He's not going to run me down. I was wrong, and if I hadn't dived out of the way at the last minute, I'd have been thrown in the air as he sped through the line and into the car park.

I was beside myself with rage and immediately ran after him. I caught up with the car just as he had parked up and him and a few others were getting out. Jimmy saw me hurtling towards him and waved me away with his hand.

'Go away, Tommy,' he said. 'I'm not looking for any trouble here.'

I couldn't believe what I was hearing. My own mate, a scab. I was genuinely shocked.

'Well that's easy then,' I replied. 'Just get back in your fucking car and go home,' I demanded.

'Not happening, Tom. I'm going to work. If you and your Commie mates want a revolution, that's up to you. I've got to put food on the table.' With that he turned away from me and started walking towards the plant.

I was livid, but still convinced I could reason with him. I was wrong again.

'The strike will be over soon, Jim. The company will cave. You and I know that the deal on the table is no good. It will barely make a difference.' I was pleading with him, trying to get through as a mate, but he kept on walking.

'The rest of the country disagrees with you; they've accepted the deal. Even Jones and Scanlon have told us to go back,' he replied without turning around. His group kept moving and I was jogging alongside them.

'They have to listen to us,' I said. They can't sell their motors without us, can they?' I could see I was getting nowhere.

'That's it with you, isn't it,' he answered, practically spitting the words at me. 'All you care about is your bleeding union. While the rest of us are worried about the rent, you're enjoying yourselves, playing at being revolutionaries. Big Flame my arse. More like big fucking divvies.'

He picked up the pace and strode off. His mates were laughing and that was it for me. Their laughter was like a red rag to a bull.

I don't remember much after that, but Jimmy would later tell me that I'd run at him and rugby tackled him to the ground. We'd exchanged blows and wrestled on the tarmac for a while before his mates dragged him away.

The rest of the pickets pulled me off him. Apparently, we were both still swinging at each other as we were wrestled away in opposite directions.

I didn't set eyes on Jimmy again for several weeks, and when we did see each other our wounds had healed. The rift between us hadn't, though, and it would take a long time and a horrific tragedy before it would.

We'd bruised each other up pretty badly that day. Elaine had told Marie that Jimmy had two black eyes and I'd knocked his front tooth out. For his part, he'd burst my lip and broken my nose.

Jimmy had taken exception to being compared to Charlie, the old clipboard jobsworth from our Martindale's days.

In addition, being told by me that he was doing a great job of looking after Henry Ford's purse didn't go down too well either. Maybe I touched a raw nerve.

Looking back now, I realise that I must have come across to Jimmy as a great big know-it-all. To him, I had a superiority complex, as if I had this divine insight and he was just a simpleton who couldn't see the truth. I know this partly because he told me that, in exactly those words, and partly because, if I'm honest, that's probably how I felt at the time.

I didn't think my interpretation of the world was heaven sent, but I did think I could see things differently to the likes of Jim and the people I had grown up with or come to know. I had begun reading a lot in those days, and it wasn't your detective novels or James Bond that gripped me.

Thanks to the likes of Albert and others in Big Flame and the union, I had been exposed to Trotsky and Marx. In truth, I found some of it difficult to get my head around and I was no scholar by any means. But I managed to see what I thought was the problem facing British workers and the unions.

In the late sixties, the movements that emerged across the world were obsessed with change. The older more conservative generation were responsible for all the world's ills, we thought. We wanted a revolution, a social revolution: better pay, housing, health and welfare. Life had to mean more than the drudgery of work and the permanent terror of war.

All those individual battles, going on peace marches, demonstrating and striking, they were all necessary and very important. We wanted to live without fear, to be free from poverty wages and slum housing so that we could enjoy our lives. We wanted to listen to music, play and watch football and travel the world with our teams.

So we fought and we struggled for the petty stuff, like pay rises and, in some areas, we broke the law to defend our communities.

The rent strikes in Kirkby were an example of all that. In my view, though, we'd become so embroiled in the little stuff, the day-to-day mundanity of living, we'd lost sight of the bigger issues.

It was as clear as the nose on my face. It still is. We can't make progress on all of that unless we have real change at the very top. I believed that we needed a socialist revolution, not just a social one.

I wanted what Marx and for that matter what Shankly wanted, too: socialism. Liverpool's manager, having come from the mining town of Glenbuck, understood intuitively that to have real success, for life to have real meaning and purpose, you had to have collective effort and for the fruits of your labours to be shared equally. He would famously say,

'The socialism I believe in is everyone working for each other, everyone having a share of the rewards. It's the way I see football, the way I see life.'

Trouble was, Jimmy didn't see life like that. I would never have called him a Conservative, not even with a small 'c'. It's just that he wasn't even remotely interested in political thought. That stuff just wound him up.

So, like the governments of the day, and the trade unions, he was heavily focused on the here and now, on the bread and the butter. Meanwhile, me and people like me wanted the main course, the dessert and everything else. We wanted the whole bloody banquet.

That's why we had the dock strikes in 1972 and 1974; that's why rubbish piled up on the streets and bodies didn't get buried. It wasn't because the workers had too much power, it was because we had become embroiled in a fight for the crumbs that rolled down from the bosses' tables while they dined out on all the rest.

They could do that, because no matter how many times we went on strike, the same people would be in charge. No matter who was in Number 10, the same rules of the game applied. Change that, and we could have it all, I believed. I still do.

That probably reads like a lecture. Does it? I suppose it does, and I know that's exactly how the likes of Jimmy would have taken it, too. I wasn't so much a master of persuasion back then, as a self-appointed oracle, convinced that I was in possession of 'the truth', and that it was my job to convince everyone else of that fact.

If I went back in time and bumped into my 30-year-old self, I probably wouldn't disagree with much of his analysis of the world. He would, however, annoy the hell out of me. I guess Jimmy had the foresight to be irritated by me in 1970, rather than wait until 2012.

We had clashed on these matters many times before. In truth, the scrap we had in the Ford's car park was simply a culmination of minor squabbles and a simmering tension that had existed between us for a number of years. Our lives had diverged a lot since that cold morning outside the coal yard. So, too, had our ideas and aspirations.

We didn't speak to each again for almost 20 years. The wives kept up their friendship for a while, but eventually it became impossible. Inevitably each would take their husband's side and they drifted apart, too.

It was an awful waste, especially as we'd become so close as a family. Even our kids who had played together were separated by the feud. At least for a while they were, anyway.

I couldn't have let it go, though. Not back then. To my mind, Jimmy had scabbed and that was unforgivable. To him, I'd put my beliefs and principles before common sense and food on the table. I'd lost the plot.

Maybe there was some truth in that. However, I would argue that if it wasn't for people of principle who were prepared to fight, the bosses wouldn't be handing out pay rises for the good of their health. Pay rises do put food on the table.

Nevertheless, Jimmy's stubbornness meant that, unless I 'saw sense', made the first move and apologised, our friendship was over. I wasn't about to relent, so that was it.

We both settled in for that quintessential 70s thing: the long stalemate. Sadly, we would learn the hard way that life is too short for such divisions and that at the end of the day, solidarity is all we really have.

Chapter Eleven

Tales from a Hospital Bed: The Bell, The Doll and a Historic Shoot-out

1

Researching and telling this story has been both a joyful experience and a painful one. I have relived my own journey and I've confronted things I'd rather have left in the attic. In addition, there have been some great discoveries along the way.

One involves a trip Jimmy had taken to Germany more than 40 years earlier. It took place on Wednesday 21 October 1970. Both Liverpool and Everton were taking on European opposition in different competitions on the same night.

For the Reds, there was a relatively low-key tussle with Hungarian side, Ferencváros. Shankly's men would win the game 1-0 thanks to a thundering strike by Emlyn Hughes.

I remember the game well, but I never knew that while I was at Anfield that night Jimmy was also having an adventure on foreign shores. He told me about it during a hospital visit in 2012. His memory of the trip was still strong.

The visit took place on a beautiful spring evening in April. I had been anxious about seeing my mate. For almost a year he had deteriorated before my eyes, and I simply hadn't seen it. His body was withering under the onslaught of his cancer. How could I have been so blind? I guess I just didn't want to see it.

Elaine and Eve had been nagging him for months to go to the doctors but he had fobbed them off. They could see the weight loss, noticed the persistent nagging cough, and although he had hidden the bloodied tissues from them they knew something was wrong. Badly wrong.

The ward looked tidy and organised. Everything was in its rightful place, except my mate. He didn't belong there, in a bed, in pyjamas bought specially for his admission, pristine and with a razor-sharp crease in the sleeves.

As I walked past an empty nurse's station, a radio was playing. The singer was serenading 'somebody that they used to know' and I thought about Jimmy and the man he used to be when we were young. The contrast couldn't have been sharper.

Jimmy belonged back in those days, in the pub, on his couch watching a game, or at the match, home or away. Anywhere but here, frail and tired and in bed at tea-time.

It broke my heart to see him in this state but I twisted my face into a smile anyway.

'What are you doing in bed lazy arse,' I shouted and tossed a copy of that night's *Echo* on the bed.

He looked startled, like he'd been shocked out of a daydream. On the table next to his bed was a collection of half-eaten sandwiches and cold cups of tea. The remnants of that afternoon's visiting were left on his locker. More sandwiches wrapped in tin foil, a couple of books and a bottle of shampoo.

He was in a room with three other patients, all of whom looked gravely ill. Anxious loved ones maintained grim vigils at their side. It was a troubling tableau and I knew it would have affected Jimmy, made him feel closer to the end.

I love the National Health Service; no other institution does more with less.

However, for all the great work it does, for all the compassion and care, this was no place to end your days. As I stared at my mate in that bed, dazed and exhausted, I knew we had to get him out of there as soon as possible.

'Alright lad,' he said, as he recognised me. 'You didn't have to bother coming in here.'

'Shut up. There's the *Echo*. You might enjoy the back pages; I can't.' I sat down on the edge of his bed.

He smiled and seemed to brighten up a little. 'Not nice living in our shadow is it, Tommy lad?' he said with a wink.

I let him have that one. I could have pointed out that we'd got the better of Everton in both derbies already, that we had put a total of five goals past them without reply, but the league table made a mockery of all of that. Liverpool were in eighth place, one below the Blues.

Neither side was a force anymore. Liverpool's rampant cup success of the noughties was a fading memory.

We'd also lost a European Cup-winning manager and one I personally adored, replacing him with a man not fit to lace his shoes.

To make matters worse, the club had flirted with administration after a couple of clowns from America persuaded David Moores, the club's chairman, to hand them the keys to Anfield. He had dutifully obliged, after he had rejected an inferior offer from investors with far deeper pockets. It was an act that plunged Liverpool into almost perpetual crisis.

All of that was over now, but the club had swapped one set of American owners for another. They promptly dismissed Roy Hodgson, a darling of Fleet Street and an anathema to the Kop, replacing him with Kenny Dalglish. Hodgson's reign may have been the shortest in Liverpool's history. We still felt he'd hung around too long.

Kenny was king, and he had an immediate effect on the mood around the club. He brought back hope, too, steering us to our first trophy in six years.

By the end of February 2012, under his stewardship, Liverpool had beaten Cardiff at Wembley to lift the League Cup. It had taken a penalty shoot-out, but Kenny was back and he'd delivered silverware at his first attempt.

Now we were in a semi-final of the FA Cup and facing another trip to the capital. There we would face our oldest and greatest rivals, Everton.

Liverpool's new owners had labelled the defeat of Cardiff as 'just the beginning'. They meant it as a rallying cry, I think. To me it was a reminder of how far we'd fallen. Getting back to the summit was going to take years.

Liverpool's squad was a shadow of the ones assembled by Houllier and Benítez. It was light years from those who had dominated Europe for decades in the 70s and 80s, but we still had a few gems.

The madness and genius of Luis Suarez arrived to add real quality to the magnificence of Steven Gerrard and Jamie Carragher. I also loved Dirk Kuyt, who was like a machine. However, the rest were either past their best or simply not good enough in the first place.

Our league form was terrible. Prior to the FA Cup semi-final, the Reds had won just 12 games out of 33, drawing ten and losing 11. We were as far away from winning the title as we had ever been.

The only thing that had kept most of us sane since the last title win in 1990, was the regular procession of cup finals and silverware in the years that followed. For Everton supporters, it had been even slimmer pickings.

Finishing above the Reds and knocking us out of the FA Cup would be a decent season for Jimmy, irrespective of the result in the final. However, to win the competition would have ended 17 years of hurt for the Blues. There would also be the opportunity to laud the fact that, while Liverpool had won a trophy often called the 'Mickey Mouse Cup', the Blues would have won the more prestigious FA Cup.

There was so much at stake for both of us, again. We wanted evidence of continued progress and hope that the recent dark days were over. Everton supporters had a genuine shot at claiming parity with their neighbours at the end of the season, and a potential springboard to a more prosperous decade.

'We need this one more than you, Tommy.' Jimmy said.

'What do you mean?' I asked, even though I knew what he meant. 'Have you not been reading the papers recently? We're a fucking mess mate.'

He smiled. 'Well, I won't argue with that, but you've won a trophy and for us it's been too long. For a club with our history to go this long without silver, mate, it's not good enough.'

As with all clubs, all it takes is a spark, a catalyst that propels you forward. Players often talk about the first time they won something and how that made them want it more. Silverware is like a drug and once you've tasted the high, you'll push yourself to extraordinary lengths to taste it again.

'That's what winning this cup could do for us,' he said. 'It would say the slump is over and we could start to look to the future again. Not me like, but for my little Eve. I won't see it.'

'Don't be talking like that, Jim.' I said, stopping him in his tracks. I was never comfortable talking about death.

Jimmy realised I wasn't going there. He smiled awkwardly, then waved away the subject with a waft of his hand, saying, 'Look, all I'm saying is winning this game is a bigger deal for me than it is you.'

'Not having that,' I said defiantly.

He ignored me and carried on. 'I'd love us to get back into Europe, too. I always loved playing teams on the continent. Those games are different, special like. I know our Eve regrets not going to Rotterdam.

'Her mother pleaded with her not to go. She was convinced there would be trouble. In the end I saw none and when I got home she was devastated to have missed us win our first European trophy.'

'I can imagine,' I said.

He was right. Winning the FA Cup would see both Liverpool and Everton in the Europa League, or UEFA Cup as I prefer to call it. It was our only realistic chance, and, while it was less lucrative than the Champions League, it was another possible springboard to better days. Jimmy went on, 'I felt really guilty about it. I'd already been on a European away day, back in 1970. But she'd never experienced anything like that.'

My ears pricked up at that, sensing there was a story or two lurking in that sentence. I knew he'd been to Holland in the 80s. A mate had told me that. I knew nothing of his earlier expedition though.

'Hang on a minute,' I said. 'You went away with the Blues in 1970?'

In 1970 the Blues were in the European Cup, as English champions.

'Yeah, we should have won it that year, too,' he said.

His eyes were far away now, as he recalled the season. 'We had a great team. Those players deserved a winner's medal in that competition. I can't believe we went out to the Greeks either. Shocking.'

'I just had no idea you'd been away with them,' I said.

'Yeah it was when you weren't speaking to me,' he laughed, and for a moment the ravages of his illness were stripped away.

'Well you did scab, Jimmy lad. Unforgivable, that.' I replied.

'Yeah well, somehow you managed to forgive me, eh?' he winked. 'Plenty of bad blood between us back then, kid. Don't think we thought much of each other for a while did we?'

That was an understatement to be fair. We hated each other.

The scabbing incident was bad enough, but later we would be embroiled in another row that made the rift between us far worse. It cost me my job and I would blame Jimmy.

In the summer of 1973, I had been leaving work at the end of my shift. I was in high spirits. The Reds had won their eighth league title and had capped that feat with UEFA Cup triumph.

For Everton there had been a collapse following the 1970 title win.

The sale of Alan Ball to Arsenal in 1971 had enraged Blues, with some openly protesting and demanding Harry Catterick be sacked. The manager's health issues probably contributed to the slump and before the 1972/73 season was out, he'd been moved upstairs to the boardroom.

Tom Eggleston would step into a caretaker role, but Everton's season was long gone by that stage. The Reds had done the double in the derby and the Blues had finished 17th out of 22 teams. Liverpool's joy would simply add to the storm clouds over Goodison.

For Jimmy and me, our relationship had settled into a long, deep winter. The only interaction between us was the evil eye. Aside from that we had nothing to do with each other.

I was gaining a name for myself in the union and had been elected shop steward in 1972. That would have enraged Jimmy, I'm sure. In truth it was a thankless task. You simply couldn't please anyone. The lads would always complain that you'd sold them out, and the management would have your cards marked.

As I walked out of the plant in June 1973, I was feeling pretty good about myself. I'd represented a young lad in a disciplinary hearing. I got him off with a warning, even though he had been caught bang to rights, stealing parts from the store room.

We'd concocted a story that he was having problems at home with his wife and that this was a momentary lapse. The lad basically threw himself on the mercy of the panel, and I promised as his steward to look after him and keep him on the straight and narrow.

I couldn't believe they went for it. They probably didn't fancy a strike and my reputation suggested that calling wildcat action over something like this wasn't beyond me. They didn't know that I had warned the lad that his chances weren't good, given the evidence, and that he would probably get the sack. When he received no more than a warning, he was jubilant.

The foreman who had caught him was furious, and if looks could have killed I'd have been in the ground long ago. The foremen were a strong clique back then, and my ears would have been burning as I went back to the line. Stealing parts was rife. Many of the lads would supplement their income by selling them to family and friends. It was all too easy. The only real challenge was smuggling them past security. They often received tip offs and would conduct security checks and bag searches at the gates.

I had no such concerns as I approached the guards that day. I had done nothing wrong, What I didn't know was that someone had planted stuff in my bag.

I noticed lads being stopped but just walked on whistling to myself and looking forward to getting home. As a steward you knew the company never needed much of an excuse to get rid of you, so you always kept your nose clean. I'd never give them an excuse.

As I strode confidently towards the exit, some fella leaned in and whispered, 'Looks like they've been tipped off. If you've got anything, you might want to get rid.'

'Nah,' I said. 'I'm not carrying anything mate. Nothing to worry about.' He nodded and walked on ahead of me.

I had a rucksack slung over my shoulder, so naturally I was stopped. Thinking I had nothing to hide I willingly surrendered it to the security guard and was horrified when he pulled out a fistful of sparkplugs.

I knew right away that I had been set up. I was furious, but my protests fell on deaf ears. As I was marched back into the plant I spotted Jimmy coming the other way. He was grinning, and I interpreted that to mean he'd been the one who'd set me up. I lunged at him.

I got nowhere near him, though, and I'm glad of that really. I now know he had nothing to do with it, but for many years I was convinced he'd cost me my livelihood.

As I sat in the hospital ward, looking at Jimmy, a ghost of the man I had fought for years in the 1970s and avoided thereafter, I instantly regretted all of it. It had all been such a waste, all so pointless.

So I was in no mood to have it dragged up now. Not while he was lying in a hospital bed.

'Let's not go there, my old mate,' I said with a wink, adding, 'Or I might change my mind.'

We just brushed past it and moved on to his adventure on foreign shores, back in 1970. There was no one happier than Jimmy to relive that journey.

He told me that he had gone to Germany to see Everton take on Borussia Mönchengladbach, in October 1970. Experiences like this are priceless. They're what following your team is all about. I hope you all get to tell your kids and grandkids tales like this, someday.

Here it is, just as he told it to me.

2

After clinching the championship the season before, Everton had English football at their feet. They were a young side, playing some of the best football in the country.

They had four players in the England squad and all of Fleet Street seemed obsessed with the famous 'trinity' of Kendall, Harvey and Ball. Evertonians knew that they had a team of 11, not just three players, but few would argue that the trio had not been hugely influential.

There had been talk of Everton becoming the team of the 70s. However, the promised new era of domination didn't survive first contact with the enemy, and the Blues would struggle to get their 1970/71 season going.

In the league they laboured in mid-table. Fortunately, though, the cup competitions offered a little respite. Everton would later progress to the semi-final of the FA Cup, and in Europe they reached the quarter-finals of the continent's elite competition.

As the tournament got underway, most people would have agreed that Everton and Mönchengladbach were the two best sides in Europe that year. The German side boasted the likes of Berti Vogts and Juppe Heynkes, players who oozed class and would go on to have stellar careers.

If there was one side Everton wanted to avoid, after they had dumped out Icelandic champions Keflavik 9-2 on aggregate, it was the German outfit. That meant it was an absolute certainty that they would get them.

They did, of course, and to makes things worse their opponents had just dispatched Cypriot side Larnaca 16-0 over two legs. If Everton were going to conquer Europe, they would have to get past a team that was defensively ruthless and utterly lethal up front.

The first leg meant a trip to Germany, which offered some comfort. Most Evertonians were confident that if they could get any kind of result away from home, Goodison would be an absolute bear pit in the return leg.

Today, Anfield is famed for its European nights, and rightly so, but back in the 60s and 70s the ground on the other side of the park could generate one of the most intimidating atmospheres in English football. All the Blues needed to do, they reasoned, was contain the Germans on their own turf and Goodison and the 'trinity' would do the rest.

Jimmy was one of the Blues who made the trip out there. He would go with two of his mates, one of whom was a Red. Shawn Kelly was an Irish lad from the Scotland Road area of the city. Making up the trio was an old school-mate, Davey Mills. It turned out to be a memorable trip for so many reasons.

Shawn Kelly was an interesting character. Despite being a Liverpool fan from a family of staunch Reds, he had jumped at the chance of a European away day, despite it being with Everton. He was a bit of a scally, always in bother and from the type of family you wouldn't want to cross if you could help it.

There were rumours that they had links to the IRA and all sorts of stuff like that. The Kellys could have put those stories out there themselves, though. The Scotland Road area could be a tough place to live, and a reputation for being from a hard family did you no harm at all.

Scotty Road had another side, too. It was also a great community and a fertile ground for poets, writers and musicians.

Davey, or 'young Davey' as he was known, even though he was the same age as Jimmy and only a year younger than Shawn, was a quiet lad with a passion for photography. He was a devout Evertonian and followed them home and away.

Young Davey worked for the council and he had a sister who worked in the ticket office at Goodison. When the draw for the next round of the European Cup was made he'd sorted the three lads out with a ticket. All that remained was the small question of getting over to Germany.

They thought about driving over there in Kelly's dad's van, then taking a boat ride from Dover over to the continent. Shawn's father was a builder, but he was off on the sick and still had the firm's motor parked up outside the house. In the end none of them fancied the long drive and they decided to book flights out of Speke Airport.

It was the first time any of them had left the country and the thought of the journey was as exciting as the game. Jimmy and Davey hadn't realised that Shawn had a very peculiar habit on away trips.

Everywhere he went, he would carry this bloody big bell with him. Apparently, he'd smuggled it into loads of grounds and when Liverpool scored he would attempt to get on the pitch and ring it. I kid you not.

The story he told was that his father was a merchant seaman during the war, in the battle for the Atlantic, and that he had survived being sunk by a German U-boat. When he was rescued, all he had on him were the clothes on his back and this bloody bell, which he'd rescued from the wreckage.

That was the story he told. The truth was a little less heroic but no less dramatic. He had lifted the bell off the bar in the Lusitania Pub on the Dock Road. It was no more than an ornament and had never once been to sea.

He had been in the Lusitania one afternoon. There couldn't have been more than a handful of people in there with him when they heard screams from the street outside. He stood up to see what was going on when there was an almighty smash and a wagon came crashing through the front of the pub. Miraculously nobody was hurt, and it had been a blessing that the place had been so empty at the time.

Mind you, by the time the police and fire crews arrived, it seemed like half the city was in there, rolling around in the dirt and rubble. People had run from nearby establishments and even passers-by joined in. The city's accident solicitors must have done a roaring trade after that episode.

Shawn had taken his share of the compensation on offer. He'd also grabbed the bell from the bar and shoved it under his jacket. If you asked him today, I'm not sure he'd be able to tell you why. It was just there, and he wanted it.

When Davey and Jimmy called at Shawn's house on the morning of the trip they couldn't believe their eyes, as he answered the door with that thing in his hand. Jimmy was the first to bite.

'Where the fucking hell are you going with that?' he asked, not knowing whether it was a wind-up.

'You can't bring that with us,' said Davey, joining in. 'They'll never let you in the stadium with it, never mind on the plane.'

In them days, stadia around England had started pinning up posters at turnstiles with a list of prohibited items on them. They would include the usual stuff: darts, knives, etc. I'd never seen a ship's bell on one of those notices, but Davey had a point.

'They can fucking try stopping me,' he replied, defiantly.

Neither Jimmy nor Davey were brave enough to argue, so they just swallowed their objections and headed for the airport. They had booked a day trip, which meant they would be in and out of Düsseldorf on the same day.

Nevertheless, it would be more than enough time for them to leave their mark on the town. They had an impact on the game, too.

Jimmy spent most of the ride to Speke worrying about whether they would even be allowed on the plane. To his amazement nobody said a word to them. It was already packed with supporters making the journey to Germany; one of them had a guitar and another had a banner on two poles that read 'EVERTON FC THE GEAR'.

Suddenly a relatively small bell didn't seem that big a deal. They took their seats and Jimmy finally relaxed. It was happening. They were going to Germany to watch the Blues.

Davey was clutching his camera. Earlier he had been taking snaps of fans as they milled around the airport and he was at it again on the plane. Jimmy laughed at him doing his 'boy reporter' bit. 'What are you going to do with all these pictures anyway, soft lad?'

'Memories, isn't it,' Davey replied. 'Besides, you never know: if I get some decent pictures, the *Echo* might buy them.'

He was serious. Davey had harboured ambitions to be a press photographer, and if he could have afforded to, he would have studied journalism at university. Sadly, he needed to work for a living.

Shawn and Jimmy sniggered. 'Don't you think the *Echo* will have their own people out there?' mocked Shawn.

'Suppose so. But they're not as good as me, are they?' came the reply. There really was no answer to that.

The three of them flew into Düsseldorf Airport at around midday local time. That left several hours to kill before kick-off, meaning an inevitable exploration of the local hospitality.

The area had a large military barracks and a significant number of the English servicemen were turning out to support Everton. The area was full of off-duty servicemen and there were English accents all around.

Newspapers would later run photographs of the Everton team posing in front of and on top of tanks. Gleeful English servicemen mobbed the team and the mood among the players and the supporters couldn't have been better.

The army was stationed in West Germany, along with their American counterparts, to deter a Soviet invasion of western Europe. Over the years, I suppose they managed to do that. But, on 21 October 1970, in front of almost 30,000 people in the Bökelbergstadion, they were utterly powerless to prevent the most bizarre Anglo-Irish pitch invasion from taking place.

Before kick-off the lads entertained themselves by sampling the very best that Düsseldorf's breweries had to offer. However, before they could drink a single drop of the local beer, Jimmy had a mission to complete. It would see the trio patrolling the various shops along the high street looking for a gift for Eve.

He was conscious of the need to bring something back to Liverpool. Marie wouldn't expect anything, but if he came home with a present for the little one, any grief he had earned by taking the trip would soon be forgotten.

They wandered in and out of various shops before they came across what looked like a toy store. As they barged in, Jimmy, wearing a big blue and white rosette and matching hat, Shawn, carrying his bell and Davey pointing his camera in all directions, they startled an older-looking woman who had been, up to that point, sat behind the counter smoking a cigarette and looking bored to death.

They nodded towards her and immediately started browsing. The click and whirr of Davey's camera filled the air, as he photographed every angle. He was a prolific snapper and his ambition had been to photograph every football ground in the country. He was delighted to add Europe to his already extensive collection.

Jimmy and Shawn went about picking up every item in the shop, searching for the price. The woman must have got very nervous, because she shouted for someone in the back of the store. A burly-looking man emerged from a doorway behind the counter. Jimmy assumed it was her husband, as the man placed a reassuring hand on her shoulder and muttered something calming in her ear.

As far as the lads were concerned there was no need for any drama; they were just there to buy a toy for Jimmy's daughter, after all.

Shawn was holding a huge porcelain doll in one hand, and still had the ridiculous bell in the other. He shouted across the store to Jimmy in his broad Northern Irish accent,

'Here you go, Jim. This'll do you.'

The lady had disappeared into the back of the shop, leaving her husband to deal with the 'problem'. He showed none of his wife's nervousness.

'Can I help you, gentleman,' he said in flawless English. 'You like the doll?'

'Yeah, it's for my daughter,' explained Jimmy.

'That is good. I was just thinking that was a strange purchase for a football supporter, yes?'

Jimmy and Shawn laughed, a little embarrassed. Jimmy wandered over to the counter to discuss the price. He had changed some money at home but had no real idea of exchange rates. Fortunately, this guy had no intention of capitalising on his customer's vulnerability.

The atmosphere was friendly and jovial, and eventually even Mrs Shopkeeper came back out to join in. Davey wasn't so happy with proceedings, though. He was busy muttering to himself in the corner of the shop.

As far as he was concerned, they had just made getting into the ground even more complicated. Not only did they have to negotiate their way into a German football stadium with a 'ship's-fucking-bell', as he put it, they now had a 'giant scary-arsed-doll' to smuggle in, too.

They left the store, Shawn walking out in front, ringing his ridiculous bell, Jimmy clutching his new purchase and Davey still moaning.

'What's the matter with you?' said Jimmy, angrily.

'What do you think?' Davey replied, attempting to whisper, but not doing a very good job. 'It's bad enough soft lad there brought the fucking bell from the Titanic or whatever it is. Now you got that horrible fucking thing.'

Jimmy laughed. 'I'll tell you what, la, you are one miserable git, you.

'I've seen fellas going into grounds with huge flags and banners, never mind darts and other stuff. It's hardly an offensive weapon, is it.'

'Well it's offending me like.' Davey knew he was getting nowhere and just muttered something else under his breath, before going quiet.

In fairness, he had a point about that doll. Eve still has it, and one day, years later, when our two families got together for a summer barbeque, she brought it down from the attic. All I will say is that it wouldn't have looked out of place in a horror film.

Shawn had heard Davey's whining and stopped ringing the bell. He wandered back to the pair and placed an arm around Davey's shoulder, saying, 'Come on lad. What you need is a beer.' With that they all went off in search of a German boozer.

They would find that the drinking culture in Germany was very different to the one back in Liverpool, where standing at the bar all night was commonplace. Here, people went to the pub for food and conversation as much as for beer.

The three of them stumbled across a bar, down a side street off the main road. A group of Everton fans were standing around a couple of small tables in the street. You could have easily missed the place, had those Blues not been there with their giant glasses of beer in hand and puffing away on their ciggies.

The trio went inside and found the main bar area down a flight of steps, which led into a spacious room that looked more like a restaurant than any pub they had ever seen. The construction reminded Jimmy of the Cavern back home, with the place divided into sections and separated by big stone archways.

On the back wall there were giant beer barrels stacked up, one on top of the other. All around them, the sound of what the lads would refer to as 'umpah' music filled the air. It rose above the chatter of families gathered around the tables and the clink of glasses.

This was a world away from Liverpool. It felt relaxed and comfortable and Jimmy thought it would be easy to forget all his worries and continue to soak up that mood forever.

To their left, was a long bar with plenty of activity going on behind it. However, it didn't look like anyone was serving and there were no customers waiting there. The staff were busy enough like, running around filling huge glasses with amber and dark liquids.

They made sure each one had a giant head of froth on top, before loading them on to trays, for men and women in traditional German wear to ferry them to their destinations. Jimmy marvelled at the improbable loads they were carrying. Even the daintiest of female staff would carry up to nine steins on one of those trays, in one hand. Not a drop was spilled.

Shawn spotted someone he knew sat at one of the tables. He shouted and waved, before making a beeline for him. Jimmy and Davey followed in his wake.

A group of supporters, who had obviously been there since very early, had ensconced themselves around a bench littered with empties and huge slabs of what appeared to be salted bread. The lads seemed happy to see Shawn.

'What the fuck is a Red doing over here? Shouldn't you be at Anfield watching your own team? Or, have you converted?' shouted a lad in a white shirt and giant rosette pinned to the front of it.

'Aye that'll be the day,' said Shawn, before adding. 'How the fuck does a man get a drink in here?'

On the table next to them a family were enjoying a meal and a woman looked up to see what the commotion was. She gestured towards a passing waiter and Jimmy thought they were about to be thrown out.

Instead, from behind them, a couple more waiters appeared, one carrying a small table and the others some chairs. They gestured to the men to take a seat before disappearing behind the bar.

'Shawn!' shouted another Blue, who had a huge tankard in front of him. 'Tell you what lad, it's not easy. If you're not careful you can sober up between pints.' There were nods of agreement all around the table.

'We've been here hours,' said another lad, 'and we've only had three pints.'

Shawn looked horrified. 'Jesus you're joking, aren't you?'

Jimmy told me that the beers looked much bigger than the pints we got here in Liverpool. He would also testify to the strength of the stuff compared to the average beer back home. He said they were lucky the service was slow, otherwise they'd have been carried out of the place on a stretcher.

Another waiter appeared next to them, took a notebook from his pocket and said 'Drie bier gentleman, yes?'

The three lads looked at each other, puzzled. Jimmy said he hadn't a clue what the fella had said to him and had looked to Davey for help.

His mate had no idea either, but he'd developed a reputation of being the brains of the outfit and didn't want to disappoint. So, speaking with a confidence that belied his complete terror, he declared boldly,

'Erm, no mate. We want three beers, please.'

The man erupted in laughter and said, 'And for your friend?' He was pointing at the doll in Jimmy's lap.

Jimmy started to protest. 'It's for my little girl,' he said. It was no good, though, and the waiter walked off laughing without bothering to listen.

The beers arrived eventually and they got stuck straight in. Soon all were very merry indeed, the whole group becoming increasingly noisy with every passing round.

Families around them began to leave and that's when the singing started. They went through the full repertoire, starting with an old favourite:

> 'Hail, Hail, The Everton are here,
> What the hell do we care,
> What the hell do we care,
> Hail, Hail, The Everton are here,
> What the hell do we care now ...
> For it's a Grand Old Team to play for,
> For it's a Grand Old Team to see,

And if you know the history,
It's enough to make your heart go
Wooooooaaaaaarrrrrr!!
We don't care what the Redshite say,
What the fuck do we care,
For we all know,
That there's going to be a show,
When the Everton boys are there.'

They moved through the songbook and as kick-off approached, it was time to attempt those stairs and venture into the street again. It was then, as he ascended the stairs with wobbly legs, that Jimmy realised that the beer they had been drinking was a lot more potent than any of them were used to.

The air outside was cool and it had started to go dark. It was a decent walk to the stadium, which was a relief in some ways, as they needed that time to sober up. A good few Everton fans had joined them now and soon a huge procession of blue and white-clad Scousers were marching through the town, singing as they went.

'We shall not, we shall not be moved
We shall not, we shall not be moved
Just like the team that's going to win the European Cup
We shall not, we shall not be moved.'

Flags and banners were everywhere. Jimmy's heart filled with pride. He was convinced that no foe, no matter how mighty, could stop this Everton team or its fans.

3

It turned out that all of Davey's worst fears were groundless. Stadium security was surprisingly lax. There were no searches and the police displayed a casual indifference as the lads marched towards the turnstiles.

One after the other they pushed through the barrier, flashing their tickets and then they were in. Jimmy got a rush of excitement as he entered the stadium concourse, his ticket still intact, after the man on the turnstile had simply waved him through without inspecting it. He didn't care, though. So long as he got to see the game it didn't matter. The end they were in was packed with a mix of Everton supporters and British army personnel. Some of them were in uniform.

The ground was smaller than Goodison and probably held about 30,000 supporters. Still, the atmosphere seemed intense. The crowd was close to the pitch, with only a minimal track separating the stands from the turf. The terracing behind each goal was uncovered, and in the four corners giant floodlight pylons stretched into the night sky, bathing the pitch in their white glow.

The Mönchengladbach fans had unfurled giant flags and banners in their end. Their slogans meant little to him. However, he understood they were passionate fans who loved their club and he could get behind that. European nights were magical, and he never wanted this one to end.

The first half seemed to go by in a whirlwind from Jimmy's perspective. Everton had held their own. However, this was class opposition and he hadn't been surprised when on 35 minutes Berti Vogts put the Germans a goal up.

There was no panic, though. Even a 1-0 defeat away from home was recoverable, as far as Evertonians were concerned. A hostile and ferocious night at Goodison would see to that. At half-time the three lads discussed tactics for the second half, and both Jimmy and Davey were in confident mood.

Shawn, meanwhile, couldn't care less. While he didn't particularly want Everton to lose, he was along for the ride. The sight of that lush green grass, bathed in artificial light, excited him and he longed for the chance to get out there and become centre stage.

Kelly was a serial pitch invader for Liverpool. He loved the thrill of it, being chased by the police and the cheers from the crowd. Sometimes they'd be booing, but in his head they were really roaring him on. The second half would provide him with just the opportunity he needed, and without ever planning to be, Davey and Jimmy would be dragged along with him.

During the first half the lads had been quite a way back from pitch side, but as supporters drifted back to the concourse at the interval, they took the opportunity to manoeuvre their way to the front. It was all part of Shawn's masterplan, but Jimmy claimed he and Davey had no idea.

Within two minutes of the restart Everton had levelled, thanks to a brilliant strike from distance by Howard Kendall. The Blues in the away end erupted, and the crowd surged forward. Their team had secured a vital goal away from home. Suddenly Shawn was away and over the low wall in front of the terrace.

Without a second thought, Davey, camera swinging around his neck, and Jimmy screaming at the top of his lungs and waving his arms about frantically, were right behind him. It wasn't until the Irishman was near the centre circle and swinging his bell for dear life that the other two realised what they had done, so caught up in the moment were they.

Panic quickly set in and Jimmy was expecting to be tackled to the ground at any minute. Instead, at first, it seemed like nobody was bothered. He told me much later that the only thought going through his mind at that point was, 'okay, I'm here, what do I do next?'

He looked across at Davey, who was stood near the penalty spot, and shrugged. The Everton players were still celebrating and the Germans were just milling about with their heads bowed. Had nobody seen them enter the pitch, really?

They just stood there frozen, for what seemed like an age. Davey would later describe an almost out-of-body experience, in which he was watching the chaos ensue from a distance as time passed incredibly slowly. He could see Shawn dancing in the centre circle and clanging that bell, and it was as if nobody else in the stadium had noticed the three of them on the pitch at all.

Amid it all, Davey just lifted his camera and started taking pictures. Of course, they had been spotted. It just seemed that stadium security in Germany had a very different view of pitch invaders than the ones at Wembley.

Eventually someone did arrive, as the referee was beginning to restore order on the field of play. The ball had returned to the centre circle and the three of them were just gently escorted back to their place in the away end, no drama, no fuss.

All around them fellow Blues were laughing hysterically and patting them on the back. A legend had been created and images seared into the minds of everyone who had witnessed that goal and the antics of two Blues and a Red.

That's why European football is so special. Yes, the results are important, and getting to finals and winning them is the ultimate destination, but the journey is always worth it, whether you return with the trophy or not.

Scousers of both persuasions have embarked on countless foreign adventures with their teams over the decades. The stories they bring back enrich our history. They cement the love we feel for our clubs every bit as much as the silverware we win.

In Germany, Everton would hang on for the draw, and the chance to make history back at Goodison. That game would also finish one-a-piece and would set up the first ever penalty shoot-out in European football history.

Prior to 1970, European games that could not be settled after extra time, were won or lost on the toss of a coin. UEFA ended that practice at the start of the new decade and the Blues were the first team ever to win a shoot-out.

The Blues would ultimately crash out of the competition, after defeat to the Greek champions, Panathinaikos in the quarter-finals. However, as Jimmy recounted that trip to Germany there was not a hint of sadness. To him it is a treasured memory, despite the disappointment that would follow, and rightly so.

4

The second leg had got off to the best possible start for the Everton. Johnny Morrissey had put them a goal up inside the first minute.

Goodison was a swaying, seething mass of humanity and the decibel count must have been in the stratosphere when the ball hit the net.

However, it took little more than half an hour for the Germans to silence the old ground, thanks to an equaliser by their striker Herbert Laumen. What followed was a tense affair. Both sides went for it and it was all-out attack against resolute defence.

Each team's keeper would pull off spectacular saves. In the end, it was stalemate. Only that historic penalty shoot-out could separate them.

Jimmy told me that the tension had been unbearable. He had never felt so nervous at a football match.

His reasoning was that if you lost after a coin toss, it would hurt, but there was no shame in that. Defeat after missing a penalty, however ... well that was a different thing altogether.

I could see what he meant, sort of. The lottery of the coin toss meant that nobody was to blame, really. Maybe God, if you believed in that sort of thing. Although if there is a God, I can't imagine he's too bothered about the result of a match between Everton and Borussia Mönchengladbach.

Losing because one of your heroes messed up from the spot, however, that's tough to take. That fate almost befell a young Joe Royle. He would, of course, go on to become an Everton legend, but on 4 November 1970 he would become the first ever footballer to miss a penalty in a shoot-out.

As the keeper saved his low effort to the right, there was absolute despair among Blues. It had seemed as if their dreams were slipping from their grasp. Royle had trudged back to join his team-mates, carrying the weight of the world and the dreams of his followers on youthful shoulders.

Klaus-Dieter Sieloff then scored for the Germans, putting them a goal up in the shoot-out. All seemed to be going against the men in blue. Then a miracle happened. There was a reprieve. Mönchengladbach's hero, the man who had levelled on the night, Laumen, missed his penalty.

Once more Goodison exploded, as the German looked disconsolate. It was game back on.

Everton took full advantage and wouldn't make another mistake that night. Alan Ball, Johnny Morrissey and Howard Kendall would all confidently tuck away their spot-kicks.

It was the footballing equivalent of match point and you could cut through the nervous expectation with a knife. In the away end the Germans prayed. Among the home support a great pressure valve was about to be released and pandemonium would ensue.

Up stepped a leggy-looking Ludwig Müller for Mönchengladbach. In goal for Everton was Andy Rankin. He had deputised for Gordon West, who was out injured. It had caused a few nerves before the tie, but all doubts were erased when the youngster dived to save low to his right. The Blues were through.

Scenes of wild celebration greeted his heroics on and off the pitch. Everton were in the quarter-finals. Their league form might have dipped, but this result would put the club on a much bigger stage. They had beaten quality opposition and now all of Europe would have to sit up and take notice.

It was a great moment in Merseyside football history, and as Jimmy finished his tale he slumped back on his pillow, exhausted. I was wishing I had taken in a tape recorder or a notebook. Instead I had to write up the conversation when I got home later.

Chapter Twelve

Silent Knights at Anfield and FA Cup Delights at Old Trafford

1

In the 50 years since the restoration of the Merseyside derby in 1962, many games could lay claim to be the greatest ever. In my view, though, you would have to go a long way to better the one fought at Anfield, on 21 November 1970, just 17 days after Everton's historic shoot-out against Mönchengladbach.

Of course, the Blues would pick a different one. Your allegiance, as well as the scoreline, always determines the choice. However, even the most myopic of Evertonians would not deny the sheer drama of that encounter.

This game would be our Joe's first game. He'd have been around eight years old. Sadly, he remembers little of the action, but his position in the Paddock (what we now call the Main Stand) afforded him a jaw-dropping view of the greatest terrace in world football: the Kop.

These days the Kop is still a magical sight on the big occasions: European nights, against Manchester United, and of course the derby. Back then it was a spectacle no matter what the occasion. The colour, the sound and the motion of the thing was simply awe-inspiring.

Observing the Kop throughout the 70s had a mesmeric effect on my son. There were no song sheets or conductors. All it took was a fella or group of mates to get something going and in no time at all it would take on a life of its own. It was magic. It really was. Simply remembering it sends shivers through my body.

I've never been one to bemoan the modern phenomena of Liverpool supporters from outside our city coming to Anfield. I've always had an internationalist outlook in life. But the Kop was undeniably Scouse back then. You could hear the accent in the songs. That's not me complaining or saying you should live in Liverpool if you want to support the team. It's just how I remember it. In any case, to my mind, to be Scouse is to be a citizen of the world anyway.

The city's population is a mongrel one, and proudly so. We have the oldest Chinese community in Europe, the first mosque in Britain was built here and our accent would be Lancastrian if it wasn't for the influx of Irish immigrants.

Indeed, the very dish that gave us our name, Scouse, is a northern European or Scandinavian concoction, brought to us by sailors and lapped up by the working class and the poor. How, then, can we complain when our gloriously historic city, with its mysterious birds and equally mythical football club, attracts followers from across the globe. It always has.

We had a slogan back then. It became a badge sewn on to denim jackets. It read, 'Supporters All Over The World'. I was always proud of that and I still am. However, back then the accent of the Kop was important. To be Scouse meant to be witty, anarchic and original.

The Kop has evolved. That's not a bad thing. Nor is it wrong to feel moved by and proud of the community and culture that gave birth to a global institution, as I do.

As I stood next to Joe that day my heart was bursting with pride. I felt I had passed the torch to the next generation. I sensed it as I walked up Walton Breck Road with him. I was even more convinced when I saw the look of wonder on his little face, as he stared at that huge terrace.

Those feelings, written so clearly in his eyes and by his open mouth, would live with him for the rest of his life. It would be the same for any Blue who attended their first game at Goodison or sampled the heart-pounding tension and soaring ecstasy of a Merseyside derby. Once you're in, you're in, and there's no turning back.

I've since learned that young Eve was at that game too, with her mum and dad. We never saw each other, but I'm sure the experience was the same for her. Despite being on the losing side, she would have watched her parent's reactions, heard the Everton fans singing and sensed their passion. She'd also become hooked for life.

That's football. Its appeal goes beyond notions of success and silverware. If it was all about that, well, 99 per cent of football supporters would give up. They don't, because again it's as much about the journey as it is the destination.

Football is about belonging; it's about shared stories and common purpose. You keep going through the bleak times because in the end these are your people, whether they're on the pitch or in the stands. You win together, and you lose together.

In my life, there are people and things that mean more to me than football. My wife, my kids and my beliefs and values, to name a few. But my sense of community and my belief in the power of collective effort, of fairness and hard work, owe their origins as much to the Kop as to anything else.

I know that's the case for Evertonians, too, and the thing that bothers me most about the way our rivalry has evolved is the feeling I get now that some of us have started viewing the other as something different. I don't remember having that sense of 'otherness' in the old days.

We stood together in derby matches and yes, like any family, we fell out, argued and even fought. We may have thought our team was superior to the other, but we never viewed ourselves as better than them. We were Scousers, who just happened to be Red or Blue.

It was like that in the Paddock, as I stood next to my son flanked by Reds and Blues. In the top right-hand corner of the Kop, I could see a dense pocket of Everton supporters, stood together and attempting to out-sing tens of thousands of Kopites. There were smatterings of Blues all around the stadium and it felt the most natural thing in the world.

I wanted us to beat them and do it in style. Not because I hated them, but because I wanted Joe to see us do it and be able to hold his own in the playground. I wanted the win for Shanks and, most of all, I wanted to walk into work on Monday and rub their noses in it. They wanted the win for much the same reasons. That was okay by me.

I thought we had a real chance of upsetting them, too. Everton were having a bad season in the league. We were still building. The distance in terms of points between us wasn't that great either.

They had the more experienced side, and they'd taken the league by storm the season before. So, we respected them. There was no fear, though. Shankly always made us feel we shouldn't be afraid of anyone.

The Scot was creating something special. You could sense it. Gone were St John and Hunt, Lawrence and Yeats. The men who had served him with distinction and were still living legends to the supporters had been moved aside. Shankly would not let sentiment stand in the way of his relentless pursuit of glory.

In their place we now had Clemence and Hughes, Smith and Lawler. Add to those a young Steve Heighway and John Toshack. We had the spine of a team that was going places.

We couldn't have possibly known this back then, but these were men who would go on to write new chapters in the story of the club. Three of them, Steve Heighway, John Toshack and Chris Lawler would have a defining impact on this, the 103rd Merseyside derby, too. In doing so, they'd create one of the most magical derby memories in the history of the fixture.

The first half was carnage. Tackles flew in and players went down on both sides.

One report suggested there were 21 fouls apiece in the opening 45 minutes, and the referee ignored a few, too. The players looked edgy and were so afraid of making a mistake or conceding ground that they simply allowed the game to descend into open warfare.

I remember reading one column that said something like, 'both teams played as if the stands were full of snipers'. It was a decent description, and nobody was being entertained.

As both sets of players headed for the tunnel at half-time, the whole ground started chanting 'We want football, we want football.'

Joe looked up at me and asked, 'What do they mean, Dad?' His eyes were wide and innocent and he was too young to appreciate that what he had just witnessed wasn't normal fare. I smiled at him and replied,

'I suppose they want to see the players kick the ball and not each other, son. If it carries on like this, we'll be playing five-a-side.' He nodded, and I think he understood.

In the second half it was like watching a different fixture altogether. Both managers must have got into their players, because when they came out they immediately remembered they were footballers, not boxers.

Liverpool went on the attack, running towards the Kop end, which in no time had become a pulsating and feverish pit of emotion and noise. As I looked over, it seemed to be busting at the seams and I noticed there were people spilling out at the front and fainting. St John Ambulance crews rushed to their aid and it seemed like there was a procession of stretchers parading along the side of the pitch, directly in front of us.

Meanwhile, the sight of supporters being passed from the back of the terrace to the front, over the heads of fellow Kopites, made me realise that it must have been incredibly uncomfortable in there. I was glad I hadn't taken my son there.

Then disaster struck. It was like a thunderbolt, or a great tidal wave that sucked the life out of you and left you breathless on the ground. Everton went 1-0 up.

The sight of Evertonians celebrating all around the ground was like an arrow through the heart. Joe was staring in amazement at the sight of people celebrating as Liverpool went a goal behind. I could tell he was confused and conflicted.

We were only ten minutes or so into the second half and Johnny Morrissey had robbed Tommy Smith in the middle of the park and whipped it out to Alan Whittle on the wing. As he closed in on goal, we could see Clemence was way off his line. One lad near me shouted at him to get back. Of course, he didn't.

To be fair Whittle's goal was an act of sublime genius. He just chipped the ball over our keeper and into the net. It was a heartbreaker, but things were about to get a whole lot worse.

Within ten minutes Everton were two up and hopes of creating happy matchday memories for Joe were fading fast. Instead there was a risk this could become a complete rout.

The language from supporters nearby would make your hair curl. I gave Joe a sideways glance. I wanted him to know I had heard it, and that I disapproved. He saw me, but I could see he was pretending not to. He couldn't hide the smirk on his face either and I laughed to myself.

It was a temporary respite from the gloom. I felt like screaming all manner of obscenities. If I hadn't had my son with me, I would have. I just couldn't believe it was happening.

Their goal was another great piece of football. Alan Ball had fed Morrissey, who was giving the Reds' defence a torrid time. He dribbled past about three of our players, with the Kop screaming for someone to take him out. Then he chipped the ball on to the head of Joe Royle, who nodded it home.

It was a catastrophe for us and the Blues were jubilant. We were staring down the barrel of a humiliating defeat. This wasn't how I wanted Joe's first game to end.

I looked down at him and noticed he was crying. It broke my heart. I knew he supported the Reds. I hadn't given him much choice in the matter but I had no idea he cared this much. Putting an arm around his shoulder I leaned down to whisper some soothing words in his ear. I didn't get the chance, because he shrugged me off, wiped his eyes with the sleeve of his shirt and said, 'Dad, no!'

His tone was a mixture of anger and embarrassment. I smiled. This kid would be alright, I thought. He didn't need me to tell him it would be okay, and he understood that football was sometimes about losing with dignity.

Suddenly, he shouted 'Come on Liverpool!' His voice was tiny and high-pitched, and it took me by surprise. I still hear it now and it brings a lump to my throat and a tear to my eye. It will never leave me. He was completely immersed in the atmosphere now. Yes, he was down, but he was refusing to accept it was over and he seemed determined to do his bit to turn it around.

How could it be over? We had Shankly, we had Anfield and the Kop. He'd heard so many legends about this place, mostly from me. How could he lay down and cry, just because we were two goals down?

I didn't have time to feel proud in the moment, because the Kop seemed to roar into life as the ball was placed into the centre circle. The noise was colossal, and I know it can't be true, but I'm convinced I saw the Liverpool players physically grow in front of me.

In the Paddock, we all joined in and the noise was unbelievable. The official attendance was 53,000. You wouldn't have heard a louder cry at Wembley with 100,000 watching.

The effect was almost immediate. Tommy Smith, who had been partly complicit in Everton's first goal, hit a long pass to the left. Steve Heighway picked up the ball and raced down the wing, before cutting inside. The angle was tight, but he didn't need much encouragement, and would unleash an incredible shot that flew straight in.

The Reds had merely pulled a goal back, but you'd have thought we'd won the game, such was the roar. It felt like Anfield lifted from its foundations and crashed back into the ground. The Everton supporters had gone quiet but we were in party mood.

There was a full 20 minutes left and, as far as we were concerned, anything could happen now. The next goal would be pivotal. When it came, it would be delivered by one of Shankly's new boys.

John Toshack had only joined the club ten days earlier. He had cost Shankly £110,000 and he was about to repay every penny of that, with interest on top. His equaliser was an incredible trademark header, but again the plaudits go to the youngster, Steve Heighway.

His fine footwork and pace on the wing had the Blues on the run. Suddenly he was free in space and lobbed the ball into the box. Toshack mopped it up with aplomb and, incredibly, the Reds were level. The Kop exploded. They could sense blood and I'm sure the Blues inside the ground could, too.

Football can do that. Belief does that. A team can be out on their feet. The odds may be impossibly stacked against you, but the slightest glimmer of hope can transform the seemingly vanquished into victors and vice versa. That's happened so many times at Anfield it has become a virtue.

If the game had ended right there, we'd have all gone home entertained. Everton fans would have felt relieved and we would have been furious that we'd not finished them off. Fortunately for us, Liverpool had no intentions of taking it easy on their rivals.

Joe was absolutely loving it by this stage and I'm certain he felt he'd played his part in the turnaround. After all, he had refused to accept the arm of consolation and had roared his team on when all seemed lost. His initiation was almost complete. Almost.

With just five minutes left, Liverpool hit the winner. The goal capped a remarkable comeback. It would have seemed impossible just 20 minutes earlier, but it would live long in the memory of every Red in the ground.

Again it was Steve Heighway who caused mayhem in the Blues rearguard. This was surely a man-of-the-match performance.

The Kop was swaying and surging. Shouts of 'Liverpool', 'Liverpool', rang out loud into the Anfield air. Heighway picked up the ball and crossed it into the box. Again he found the head of Toshack, who flicked it backwards to Chris Lawler, who had ghosted unnoticed into the box.

Lawler was renowned for appearing in the right place, at the right time, often unseen by opposition defenders. His talent had earned him the nickname 'Silent Knight'.

Time seemed to slow to a complete stop as Toshack rose to head on Heighway's pass. Lawler just seemed to materialise in the penalty area and his foot connected beautifully with the ball. It flew past Andy Rankin, who only a couple of weeks earlier had been Everton's saviour.

As the ball nestled in the back of the net, there was a moment in which nobody could believe what had happened. Then there was an explosion of sound and supporters all around us leapt for joy. The Kop was a tumultuous mass of people, arms flailing and flags waving.

The Everton players looked crushed. All I could focus on was Lawler being mobbed in the goalmouth.

There was a flurry of activity on each bench. Kendall went off for Everton and I remember Phil Boersma coming on for Liverpool. The game was won, though. Everton had nothing left. They had surrendered certain victory, or rather it had been ripped from their grasp.

I picked up Joe, whether he liked it or not, and threw him on to my shoulders. He was screaming with joy. We'd enjoy work and school on Monday morning.

2

Everton's next opportunity for revenge would come on 27 March 1971, at Old Trafford in an FA Cup semi-final. It's hard to put into words how massive this game was. Let me try.

The new decade was well underway and, just as in the last, change was all around us. We were coming to terms with the end of the Beatles and the emergence of their solo careers. George Harrison had just spent five weeks at number one with 'My Sweet

Lord', and Reds everywhere were praying for a second FA Cup final under Bill Shankly.

For Blues, this was an opportunity to salvage a season that had failed to live up to expectations. They had eased past Colchester, with a thumping 5-0 victory in the previous round. A brace from Howard Kendall and one each from Joe Royle, Jimmy Husband and Alan Ball saw them through comfortably.

However, the tie against the Reds would come just three days after they had crashed out of the European Cup to Panathinaikos in the quarter-final. It wasn't the ideal preparation.

The Reds were still competing in the Fairs Cup. They'd got past Bayern Munich and faced a semi-final against eventual winners Leeds United. But any thoughts of a league championship had well and truly faded.

The FA Cup, though, was still the pinnacle of cup competition. I wanted us to win it more than anything else. It felt so close, too. I could almost taste it.

Liverpool's passage to the semi-final came courtesy of a victory over Tottenham Hotspur in a sixth-round replay at White Hart Lane. We were treated to more Steve Heighway brilliance but it was a goalkeeping masterclass by Ray Clemence that sealed the win.

As soon as we realised that both teams were through, everybody in the city was predicting we'd be drawn together in the semi-final. 'Bloody fix' was a common refrain and many of us believed that the Football Association didn't want to see an all-Merseyside cup final.

To be fair, even if we were right and they didn't want us to face off in the 70s, they clearly changed their mind in the 80s, when the two teams met in three finals.

The local press went into overdrive in the run-up to the game. Still, I can't really call it hype. To do that would suggest they were exaggerating the stakes. They couldn't possibly have done that.

Even when one paper declared it the most important derby in the history of the two clubs, you wouldn't find a single supporter of either persuasion who would have disagreed.

Whatever the result, we all knew that one half of the city would experience a world of pain. Defeat in this game, of this magnitude, would mean months of humiliation. School or work could be the best or the worst place on earth, and it all hinged on the result of 90 minutes of football.

There would be no hiding place, anywhere, for the losers. For other teams, the sanctuary of home may offer respite after a chastening defeat to a bitter rival. Not in Liverpool. Here you may have to face a tormentor under your own roof.

The game affected my every waking moment. It even entered my dreams. Sometimes I'd wake elated, then crushed when I realised I'd only imagined the win. On other occasions, I would feel great relief that the crushing defeat I'd just experienced was mere fantasy.

The only thing we could do was busy ourselves with the practicalities. The search for tickets and booking transport was a welcome distraction at times like this. Those who couldn't get to the game faced an agony that I wouldn't wish on my worst enemy. They'd have to listen to it on the radio. Only the final was broadcast live back then, of course.

I could never bear following a game that way. Stupid, I know, but I always felt I was somehow in control if I was at the game. I'm the same today to be honest and, while I'm not a superstitious or religious man, the rituals I have developed around the game still give me comfort and ease the nerves.

In the 70s I would end up with this crazy habit when listening to away games on the wireless. I'd convinced myself that if I listened we would always lose. So I would put myself through agony, before turning it on at full time to learn the result.

That seemed to work for a while, but then inevitably I would tune in, only to find that we were being beaten. Still I tried to keep faith with it and stuck with the habit for the following match. It was killing me, though, and at half-time I couldn't take it anymore.

This game happened to be on a Tuesday night, and Liverpool were facing Mansfield Town in the second round of the League

Cup at Anfield. The first round had finished goalless. We didn't take that competition too seriously as a club back then, but I took every game seriously.

I was pacing around the living room, disturbing Marie as she tried to watch telly. I think she was watching *On the Buses* or something like that. Anyway, she got fed up with me and banished me to the kitchen.

Our radio, which was on the kitchen worktop, was always tuned into 194 Radio City. It was killing me but I resisted the urge to turn it on until half-time. I just couldn't stand the suspense anymore.

As I clicked it on the presenter of *Midweek Match* was recapping the game so far. Liverpool were drawing 1-1. I was shocked.

Turns out the visitors had gone a goal up in the first two minutes but Hughes had levelled on the quarter-hour mark. It had been a tricky tie, it seemed, and I was beginning to regret my decision to switch it on. What if I killed off our comeback by turning on the radio?

My worst fears were confirmed when John Stenson put Mansfield ahead again in the 65th minute. I almost turned it off. Instead, I continued to listen but hurled a half-full cup of tea in the sink in an act of sheer frustration.

The cup broke, and I cursed as I collected the fragments from the stone sink and threw them in the bin. From the living room, I heard Marie shout, 'You alright, Tom?'

She knew I was a nightmare when following the Reds from home, and although she's a supporter herself, she preferred to give me a wide berth and leave me to it. It was probably wise.

Liverpool were facing an embarrassing exit, and it seemed to spur the team and the crowd on. From that moment, every Liverpool attack would see the commentator's voice rise and fall as chances went begging and passes went astray. It was sheer agony and I kicked chairs and door frames as the minutes ticked by.

Then, the tinny and crackly voice on the little box in my kitchen screamed penalty. I punched the air and screamed 'YES!' The door swung open and Marie stepped in. 'What's going on, Tom?'

For a moment, I thought of chasing her back out. After all, she hadn't been there when we won the spot-kick. What if she was a jinx? In the end, I suppressed that ridiculous thought and we listened intently together as Tommy Smith prepared to take it. There were only ten minutes left. We waited, at the mercy of a man who was reporting on a game we couldn't see. The tone and pitch of his voice, and the sound of the crowd in the background, would tell us everything we needed to know.

'Smith steps up. He scores!' Marie and I danced around the kitchen together, laughing.

'Oh, Tommy, have we won it?' She asked.

I realised she'd had no idea of how the game had unfolded.

'No love,' I said. 'It's 2-2. We need another.'

Liverpool pushed, but the game ended level. That meant another 30 minutes. The kitchen door opened again. It was Joe. We'd sent him to bed earlier but he'd heard the commotion and came down to see what was going on.

I couldn't send him back to bed and the three of us sat and listened intently as Alun Evans, Liverpool's young teenage sensation, smashed in the winner in the first period of extra time. It was only the League Cup against Mansfield Town, but I've remembered those moments my whole life.

The way we danced together as a family at full time; the look on Joe's beaming face. He was as happy at being allowed to stay up late as he was about the score.

Joe and I got lucky and secured two tickets for the semi-final. It would cost me the grand total of £1.50.

As far as I was concerned, though, the 30 bob I spent taking our Joe to Old Trafford on 23 March 1971 represented great value for money. It was a game that should have graced Wembley. The atmosphere and the spectacle were everything football should be.

I remember Joe and I being caught up in the crowds outside the ground as the team bus arrived. A great roar went up, and although there were plenty of Blues around us I don't remember any booing or bother of any kind.

Fists punched the air, rattles were spun and chants of 'Liverpool, Liverpool' drifted into the skies above, while the faces of the players stared back at us. Some were lapping it up, while others, like Brian Hall, looked terrified.

Our number 11 would only be in the side because of injuries, and at 20 years of age this would have been the biggest game of his life. The sight of us lot would have hammered that point home and must have heaped huge pressure on the lad. As it turned out he would use that tension and anxiety to good effect in the game.

Inside the ground there was only nominal segregation. No doubt mates and family members, divided only by the colour of the team they supported, would have hunted in packs for tickets and divided the spoils between each other. That meant they'd be stood next to each other in the game.

I don't remember much about the first-half action to be honest. It's like the game comes alive in my mind in that second period. Two moments do stand out for me, though.

The first, of course, is Everton going a goal up. It was a brilliant take by Alan Ball, Everton's maestro. I remember thinking that the Blues had no right to be playing such attractive cultured football in a game riddled with tension and in which the consequences of error were so disastrous.

Liverpool were all blood and thunder, though. The papers after the game would refer to the Reds as Shankly's lions. It was an apt description, because Liverpool immediately hit back.

I remember the ball landing at Callaghan's feet and him blasting it straight into the net. There followed a brief celebration, before we all realised the referee had disallowed it. None of us knew why at the time. When we got home, we'd find out he'd given a handball.

Callaghan had vehemently protested his innocence, and I remember reading hilarious quotes from Tommy Smith on the incident. His argument had gone along the lines of, 'I tell lies, everybody tells lies, but Cally doesn't lie, and if he says he didn't handball it, then he didn't.'

To be honest, that was probably a fair comment. Callaghan was a great player. His consistency over so many years was proof of that. He was also a gentleman and a model footballer. His one booking in 857 appearances is ample evidence of that fact.

At half-time, I wasn't down. I suppose I must have seen enough evidence to suggest we'd get back into the game. The Blues around me had also chewed their fingers down to the elbows, and match reports suggested Liverpool had given the Everton back line a stern test in that opening 45.

Joe was a different story. The thought of his dreams of a trip to Wembley being snatched away were weighing heavily on him. The build-up to the game had ramped up the stakes and his levels of expectation were in the stratosphere. Were we to lose, the resultant comedown would have been devastating.

As the teams kicked off the second half, there were no signs of the action quieting down. The Blues received a blow early on, when Brian Labone limped off injured and was replaced by Sandy Brown. Everton, who had struggled with our attack in the first half, would face a torrid time in the second.

Just ten minutes later, Liverpool were level. Alun Evans scored the goal and the joy among our supporters was unbelievable. The Blues stood silent but the looks on their faces told its own story. I believe, even now, that in that moment they could see the writing on the wall.

It would take another quarter of an hour for the game to be settled. For Joe and me and probably all 60-odd thousand supporters inside the ground, it was the longest 15 minutes of our lives. There was a guy in front of me whose face was puce. God knows what his blood pressure must have been.

With each tick of the clock the significance of a goal by either side grew. The later the strike the less time there was for a comeback. The killer blow for Everton came in the 76th minute.

Alun Evans swept down the wing and launched a brilliant cross into the box. Andy Rankin and John Toshack both jumped for the ball at the same time. It looked to me like Tosh had got to it first and headed it down, but the Blues around me screamed handball. I think some of their players did too.

There was an instant of panic, then the ball was in the net. Then came that sound. I've heard it a thousand times but I never tire of it. It's the noise of tens of thousands of souls united in unbridled joy. It's like they're all screaming 'YES!' at the top of their lungs.

My response was far less coherent. I just remember screaming, mouth agape and eyes bulging. I was rooted to the spot, arms outstretched as a wave of sheer euphoria swept through me. As I turned to look for Joe, who had disappeared in a torrent of celebrating bodies, I noticed him fighting his way through to me.

The look on his face was, well I can't find the words. I'll never forget that. For him, it was birthdays, Easter eggs, Christmas presents and every summer holiday of his little life all wrapped up together and presented to him in an instant. Incomprehensible joy and mind-blowing ecstasy.

If anyone is reading this book, trying to figure out why grown men with jobs and homes and responsibilities get so wound up about the fortunes of 11 men they don't know, then the words you've just read should explain it. It's because of moments like those, the joy on a child's face, the roar of emotion that wells up from somewhere deep inside. It's the memories of all those moments, accumulated over a lifetime that bond us forever with our teams.

It's probably true to say that the remaining moments of the game were fraught and frantic. It may be that we endured an agony of waiting for that final whistle. I remember none of that. All I can recall is the journey home, on the 'special' back to Lime Street, Joe fast asleep with his head on my lap.

I still see the fields and trees whizzing past my window and I'm far away. I'm dreaming of Wembley, of Shankly with his arms outstretched, lapping up the adulation of his people. I see the team holding another FA Cup back in Liverpool.

It wasn't to be, though. A dramatic and ultimately heartbreaking day at Wembley ended our dreams for another season. Charlie

George's winner for Arsenal was bad enough; his celebration, lying on the turf of the national stadium screaming at the heavens, his arms punching the air, like some daft fool, would haunt the dreams of all Reds who saw it.

Back then, though, we were there for Liverpool, win, lose or draw. Shanks could do no wrong and his players were just like us in our eyes. We still turned out in our thousands to welcome the boys home in defeat.

Many of you will have seen the famous, now iconic, image of Shanks on the steps of St George's Hall. His Christ-like pose against a backdrop of thousands of worshippers bears all the hallmarks of an all-conquering leader who has returned from battle carrying the spoils of victory.

Not so. That picture, which adorns the wall in my home still, is of the 1971 homecoming, when the Reds and Shankly had returned from battle empty-handed and bruised. The great man would announce from that platform, on that day, that we shouldn't be too down.

He compared us to a 'Red Army' and said we'd be back again the following year.

As Joe and I trudged away from the Plateau that day, I believed him. We all did. That was the effect he had on us. When Shankly spoke you listened, and if he told you your team would be at Wembley next year, you booked your train ticket.

Of course, we didn't get back to Wembley in 1972, but much more lay ahead. There would be unparalleled glory for Liverpool, and not even a changing of the guard in 1974 could stop the club experiencing arguably the greatest decade in its history.

For the Blues it was a polar-opposite. In all, Liverpool and Everton would meet 23 times in the 1970s, with the men from Goodison triumphant on just three occasions.

The 1980s, of course, would be very different from a Blue perspective. Success on the field would return and with it came a renewed sense of pride and optimism for the future. Merseyside's two great rivals would sweep all before them. It was an unrivalled period of glory on the footballing field, juxtaposed with great tragedy off it.

The city itself would become a brooding symbol of defiance and resistance. Gone was the bravado and swagger of previous decades. The image of the lovable Scouser had now been replaced with portraits of an angry people fighting amid post-industrial squalor and decay.

On the streets and in the council chambers, the people of Liverpool fought the system that brought them so much misery. On the football field and in the terraces, we sought escape from our battles, at least for 90 minutes. We conquered the lot and shared the treasures of battle between ourselves.

We earned respect in some quarters, and hatred in others. That wasn't our concern, though, because through all of it we always had each other.

Liverpool, the city, would develop a sense of otherness that went beyond the cockiness of the 60s and the industrial solidarity of the 70s. We had developed a siege mentality, a sense of us against them. Had someone offered us a referendum, independence from the United Kingdom in the 80s, I'm certain a YES vote would have carried the day.

Before all of that, though, Everton would enjoy one more special day in the sunshine, at Goodison in 1978. It was a day when a King called Andy ended a long dark winter, and sent Liverpool back across the park, licking their wounds. Twenty eight years later, in the same place, another Andy would have a similar impact. Let's talk about that next.

Chapter Thirteen

Tales from a
Scouse Wedding

Part One

The summer of 2006 had finally given way to autumn and I
remember a small group of smart-looking men gathered outside
a Methodist church on Oakfield Road, Anfield. They were pacing
nervously in front of the entrance. A wedding would soon be
underway.

Some drew deeply on cigarettes; others chewed on their
fingernails or gum; while one man, the groom, took a swig of the
strong stuff from a silver flask. His name was Joe Gardener, my
son, and he was about to marry the love of his life, Eve Harrington.

The anxiety on show, though, had little to do with the
impending nuptials. There was no last-minute cold feet, no fear
related to speeches or first dances. Instead, this was a display of
PMT (pre-match tension). It was, after all, a wedding taking place
in the shadow of the Merseyside derby.

Just over a mile away, in about 45 minutes' time at Goodison
Park, a football match would start. Everton and Liverpool would do
battle for the 204th time and around 40,000 people had descended
on the old stadium to cheer on their teams.

This would be the Blues fourth game of the season. Having
beaten Watford and Tottenham and securing a draw away to
Blackburn, David Moyes' men were in confident mood.

At the start of the 2006/07 season, Everton supporters had a new hero. The club had signed Andy Johnson in the summer, from Crystal Palace for the sum of £8.5 million. He'd already weighed in with a couple of goals, and by the end of the day he would achieve legendary status with two more priceless strikes.

David Moyes had become manager of Everton in 2002. Christened the Moysiah, he had immediately delighted Blues and irritated the Reds by asserting that Everton were the 'people's club', claiming that 'most of the people you meet on the city's streets support Everton'.

As his tenure progressed he would also manage to restore some pride to a team that had been struggling prior to his appointment. Moyes led his club to a fourth place finish in 2004, securing qualification for a Champions League qualifier and, as he prepared to do battle with Benítez's Liverpool, his stock was still as high as ever. It would rise to new heights at full time.

For Liverpool supporters, Rafa Benítez was still God. Having steered the club to their first European Cup win since 1984, and adding a Super Cup, FA Cup and Community Shield in his first two seasons on Merseyside, the man could do no wrong. Such was his impact, we'd all forgiven him for losing the League Cup Final to Jose Mourinho's Chelsea in 2005. Some of us had even managed to forget all about it.

The Reds had played an extra game in the run-up to the derby, thanks to their participation in the Champions League qualifying rounds. However, this was a team Liverpool fans had a lot of faith in, put together by a manager who had established a strong bond with the Kop. There could be no excuse for failure, especially as the game had come so early in the season.

Joe's best man was Steve Evans, an old workmate. The pair had met in the early eighties, while Joe was working at Royal Life Insurance, situated in what's now referred to as the commercial district of the city.

They had both joined the company as temps, and, although it paid peanuts, the money supported their two major pastimes, beer and football. Steve was a big Liverpool supporter, in every sense of the word. Weighing in at about 19 stone and with a halo of flame red hair, he was easy to spot, and hard to ignore.

Steve was unbelievably quick-witted and incredibly articulate. He would combine those qualities with an insatiable appetite for beer, football, music and laughter. My greatest memory of Steve is of him standing on a table in a boozer in London. It must have been after one of the many cup finals of the 1980s, and I just have this image of him leading the singing, high above everybody else, with the whole bar joining in, their pints held high in the air.

Sadly, we lost him a few years ago. He was taken from us far too soon, but a character like Steve was never going to fade away into the mundanity of old age. He had burned his candle too fiercely and for too long for that to happen. If ever there was an example of someone extracting every ounce of enjoyment from life, it was Steve.

I would later come to realise that his larger-than-life persona masked an inner sadness, and that he was often plagued with self-doubt. None of us had a clue. Isn't that always the way. I wish I could have one last pint with him, just so I could tell him what an impact his brief life had on my son and me. I know Joe would want to do that, too.

It didn't take too long for Joe and Steve to become inseparable. They would follow Liverpool together, home and away throughout the 1980s. Their stories from football grounds around Europe would fill several volumes. Maybe Joe will do just that one day. I hope he does.

Working alongside them in those days was another lad called Keith Dolan. Keith was a staunch Evertonian who held a season ticket for both the Gwladys Street and the Kop.

Today that would be unthinkable, but nobody thought anything of it back then. Keith's dad had been a Red, and when he died his son just kept renewing the ticket. He did that until the advent of the Taylor report in 1990. That meant that the old stand would eventually become all-seater, and more expensive.

Keith had joined Joe and Steve as they paced back and forth outside the church. They each looked nervously at their watches. It was 12:15 now and kick-off was just half an hour away.

'Of all the fucking days to book your wedding, lad. Can't believe it.' Keith hadn't stopped whinging about missing the derby ever since the fixture list came out at the start of the season. It was tongue in cheek, but only slightly.

Of course, Joe and Eve would have had no idea what the fixture gods would do when they had set the date for their marriage. They'd realised that it would mean one side of the family missing a game but hadn't banked on the derby occurring so early in the season.

So, for Steve, the honour of being best man was tempered by the knowledge he was going to miss a derby match for the first time. He did a good job of hiding his frustration, of course, but inside he was in turmoil over it.

Joe's bride-to-be was having similar issues. She, too, had cursed her luck when the fixture list was announced, but plans were too far down the road, and rearranging the date and venue was simply not an option. Not that her dad, Jimmy, hadn't tried to suggest it.

Joe had gone through the same conversation with his mates dozens of times, and once more he felt obliged to do so all over again. They could see the fatigue of it all in his face.

'I know, I know, believe me,' he answered. 'Eve wasn't too happy about it either, but it was too late to change. We did look at it, but it just couldn't be done,' he explained for the umpteenth time.

'Alright mate. Don't worry about it. Ignore me,' said Keith, realising that his timing was a bit off. 'I'm just kidding with you.' He was lying, Joe knew he was lying but that's friendship: never having to upset your mates with the truth when a good fib will keep everybody happy.

'We wouldn't have wanted to be anywhere else, mate,' said Steve, joining in the platitudes. 'Seriously,' he added, after seeing Joe's raised eyebrow, 'I'm honoured to be your best man. Now give us a drink of that.' He pointed at Joe's flask, smirking.

Joe handed it to him. I'd given that silver flask to him as a wedding gift. I'd had it engraved with the date of his wedding along with both his and Eve's names. I thought it would be something to help him remember the day, and me too, in years to come.

He told me that when he woke up in his hotel room the next day, he'd noticed the flask on the bedside table. Eve had placed a sticker on it, under the date. It just said, 'AJ 3-0'. Of course, it referred to Andy Johnson's starring performance in the derby. It didn't go down well, and although the sticker could easily be removed, he never drank out of that flask again.

People were beginning to arrive now and the church was starting to fill up. It would soon be time for the three mates to go inside and take up their places in front of all those rows of wooden benches. Joe would feel his stomach turn over as he walked through the door and caught a glimpse of the room.

Stuart, Eve's brother, was standing in the doorway behind a child's buggy. In it was little Robbie. He was just two years old then. Thankfully he was sleeping; something that wouldn't last throughout the ceremony.

Stuart was born in 1975. Marie and I had heard at the time that the Harrington's second child had arrived. Liverpool's just a great big village really, and things like that always find their way to you eventually. Sadly, though, the split between our families had been almost cavernous and so we hadn't been able to offer congratulations or watch him grow up at all.

We eventually got to know him for the great lad he was, after Hillsborough in 1989. He was always a little bitter and twisted when it came to our footballing rivalry, having started going to games in the mid-eighties and being imbued in that post-Heysel fog. Still, like all Blues, he was four-square behind the Reds in the aftermath of the tragedy in Sheffield.

'Alright, Stu lad, did you bring it?' said Keith.

'Sorted, mate,' Stuart replied with a wink as he tapped his chest. Winding its way up from inside his jacket was a thin white cable that reached his right ear. At the other end was a mini radio. Stu was wired for sound and would be the congregation's ears on the match.

He wouldn't be the only one in the church that day with one eye on the game and the other on the ceremony, but the rest of them would keep their divided attentions to themselves. Thanks to Stuart the wedding party would receive goal updates via a series of spontaneous and uncontrollable whoops and shouts from the back of the church. It was like football's equivalent of Tourette's syndrome.

The wedding was due to start at 13:00, 15 minutes after the game kicked off. I watched as my son made his way to the front of the room, where he would stand fidgeting until his bride arrived. My stomach was in knots, for him and because of the game.

You may be wondering why the Methodist church was selected. Well, as Eve was raised as a Catholic and our Joe was Church of England, they'd chosen the Oakfield church because the minister had been very relaxed about the order of service and there would be no requirement to go to pre-wedding lessons or any of that stuff.

The couple also had some unorthodox requests when it came to the music they had chosen for the service. Joe, of course, had wanted to have 'You'll Never Walk Alone' played as his bride walked down the aisle. I'm told her response had turned the air blue. His attempts to explain that it symbolised the fact that they would always have each other, from that day on, fell on deaf ears.

Eve had countered that if he had his song, she would have *Z Cars*. In the end an unbelievable compromise was struck. They each agreed that the bride would walk in to the 'Johnny Todd', and she would walk out to Gerry and the Pacemakers.

As a result, both sides would experience great delight and suffering in equal measure. In the end the stunt was greeted with a mixture of surprise and glee, from all who were there. It was something different and it left all of us with special memories.

Marie and Elaine hadn't been happy with the arrangement, though, and there had been one or two heated exchanges when they found out. In the end Jimmy and I had persuaded them that this was the kids' day, not ours. If that's what they wanted, so be it, we argued.

The two mothers would eventually relent and we would all be treated to a uniquely Scouse occasion. I always think these celebrations should reflect something of the personalities of those involved. This one certainly did, more so than the traditional 'Here comes the bride' dirge.

Across the city, Jimmy and Eve were speeding their way to the venue in an old wedding carriage. They were running hopelessly late.

Earlier, the father of the bride had been stood outside his own home, along with the driver and the photographer, anxiously staring at his watch and debating whether to go in there and hurry up the bridal party. The photographer had cast him a doubtful glance.

'Skin and hair flying in there, mate,' he had warned.

It was a slight exaggeration, but not by much at all. The women had strayed dangerously close to all-out warfare, as they vied for access to mirrors, hairdryers and curling tongs. If you look at the carefully staged pre-ceremony photography in our Joe's wedding album, you would be left with an impression of deep serenity. The images of smiling bridesmaids hide a tale of gritted teeth and raised voices.

Somehow, though, calm had eventually been restored and Jimmy ventured inside to see if his daughter fancied getting married that day. I've always marvelled at the way women can be brought to the brink of all-out war before instantly signing a peace treaty in the name of getting the job done.

Fellas are completely different. We'd have been rolling around the front garden, punching seven kinds of shite out of each other.

As he poked his head around the living room door, Jimmy was stunned by the sight that greeted him. It was a picture of total calm. If a Renaissance painter had created it, you would have gazed in wonder at the sight of doting bridesmaids staring lovingly at their friend, and a bride brimming with joy, bathed in a halo of heavenly sunlight.

You could not have found a starker contrast to the mental images conjured by the shouts and screams of just a few moments ago. Jimmy was flabbergasted.

'Oh, Eve, you look amazing!' said her maid of honour, all sweetness and light. Just moments earlier she had been ready to kill or at least maim the bride, for just a few more minutes in front of a mirror.

Jimmy felt a great well of emotion as he saw his daughter in the dress for the first time. It almost overwhelmed him. 'Cars are ready, ladies,' he said, wiping a tear from his eye.

'Mr Harrington, you look so handsome,' said one of the girls. At least that's how Jimmy tells it. Then the women left to make their journey to the church, leaving Jimmy and Eve alone.

'You look amazing, girl,' he said. 'You ready to do this? It's not too late to back out you know.' He smiled and winked.

Eve took a deep breath. He could see the stress in her face, but he knew this was everything she wanted and he was so proud of her, so pleased that she had found happiness and that he had lived to see it. She reached on to the mantlepiece and grabbed hold of a bottle of champagne. It had already been opened but was still half full. To Jimmy's amazement she lifted it to her lips and took a big swig from it. The sight of her, with her hair and make-up immaculately done, dress beautifully crafted and fitted perfectly to her frame, swigging from a bottle like some wino in the street, made him laugh out loud.

'Rock and Roll, girl,' he said, chuckling.

'I'm ready now, Dad.' She failed to stifle a burp and they both laughed some more. Then they were off on their way to that church in Anfield. As the streets and houses flashed by the window, Jimmy turned to his daughter and spoke softly.

'Listen, love. There's a few things I need to tell you. This is going to be the last chance I get before you're a married woman,' he said.

'Dad! I'm not turning into a different person you know.' Eve smiled and put her hand on his. She knew what he meant but wanted to reassure him anyway. 'I'm still going to be your daughter. You'll still be my dad. I'm not going anywhere.'

Jimmy took a deep breath and pressed on. 'I know that, girl, but trust me, as life takes over there'll be less chances for me to talk to you about the things I want to say. This seems like one of those rare moments, when a father gets to be serious, if you know what I mean.'

Eve wasn't sure what to expect, but she said, 'Okay, go on, Dad.'

His mind was racing. There were so many things he wanted to say, emotions he wanted to express and feelings he wanted to share with her. He had thought for weeks about what he would say, how he would order his words. In the end it all just poured out of him.

'I know I give Joe a hard time, love. He knows I don't mean it. I think you know that, too. He's a good lad, he's been lovely to you and he's a great father to our little Robbie. It's just as well, he's a bleeding Red, isn't he.'

They both laughed, and the tension eased a little.

'It's just, well, what I wanted to say was ...' he struggled again for a moment, and Eve tightened her grip on his hand.

'Go on, Dad. It's okay.'

He coughed and sniffed and went on. 'Well, you know, it's just that I may give him stick, but I know that the daft bugger is the love of your life, isn't he?'

Eve dropped her head. 'Dad you'll mess up my make-up,' she scolded.

'I know, love, but he is, and I could see that in Sheffield that time, when Tommy and I saw you and our Stu with him. You were holding him so tight. He looked like he would collapse if you let go. I know now that he would have, because he was so broken. You put him back together.

It was the love in your eyes, though, the relief that you had found him, and he was in one piece. That's when I knew it.'

He paused and then stammered.

'This man would be the one who would take over from me.'

'No one could ever do that, Dad,' said Eve. 'You know that don't you?'

'No love, not like that. I'll always be your father. I mean, well, I don't know what I mean. Point is I could see he was the one, and I knew in that second that you two would be together forever. I still believe that.'

Eve was fighting to hold back the tears now, terrified her mascara would run. She dabbed at her eyes with a tissue.

'There's more, though, love.'

'Frigging hell, Dad! You're killing me here.' She laughed and sobbed at the same time.

'Bear with me, girl. I need to get this out,' said Jimmy. 'You two coming together is what made me and his old fella come to our senses. We knew that your happiness was all that mattered. After that terrible day, when we thought we'd lost your Joe ...'

'*Our* Joe, Dad,' interrupted Eve.

'Yes, love.' He smiled. 'Our Joe. How could me and Tommy keep up that stupid feud when the happiness of two of the most important people in our lives was at stake. I suppose what I'm saying is you didn't just save Joe that day, when you held him together that night. You saved me and his dad, too. You put me and my best mate back together, too, love.'

Eve leaned across and kissed her dad on the cheek. 'I love you, Dad,' she said.

Chapter Fourteen

A Long Dark Interlude: 15 April 1989

Jimmy had been referring to the night of 15 April 1989. The semi-final of the FA Cup between Liverpool and Brian Clough's Nottingham Forest had been abandoned just hours earlier, after a horrific crush in the Leppings Lane pens. The resultant carnage is now a matter of public record. The lives of many people and indeed an entire city would never be the same again.

Everton, meanwhile, were 92 miles away, at Villa Park, in the other semi-final. That meant there had been a huge exodus from Liverpool on the morning of the games.

Both teams were fighting once more to meet each other in a cup final at Wembley, just as they had in 1984 and 1986. It had been a glorious spring day, as supporters set off from their respective pick-up points early on the Saturday morning.

Eve and Joe had been a couple for some time. Neither Marie and I nor Jimmy and Elaine approved of their relationship. Our disapproval had been devastating for them both, but they had got on with it.

When they moved into a flat together in 1987, they'd had to transport their bin bags and boxes of stuff to the new place by themselves. Neither of them wanted an uncomfortable standoff between Jimmy and me.

I was still convinced Jimmy had got me the sack, by planting stolen car parts in my bag before I left work in the 1970s. He had robbed me of my livelihood and a future in the union, and maybe in politics. I hadn't forgiven him for being a scab, either.

For his part, Jimmy had come to regret crossing the picket line that day, but he was still furious and deeply insulted that I could accuse him of getting me sacked. I had tarred him with the same brush I used on the entire Ford management.

I'd later find out who the culprit was. It had been another foreman, who'd had enough of me agitating on the lines. It seemed my cards had been marked from the moment I was elected shop steward. I'd bumped into this fella years later. He recognised me instantly and his face went pale as I had to be restrained from punching his lights out. Thanks to my mates, he was able to make a speedy exit. I never saw him again.

As children, Eve and Joe both went to the same school and hung around with the same people. They got together after a mutual friend's 18th birthday party and have never parted in all the time since. They kept it from us at first, knowing we wouldn't be happy, but Eve's brother Stu, who was just a kid at the time, spilled the beans.

Both Jimmy and I had offered dire warnings and did all we could to sabotage the relationship before it could get going. Neither of us is proud of that. We were idiots. Ultimately, though, we didn't stand a chance. They were too much in love.

On the day of the semi-final, Eve and Joe had kissed each other goodbye and headed off to their respective meeting points. Joe was heading to Priory Road, next to Stanley Park. Eve's bus would leave from outside Barnes Travel on County Road, Walton.

There were no mobile phones back then so that would be the last time they would speak to each other until they returned home later that evening. Both were in high spirits and looking forward to the football.

The venues were the subject of a lottery, the toss of a coin. Everton could just as easily have ended up in South Yorkshire. The

Reds and Forest could have been instructed to go to the Midlands.

Neither of them gave their destination a second's thought. After all, Hillsborough and Villa Park were just the stages, it was the football that was important. Both Eve and Joe were utterly convinced that they would be making another journey in a month's time, this time to a final in London, and they'd be doing it together on the same coach. Of course, they were both right, but they would each have to overcome more than a mere football match to get there.

Eve could recall the laughter and the songs on the journey down to Birmingham. She remembered how she found herself wondering what Joe was experiencing, whether he was having as much fun as she was. She hoped both of them could celebrate with the cans of lager and cider she'd put aside in the fridge, for when they got home. She'd set the timer on the video to record *Match of the Day* in case they got stuck in traffic and were late getting back. Stu had met her outside the travel shop and they'd sat next to each other on the ride down there. He was just 14 years old and excited to be on his first away day.

Jimmy hadn't got a ticket and had only agreed to let his youngest go if he travelled with his big sister. Their tickets were in different parts of the ground but they would meet up straight after. Stu wasn't daft, and Eve knew he would keep his wits about him.

He sat next to her on the coach, admiring his ticket, in a world of his own and no doubt dreaming of glory at Wembley and FA cups. The ticket had cost his dad £6 and it was still in immaculate condition, like some prized collector's item. Eve was reminded of her first away day, which stirred up feelings and recollections – happy memories of friendships and song, of laughter and hangovers. Stuart had it all to look forward to. However, after 15 April 1989, Eve would never again feel the same about travelling to an away ground.

She had seen Joe's tickets but hadn't really taken any notice of what end of the ground he was in. Why would she? It was just another game; nobody expected there to be a problem. She was more worried about him being caught up in a traffic accident. The idea of him being close to death on a football terrace wouldn't have even entered her head.

So she knew exactly which coach company he was travelling with but not the fact that he was in the Leppings Lane end of the Hillsborough Stadium. He'd travelled up there with his mate, Steve, and a few others that she didn't really know that well.

They arrived at Villa Park early and sat outside eating the sandwiches that Elaine had made the night before and drinking tap water from a lemonade bottle. They watched the crowds build slowly and basked in the spring sunshine. It was a beautiful day for a game of football.

Back home, Marie and I were sitting down to our dinner. We had the radio on in the kitchen and we were listening to the big game build-up and hoping Joe was having a great time. I now know that Jimmy and Elaine were doing the same, both sets of parents oblivious to the fact that our whole worlds were about to be turned upside down.

For us, the terror was short-lived. For so many others, it would never end. My son and all his friends came home. Ninety-six others didn't. We had no idea, but the Harringtons knew our Joe was at the match. Stuart had mentioned it. So, when news broke of the disaster, their first thoughts were about us and what we were going through.

In the end, it was a good job they did know, as I would later urgently need transport to get me to Sheffield – and my car was off the road. Jimmy was one of the first people to turn up at my door.

He wasn't alone, though. As the decision was being made to abandon the game and the radio was announcing grimly that 72 people were confirmed to have died, there would be a crowd of people at our door offering help.

Seventy-two dead! The number seemed incomprehensible. You'd expect that sort of body count in a bombing or a plane crash. But at a game of football? It made no sense. The number would, of course, climb higher.

As I opened the front door, a group of concerned neighbours had gathered on our path. Jimmy was at the front of the queue, his eyes full of tears and holding a set of car keys in his hand.

'I know your lad is at the game, Tom. I take it you haven't heard from him yet.' I shook my head silently.

He looked at me and I couldn't see an enemy anymore. All I saw was another father who knew my pain. All the rest didn't matter. I just nodded.

'Listen, my car is in good nick,' he said 'and the tank's full of petrol. Can I drive you across to Sheffield, mate? We'll bring him back together, eh. Come on lad.'

I knew Joe was in that end of the stadium, the one where so many had their lives squeezed out of them, and I felt sick to my stomach. Marie, who didn't smoke anymore, hadn't done for years, had accepted a cigarette from the girl next door and was puffing away anxiously. Her face was stained with tears. I had never seen her like that before and I never want to again.

Her baby was at Hillsborough and she had no idea if he was alive or dead. The pain was unimaginable.

She saw that I was headed out of the door and jumped up to come with me. I turned and put my arms around her, holding her tightly for a moment. All around us the neighbours just stared, helplessly. What else could they do?

'I'm coming with you,' she said bluntly. 'He's my son. I need to see him, Tom.' Her eyes were streaming, and her cries of anguish ripped a hole right through me.

We could have all gone together, but we needed someone at home in case Joe rang, or worse still the police. I could have let her go with Jimmy. There was no reason why I deserved to go instead of her, apart from selfishness. I didn't admit that to myself then, but it was the truth. I wanted to find him, to bring him home and know that he was safe. I didn't want to be the one waiting by the phone, my guts churning and my head in bits.

So, I persuaded her he'd be okay. That I'd find him and bring him back to her, safe and sound. Thank God he was, and I could honour my pledge. If he hadn't been alive, then I don't think I could have lived with myself. I'm not sure I could have even come home. Marie may never have forgiven me.

'You stay by the phone, love. He'll call us as soon as he can. I'm certain of it. He'll be worried if there's no answer. I will call you from a phone box when I get there, and what's the bets he's already rung you by then,' I said. To this day, I'm not too sure if even I believed that.

Marie was in a daze, but I still think if it hadn't been for the woman next door, who put her arm around my wife and ushered her back into the house with promises of tea and sympathy, she'd have been fighting me for the passenger seat.

Instead, Jimmy and I drove to Sheffield together, and to this day I thank the gods, the universe or whatever force there is that I was able to bring my boy home.

We barely said a word for the first 30 miles. When the silence was finally broken it was by me.

'Wait, Jim, your Eve, does she know. Have you spoken to her?' It hadn't even occurred to me, until that moment, that Joe's girl would have been out of her mind with worry about him. I was too wrapped up in my own thoughts.

'She was at the other game, mate. She's with our Stuart,' ee said. 'We haven't heard from her, but Elaine will be waiting for her at the flat, when she gets back.'

Eve was in the Holt End. Stuart was in the Witton End. The ground was divided in half longitudinally, between Everton and Norwich fans. In Eve's end of the stadium, Blues and Canaries were separated by metal fencing. In Stuart's the Blues had the lower tear, the Norwich fans the upper. Fencing also separated both sets of supporters from the pitch.

No one knew it but fencing at football grounds was entering its final days, and the terraces would soon be replaced with more expensive seating. The game was about to change forever but not soon enough. After the game at Villa Park got underway, Eve recalled seeing an announcement on the scoreboard. She couldn't really remember if that was early in the game or later, but it had said the kick-off at Hillsborough had been delayed. She didn't suspect a thing.

Stuart remembers seeing it too, and he recalled how his first thought was about being able to listen to the final moments of Liverpool's game on the radio, as they sailed down the motorway towards Liverpool. They'd cheer and sing if Liverpool went out and they'd do the same if they got through. It would be a no-lose situation, so confident had he been of Everton's progress.

Everton's goal came in the 26th minute of the game. Eve was already getting tired. It had been a long day with an early start. The constant pushing and shoving on the terrace was taking its toll and only the excitement and adrenaline was holding her up.

Suddenly, Pat Van Den Hauwe had the ball at his feet. She almost lost her footing as the crowd swayed to the movement of the action. The ball sailed into the penalty area. She lost sight of it momentarily as heads went up to clear. Then it seemed a Norwich player had hit it against his own bar. There was a scramble near the goal line, and just like that the ball was in the net.

Supporters all around her jumped in wild celebration. She heard a fella behind her asking his mate 'Who got it?' She didn't know either. 'Nevin,' came the reply. That made it even better. Pat Nevin was Eve's hero.

In that moment all she could think about was Wembley and an unbelievable family day out. Hopefully, she thought, Everton could exact some revenge for 1986. Her confidence that Liverpool would beat Forest was absolute.

At the other end of the ground Stu was in his own little Blue heaven. He, too, had no idea who had scored, but he didn't care. He was insanely happy. Sadly, the sights and sounds of those innocent joyous moments have been forever tainted by events that happened on the same day, miles away from him in South Yorkshire.

There, the scenes were very different. Joe was in hell. Later, he would have only fragments of memory and the accounts of friends to rely on, as he attempted to piece together what happened to him that day.

Initially, all he could recall was the sense of panic and of feeling closed in and wanting to scream but not being able to get enough air into his lungs to make a sound. There was also the sickening smell of urine and vomit that would linger in his mind for a long time.

The next thing he remembers is being on the pitch, wandering around and looking for his mate, Steve. It was like a dream. At times he felt as though he was outside his own body watching himself as he drifted one way and then the other. It was so warm, and the sky was so blue, the lush grass beneath his feet so soft, yet all about him was sheer mayhem. It all seemed insane to him, surreal.

Given Steve's size and general state of fitness, Joe later told me that he didn't think his mate would have stood a cat's chance in hell of getting out of that hellhole alive. Miraculously, though, he did, though it would be the following day before they were reunited. They went to the match together, they would each return alone and carrying their own scars.

Back in Birmingham, Eve had caught up with her brother about 10 minutes after the final whistle. They were both deliriously happy and hugging each other, as they danced a small circle outside the ground.

'Did you enjoy that, mate?' Eve said to her little brother. 'Great, wasn't it?' She ruffled his hair and he laughed. Normally he would have moaned at such a patronising gesture, but he was so happy in the moment that he couldn't care less.

'Can we go to Wembley?' he asked immediately.

'If we can get a ticket, definitely,' she replied, adding, 'Come on or we'll be late for the coach and we'll never get back in time for *Match of the Day*.'

As they walked, Stuart kept asking passers-by if they knew what the Liverpool score was. Nowadays we just check our phones, but back then there was none of that. People kept saying they didn't know, and then one fella told him that the game had been delayed and was still going on.

That made the pair of them quicken their pace. If they got a move on they'd get to the bus in time to hear the last few minutes of the other semi-final. They passed a newsagent's store. Outside was a billboard. Written in black marker pen on white background were the words:

'FOOTBALL TRAGEDY 72 DEAD'

'Oh my God. Have you seen this, Eve?' said Stuart, pointing at the sign.

Amazingly it didn't register with either of them that this could have been in England, never mind Sheffield and involving people they knew. After all they had just been told the game in Yorkshire was still playing.

'Terrible,' replied Eve. 'Those poor people and their families,' she said, not really taking it in, and on they both rushed.

On the motorway, miles away, a car was speeding towards Sheffield. In it was Jimmy and me.

The radio in Jimmy's car had been stolen. In its place was a gaping hole with two wires, one red, the other black, poking out from inside the dashboard. It meant we had no contact with the outside world, no way of knowing what was happening at Hillsborough.

My frustration must have been obvious. I remember I was shaking in my seat, fidgeting nervously. I felt sick to my stomach.

It's hard to put into words the worry. We all fret over our kids. It never ends, no matter how old they get, but that's normal stuff, like will they have enough to eat, can I afford Christmas or will they get a job. In that car, bombing down the M62 on 15 April 1989, all of that seemed so trivial, compared to the clear and present danger hanging over my son's life.

'I know this must be murder for you, lad,' said Jimmy, trying something, anything, to ease the crushing weight of the situation, and apparently reading my mind. His voice sounded loud, and it made me realise just how quiet the car had been for most of the journey. 'We'll be in Sheffield in about an hour or so. There'll be a phone box somewhere, we can stop and you can phone Marie. You watch, mate. He will have phoned her to say he's safe and we'll be heading straight back to see him.'

His words had some effect and I snapped out of my stupor. 'Jesus, I hope you're right, Jim,' I said. 'If I go home without him, well I just don't know how I'm going to look Marie in the eye.'

'We'll find him, kid. I'm sure of it,' replied Jimmy.

It felt like we'd never been apart, and the years just melted away. It was good to have my mate back. Now I just needed my son and I could move past this horrible day, I thought. Of course, none of us would be able to get past that day for decades. Some still can't.

In Sheffield the sun was finally going down and Joe found himself wandering the streets. He walked past locals who stared at him, their faces full of sadness. They were like phantoms to him, coming into view and then disappearing as he drifted by.

No one spoke to him. They just walked on by, burying their concern, perhaps too afraid of how he might react if they attempted to reach out.

Though he was unaware, he looked a sight. His red polo shirt was covered in muck, a thick grimy residue of the terrace. His jeans were bloodied from the knees down and his hair was matted with sweat and who knew what. Back home, later that night, he would bathe away the remnants of the day. His mother would bin his clothes. If only we could wash away and discard the rest of Hillsborough's legacy.

But on the streets of Sheffield, Joe just kept walking. He didn't know where he was going. He just knew he couldn't stop. If he had, he feared the pictures in his mind would take over. He wouldn't be able to stop them, so he just kept walking. Little did he know, but he had orbited the ground several times before eventually managing to escape its dark gravitational pull, careering off down Leppings Lane.

He went past houses that had queues of people lining the streets, from their front doors and snaking along the pavements.

He would later learn that these were fellow supporters lining up to use telephones, kindly offered for free by the people of South Yorkshire. If he'd had had the presence of mind back then, he could have phoned his mum and put her out of her misery, but he just kept walking until his legs would carry him no more.

Eventually he sat down on the ground, under a bus shelter. He'd reached the end of Leppings Lane itself. He was exhausted, his feet were sore and his legs ached. He rocked back and forth, sobbing uncontrollably. As he pulled his legs up to his chest and formed an upright foetal position, he felt a stinging under his jeans.

Joe didn't need to look to know what the source of the pain was, but he couldn't help himself. Reaching down he pulled the left leg of his trousers about halfway up his shin to reveal a series of deep scratch marks. His brain raced back to the pens and he remembered his desperate scramble for survival, his yearning to be released. He saw himself lifted over the fence, turning to see those faces pressed against the wire, and his mind screamed.

It still screams today. In the small hours of the night, when sleep is hard to come by, Hillsborough still finds him, and he is forced to battle its demons once more. All he had done was go to a bloody football match back in 1989. In many ways he has never left that stadium.

Chapter Fifteen

The Search for Joe

Back in the Midlands, Eve and Stuart clambered on to their coach. The radio was already on, but instead of the match, all they could hear was the voice of a newsreader. It was the only sound on an otherwise completely silent bus. The driver was slumped over the wheel and barely looked up as she got on.

Passengers Eve recognised from earlier, men who had been swigging from beer cans and singing merrily on the journey over, now had their faces pressed against the windows, staring into empty space. Two seats in, a woman decked in blue and white was sobbing uncontrollably and being consoled by her friend.

Eve looked at her blankly, and the woman's pal smiled awkwardly. 'Her sister is at Hillsborough,' she explained. The response made no sense to Eve. *So what*, she thought. *Why is she crying?*

Stuart tugged on her arm. 'What is it?' she said.

He just looked at her. His face was ashen and he looked as if he was about to cry himself. His bottom lip was trembling. 'The man on the radio, Sis ...' His voice trailed off, and now tears were streaming down his cheeks in floods.

'What's the matter with everyone?' screamed Eve. 'Is this an episode of the *Twilight Zone* or something. Stu what's wrong?' Then, Stuart spoke again.

'He said there's more than 70 people dead, Eve. There's Liverpool fans dead, at Hillsborough.'

The next thing she remembered was being carried to the back of the bus. She'd fainted, and a couple of men had jumped up to help her. As she came around she could hear Stu explaining to them that Joe was in Sheffield, as they placed her longways on the seat.

'Grab us a bottle of water, Tony,' said one of the men who had helped her up off the floor. Tony produced a bottle of cola instead. 'Sorry mate, none left,' he apologised.

Eve had a bruise growing on the back of her head and she reached up to rub it. She was trying her best to sit up. 'Easy, love,' said the stranger, 'You've had a nasty fall.'

The coach was moving now, and Eve felt a wave of panic. She couldn't stay on this bus all the way back to Liverpool. She had to get to Hillsborough, to see Joe. He needed her. She needed him.

'I'm getting off,' she shouted and jumped up, shoving the soft drink aside.

Stuart was still crying, and her heart ached as she looked at him. He was confused and terrified. 'Where are you going, Sis?' he said. The sheer panic in his voice was jarring, but she pushed past it.

'I don't know how, Stu, but I've got to find Joe.' She was wobbly on her feet but at least she was standing. Holding on to the back of the seats, she barged her way to the front of the bus and the driver.

A woman stood up in front of her and placed her hands upon Eve's shoulders, attempting to slow her down. 'Who's Joe, love? Is he your boyfriend, your husband?' The woman's voice was calm and soothing. Kind of the way you hear a doctor or a nurse talking to a patient. Eve shrugged her aside and made a beeline for the front of the vehicle.

'Stop the coach.' She demanded.

'I can't, love. I'm on a motorway. Go and sit down,' said the driver, irritated.

'Look, mate. I've got nothing against you or anyone on this bus, but if you don't pull over and let me off now, I swear I will make your life a living hell all the way home.' Her eyes were wild and she was raging.

A couple of lads appeared at her shoulder and tried to calm her down. It was obvious she was having none of it, though. One of them spoke to the guy at the wheel.

'Look, lad, I think she means it like. Her fella is at the other game, you know. She wants to get to him. To be honest mate we'd all do the same. You would too, if it was one of yours who was affected.'

The driver looked at them in the mirror and said, 'I know, mate, but I'm on the fucking motorway here. I can't just stop. I'll cause an accident.'

'Eve saw her chance and shouted, 'Look there, it says services, three miles ahead.' She pointed at the road sign on the side of the motorway. 'Just pull in there. I'll sort myself out. I can hitch a ride from there to Sheffield.'

The driver had no answer. One of the other men standing behind her spoke up. 'Wouldn't you be better going home, love, with your little lad here?' He pointed towards Stuart. 'For all you know, your fella is on his way home anyway. He's not going to be hanging around in Sheffield, is he?' He was speaking sense to a point. His argument of course didn't consider the possibility that Joe was incapacitated in some way. Eve's mind was in turmoil and she had very much considered the possibility that he could be lying in a hospital bed or, worse still, a morgue, all alone. She shook the thought from her mind and carried on.

'I'll phone me mum from the service station,' she said. 'If he's home, then I suppose I'll be hitching a ride back to Liverpool, or my dad can come and get me. He's got a car.'

The man looked at her. His eyes were full of concern and he could see she wasn't budging. He tried one last tactic, desperate not to let this vulnerable woman, young enough to be his daughter, get off the coach in the middle of nowhere.

'What about this little fella then?' He meant Stuart, who at this point was beside himself with fright. He'd never seen Eve like this before. It would have been disorientating to see the person charged with taking care of him become so unglued.

Eve turned to her brother and said, 'Stu, love, you can stay on here if you like. It's heading straight back to Liverpool. I can phone Dad and tell him to pick you up from County Road. It will be okay, I promise. Or, you can come with me to find Joe.'

There was no way he was staying on the bus all by himself, no matter how friendly these people seemed. He grabbed his sister's hand and said, 'I'm coming with you, Eve.'

Jimmy and I arrived in Sheffield at about 6.30 or 7pm. I can't really remember exactly. The sun was going down. We were about 20 minutes from the stadium when I spotted a phone box.

'Over there, Jim. A phone. Pull over,' I shouted.

I slammed the ten pence pieces into the slot and hammered out our home phone number on the keypad. The dialling tone seemed to go on forever, then Marie answered. Her voice was shrill and full of expectancy.

I knew immediately that she was hoping it would be our Joe, phoning to say he was okay. I heard the disappointment in her voice as she recognised mine.

'I'm sorry, love. I know you thought that would be him. We're here now, in Sheffield. Have you heard anything at all?' I said, my stomach in knots and praying she would say something positive. She didn't.

'No, Tom. There's been nothing at all. I'm going out of my mind here. They've put this phone number up on the telly for people to ring, but it's just engaged all the time. Tommy, what are we going to do?'

I could hear she was crying and it broke my heart. Tears started to pour down my cheeks, too. I didn't know what to say to her, so I made another promise, a cheque I might not be able to cash.

'Look,' I said firmly, 'I'm here now, Marie. I'm going to find our son, and I'm going to bring him home to you. I swear, love.' I hung up and got back in the car.

'No joy?' said Jimmy.

It was a common phrase, and I knew exactly what he meant. However, it struck me as an odd thing to say in that moment. In my mind, I was shouting, *No mate, there's no frigging joy, no joy at all!*

Instead, I replied that we should head to the hospital. I had no idea then that the stadium had been turned into a temporary mortuary. Many of the families of those who had lost their lives had made their way there, searching for their loved ones. I didn't know. I'd left the house with very little information, and had one thing on my mind only: get to Sheffield.

With no radio, there was no way to find out what was happening. It would have made no sense for me to go to Hillsborough, in my mind anyway. If Joe was safe, I thought, he wouldn't have hung around at the ground, and, if he wasn't, they'd have surely taken him to the nearby infirmary. The idea of a football stadium as a place where you store the victims of a disaster never entered my head. It still sounds crazy to me today.

'Okay, mate. Have a look in the glove compartment. There's an AA map of the road in there. Should be able to find our way to the hospital using that.'

Back in Liverpool, Elaine was pacing up and down in her living room. She had agonised about going to see Marie. She would later, she had reasoned. The poor woman would have enough on her plate, without having to make small talk with someone she hadn't spoken to in years. God only knew what she must be going through, she told herself.

It was an excuse, though, and she knew it, deep down. There had been so much water under the bridge between them, and Elaine was struggling with so many emotions. Guilt was one of them; also regret that she hadn't done more to repair the rift between their families, as well as terrible shame that it should take something of this magnitude to bring them together. Going around to see Marie would mean facing all of that, and, yet, how could she not?

She was incapable of deciding what to do. So, she just stared at the phone beseeching it to ring. Hoping it would be Jimmy to say Joe was safe and she could put off making that ominous trip to Marie's house. When it rang she almost leapt out of her skin. Her heart raced, as did her mind, as she reached for the receiver.

She hadn't even considered it would be Eve or Stuart. After all they were safe, and probably on their way back, oblivious to the terrible drama unfolding at home and across the country. She lifted the phone slowly to her ear, and said, 'Jim. Have you found him?'

'No. Mum. It's me, Eve. Have you heard the news?' The voice on the other end of the phone was anxious and the words were fired down the line like bullets from a gun.

Elaine's thoughts were swirling around in her head. News? What did she mean? Hadn't everyone heard about it? Or did she mean Joe, had she heard something about Joe?

'Oh, Eve love, sorry. Erm yes, I mean, what news is that, love?' She was stammering and her voice was trembling.

Eve was silent for a moment. Then Elaine heard money being placed into the slot. 'Sorry, Mum, it was going to cut me off. The pips were going. Erm, the footy. Have you heard about the fans at Hillsborough?'

'Of course I have, Eve, I've heard about nothing else for the last few hours. Your dad is on his way there, with Tommy, now.' Her tone was blunt, unnecessarily so, and she regretted it instantly.

'Mum, I'm so sorry. I've just found out. I'm with our Stu in a service station. We're going right now to find him.' The tears were in free flow again and her mother's heart was breaking at the sound of her child in such distress.

'Eve. Listen to me. You get back on that coach. Your father has taken Joe's dad to Sheffield. They'll find him. I need you and Stuart home here with me.' Her hands were shaking and she felt like she might collapse.

'Mum, I can't. The coach is gone. We got off it and we're going to hitch a ride to Sheffield. I need to be with Joe.'

The situation felt like it was starting to unravel and she was powerless to control it. She sat down on the floor, unable to think of anything meaningful to say. Her husband and her two children were now miles away, looking for someone else's child. Dozens of mothers were waiting to hear the worst news imaginable and she had no idea whether there was worse to come for her own family.

How would her daughter cope, if she lost Joe? How would any of them manage? It was just a bloody football match. How could this be happening?

Eve replaced the receiver. Her mother had pleaded with her to come home and, in the end, she had no choice but to hang up on her. The situation was desperate and, despite her brother being at her side, hanging on her every word, she felt so alone.

'What are we going to do now, Sis?' Stuart's scared little voice pleaded.

Eve slumped against the wall and slid slowly down it, landing on the cold tiles in the service station lobby, with her knees hunched up against her chest. She rubbed her temples slowly. A headache was beginning to blossom and she realised they'd had nothing to drink for hours.

'I don't know, Stu love. I just don't know.' With that she began to weep again.

Neither Eve nor Stuart had noticed a middle-aged couple sitting at a table a few yards away. The man and woman had noticed the pair getting off the coach and spotted the colour of their scarves. They'd also overheard the entire phone conversation.

The woman stood up first and walked over to Eve and Stuart. Her husband was a yard or two behind her, maintaining a non-threatening distance.

'Excuse me, dear,' said the lady. We couldn't help but overhear. Your accents, you're from Liverpool, aren't you?'

Eve looked up at her through tear-drenched eyes and nodded. The woman had a kind smile and she looked genuinely concerned.

'I thought so. I'm sorry for listening, but were you saying you know someone who was at Hillsborough today?'

Eve pulled herself up awkwardly. She was nervous but sensed that this could lead to something positive. These people might have a car, she thought. If they could give her a lift at least part of the way, it would give her at least a chance of finding Joe. They both looked normal, too. When she told me that later, I thought it sounded ridiculous. If only it was really that easy to tell serial killers apart from the rest of the population. How could she take such a risk and get into a car with complete strangers?

In truth, if that couple had not come forward, she'd have taken an even greater risk of thumbing a lift on the hard shoulder. She'd done that before when travelling to away games. I suppose she'd have done anything, taken any risk necessary, to find her love.

Eve nodded. 'Yes. My boyfriend. He was at the match. I don't know if he's okay. This is my brother Stuart. We were in Birmingham, at the other game,' she told the woman.

There was real concern in this lady's eyes and her voice was fully of pity when she said, 'Poor things. Can we do anything?'

At that point her husband stepped forward. He was a tall thin man. Eve thought he was probably in his late 40s. His voice was hesitant, but he sounded like someone who genuinely cared.

'I'm sure your boyfriend is going to be okay, dear. I mean the odds ...' He trailed off, realising that the last thing this young girl and her brother needed was some stranger playing the numbers game. Fellas have a habit of trying to be practical, sometimes even scientific, in a crisis. It's often the last thing people need to hear, but we can't help it. He changed tack.

'We're on our way home to Manchester,' he said. 'We can take you that far, if you'd like.'

Eve would have jumped at the chance. In her mind she was already on her way out the door and looking for their car. Manchester would take them that bit closer to Joe. Then the man's wife intervened.

'No, dear,' she said firmly, turning to look at her husband. 'We'll take them all the way there. We'll take them to Sheffield.'

It had been hours since I left Marie and drove away with Jimmy. She had got rid of the last of the neighbours and was busying herself around the house, needlessly tidying things that were already tidy and washing cups that could have been left for later.

The television had been turned off. It was nothing but a harbinger of doom and every utterance from a news anchor or on-the-scene reporter brought fresh horror.

The radio was no better. She couldn't listen to anything as joyous as music when she didn't know if her son was alive or dead. So she just pottered away in silence.

Her peace was eventually broken by the ring of the doorbell. It made the sound of a Maserati horn, like on that stupid cowboy show on telly, the one set in America's deep south. It felt wholly inappropriate and she wanted to take a hammer or her shoe to the bell-box above the living room door that led into the hallway.

It had been Joe who had programmed that tune and he thought it was funny. She had, too, until now. Now it was just a reminder that he was missing.

Marie pulled the front door open and gasped. She had been expecting yet another well-meaning face, full of platitudes. Instead it was Elaine.

She looked almost embarrassed to be there and, as she started to speak, Marie just stepped on to the path next to her and threw her arms around her visitor. Elaine had been startled at first, then she just surrendered to the hug. They both cried as they held each other for a moment, and then Marie broke the ice by inviting her old friend inside.

As is the custom, the kettle went on and the two old friends moved past the pleasantries and ignored all the elephants in the room. Instead they became just two mothers in despair and leaning on each other for support.

Elaine explained that Eve and Stuart were on their way to South Yorkshire. The pair of them would have to share the same sense of powerlessness. All they could do was drink tea and cry, while their loved ones were out there doing something about the problem.

'I should have gone with him,' Marie was saying. 'If something's happened, I should be there. Can't believe I let him go without me.'

Elaine smiled and held my wife's hand. 'You probably weren't thinking straight, love. Neither was Tommy, I'm sure. Besides, what if Joe rings, or turns up at the door and there's nobody here to let him in or speak to him.'

Marie let out a deep, mournful sob. She wanted more than anything in the world to hear a knock at the door and see his smiling face again. She'd give literally anything for that, even her own life.

'You're where you need to be. Tommy is, too. Have faith, Marie.' She continued.

Marie looked up at her, disbelief written right across her face. 'How can I have faith, Elaine. Faith? What sort of God does this? Kids, fathers, mothers, sons and daughters.' She stopped for a moment, then went on, 'Dead. They're dead, Elaine. They're at a football match and they're dead and maybe my son is too.'

The tears came hard and her whole body rocked as she wailed in despair. Elaine didn't know what to do or say. What was there to say? How could she salve her friend's pain? There were no words or actions capable of lifting the burden from Marie. Only the sight of her child, safe and intact, could do that.

Elaine's faith had been tested many times during her life. She hadn't shared Jimmy's Catholicism, but she had believed, and, as she grew older, she had gone to church. She had done so especially when her father died.

That had been the sternest test, she thought. In her mind, either God put the aneurysm in his head, or chose not to do anything about it as it grew. How could she pray to a deity that was capable of that? Worse still was the growing sense that maybe we were really on our own, and there was nobody up there looking out for us.

She'd been pacified by the vicar, who told her that God's plan was his and his alone. He had a higher purpose for her father, who was now enjoying heavenly delights, free from the pain down here on earth. It had worked, then. She had wanted it to work. The alternative explanation was too unpalatable to consider while still wrestling with her grief.

Now, as she contemplated the utter senselessness of Hillsborough, she found herself mulling over the same doubts. Why would an all-powerful and merciful God allow innocent people to go to their deaths in such a cruel and brutal way? She understood that people had to die, even children, sometimes. Why like this, though? Why the pain and the fear? What purpose could that possibly serve?

As she cradled her weeping friend in her arms, she felt, perhaps for the first time in her life, that there was no purpose or point to any of it. How could there be? Instead, she realised that we were all alone with the decisions we make: to love or to hate, to fight or to give in, to despair or to hope. When you boil it all down, that's what you're left with. That's all we have, and sometimes, that's all we really need.

The sound of the phone startled her out of her thoughts, and Marie jumped up, almost stumbling as she raced to it. Elaine watched her rush to answer it.

In Marie's head, a voice was repeating the same mantra over and over, *Please be him, please be him.*

Hands shaking, she placed the handset against her ear and said softly, 'Hello.' It was almost a whisper.

The voice on the other end of the phone was more emphatic. It was me. 'Marie. It's me, Tommy. We've found him and he's okay, love.'

Jimmy had driven me to Sheffield Northern General Hospital. He hated hospitals at the best of times, but this was a very dark place indeed. As we walked through the main entrance we noticed that there were other families already here, waiting for news.

I had gone to the desk at reception to see if they had any record of Joe being admitted. I returned a few minutes later, not knowing whether to be relieved or more worried. He wasn't on their list.

Jimmy looked at me hopefully, but then when he saw my blank expression he just asked, 'Nothing, kid?'

I shook my head. What now? I thought I could search the streets, but where would I start. Next to me was a couple. They looked worried sick and exhausted. I smiled in their direction and caught the man's eye. He nodded, acknowledging the unspoken gesture of sympathy.

'We're looking for our daughter,' he said. His tone was so matter-of-fact. They were the words of a father who'd travelled way past despair and was now entering unchartered territory. He had nothing left; his emotions were flat.

The woman next to him spoke up. I assumed she was his wife. 'They've told us some of the injured are at the stadium, still. We're going there now. Are you looking for someone, too?'

'My son,' I replied, before adding, 'The stadium? Why would the injured still be at the stadium now, at this time? Surely they'd be here.'

The woman just shrugged, and I noticed the man next to her bow his head and close his eyes. I don't know if someone had told her that the injured were being cared for at the football ground, or if that's just what she wanted to hear. The man I assumed was her husband seemed to know the score, though.

We said our goodbyes and parted company with the couple. The stress was starting to really get to me but at least I was doing something. In that moment I thought of Marie. How was she keeping herself busy, was she ok? I couldn't linger there too long, though. It would have stopped me focusing on the task in hand.

'The stadium then?' asked Jimmy.

I didn't think it was worth it but had no alternative to offer. 'Yes. Let's go there,' I said.

The stadium was only ten minutes away by car but in my mind it seemed like it took us ages to get there. I remember having the road map on my knee and trying to feed Jimmy directions. If I close my eyes, I can still see those streets, the houses and the shops flying past the passenger-side window, as we wound our way to Hillsborough.

We'd just come off the main road and were about to turn on to Leppings Lane. The name still sends a shiver down my spine. To our right was a bus shelter. It was in complete darkness by now and I've no idea how Jimmy spotted him, but there was our Joe, slumped on the floor.

It was a bit of a miracle, really. I was staring out of the passenger-side window and would never have seen him, but for my mate.

Suddenly the car slowed right down and I lurched forward. I wasn't wearing my seatbelt. It had been the law since 1983 but back then I often didn't bother. Jimmy realised he'd slammed on too quickly and reached out his arm to stop me. It didn't prevent my head glancing the dashboard, though.

I felt a sharp pain and winced. It hurt like bloody hell but the words that came from Jimmy's mouth made all that go away. 'Tom, what's that? Is that him? Jesus, I think that's your Joe!' he shouted.

Eve and Stuart sat in the back of the couple's car, as it sped along the M42. At the service station, they'd introduced themselves as Colin and Margaret. They'd also established that the pair hadn't eaten or drunk anything for several hours. Eve only had coppers in her pocket and Stuart had a pound note that his dad had given him before he left the house that morning. It would have bought them little, given the prices on display.

Colin had bought them some sandwiches and a packet of crisps each. He'd also got them some bottles of juice. Stuart was getting stuck in but Eve couldn't manage anything. She felt nauseated and waves of acid reflux burned her throat.

'Can you put the radio on, please?' she asked, and Margaret dutifully obliged without saying a word. The station it was tuned to was playing songs from the charts and Jason Donovan was bemoaning the amount of broken hearts in the world.

His words washed over Eve. Her mind was elsewhere. She was thinking about Joe, obviously, and remembering that she hadn't told him she loved him that morning. He knew it, of course he did. She told him often enough, but she hadn't said it as he waved goodbye to her earlier in the day. Had he said it? She couldn't recall.

The song on the radio faded out, and a man's voice announced that it was time to go to the newsroom for an update. It was 7pm. The bulletin was of course dominated by the events in Sheffield.

Colin reached over to switch it off but Stuart asked him to leave it on.

Stuart had been struggling to comprehend how people could die at a football game. In his mind it just didn't compute. Maybe the radio could explain it and maybe whatever happened, it wasn't the place where Joe was. Then he heard it. The crush had happened in the Leppings Lane end. That was what was written on Joe's ticket. His heart sank, but he kept quiet, not wanting to upset Eve further.

In her head, Eve was back at Wembley in 1986. She was walking along Wembley Way, with Joe and Steve and a few of the gang. The sun was shining, there was Red and Blue everywhere. They were happy, deliriously so.

Barely three years had elapsed since that day, yet it felt like ancient history to her, as she stared out of the window at the fields whizzing by. They had talked of doing it all again, retracing their steps to the twin towers, revelling in the thrill of another derby spectacular in the capital, and then on into Soho or Mayfair to drink the night away.

It all seemed like an impossible dream to her now. Her aspirations now centred around one thing only: finding her man and taking him home, whatever shape he was in.

The man on the radio was reading out a phone number for anyone who had relatives at the match, and Margaret was busily jotting it down. She turned to Eve and Stuart and said, 'Maybe we can find a phone box when we get there and call this number.'

Eve took the piece of paper from her and stuffed it into her trouser pocket, without comment. Margaret went on, 'They say some of the supporters are being treated at a nearby hospital. There's also a place for families to go to at the stadium, they may have news there too. What do you think? Should we go straight to the hospital or to the ground?'

Stuart spoke before Eve could gather her thoughts. 'He can't be in the hospital. Surely if he was, they'd have contacted his family, and his dad wouldn't be out looking for him. What if he's wandering around injured or he's missed his coach back? I say we go to the ground first.'

Eve didn't argue, and Colin and Margaret agreed to go to the stadium first, and, if they couldn't find him there, they'd then go to the hospital. I have to say we owe this couple a lot. They were complete strangers to us in 1989. They became good friends of our family afterwards. Although we don't see them as much these days, we still correspond often.

Hillsborough brought people together, more than it tore them apart. If it hadn't been that way, we'd have never got the truth out.

It was going dark and the lights on the motorway took on a hypnotic quality.

Stuart fell asleep, his mind finally surrendering. Eve was wired. She wouldn't sleep for days after that night. When she eventually slept she had nightmares in which she dreamed that they had found Joe, lying on a cold slab in the middle of a vast, darkened room.

Her steps would echo on the hard stone floor as she crossed the space to be at his side. His skin was blue and cold to the touch, his face unrecognisable and still. A man in a white coat was stood over him, his features shrouded in shadow. In an ominous monotone voice, he was repeatedly saying, *He's never coming home, Eve. Your boyfriend's never coming home.*

That dream would haunt her on and off for months and not even sleeping pills from the doctor would help. In the end it just got less frequent, until it eventually vanished.

They entered Sheffield from the south and came along the A61 towards Penistone Road. Meanwhile, on the radio, Holly Johnson was singing about Americanos who wore blue jeans and chinos. His voice sounded too lively for the mood.

They had already passed a few signs for the stadium and Eve had woken Stuart up. It was quiet in the streets outside Hillsborough now. They were headed for the gymnasium turned temporary mortuary, in which the lives of dozens of people were being irrevocably torn to shreds.

Colin and Margaret hadn't discussed what they would do once they arrived. Could they just leave them there and resume their journey home to Manchester? That seemed cold and heartless. How would they get back home?

It would remain unspoken, but both knew they couldn't abandon Eve and Stuart. They were in it for the long haul.

The car continued down Penistone Road North, behind the huge Kop end that had housed the Forest fans. The gymnasium was behind the North Stand, which was accessed via Vere Road. Margaret was struggling with the map and as a result they missed the turning and sailed past the stadium.

Turning to the pair in the back seat she reassured them, 'We'll just do a left down the next road, don't worry, and come back on ourselves,' she said.

Fielding Road ran parallel with Vere. It was a long road lined with houses on either side. Margaret was telling Colin that he needed to turn left on to Leppings Lane when he came to the end. Stuart immediately recognised that name and shouted, 'That's were Joe was.'

The pair in the front seats exchanged worried glances. Eve still says she hadn't put two and two together. They would end up driving up and down, before eventually parking up in a space outside someone's house on Vere Road. It was just a short walk around to the rear of the North Stand, where the entrance to the gymnasium was. Eve and Stuart got out, leaving Margaret and Colin to wait in the car.

People were gathered around the doorway. Some were in tears and hugging each other. Eve began to slow her pace as they approached, before stopping several yards from the doorway.

'I can't go in, Stuart,' she said. Complete panic had shut her down.

'But Sis, why?' he asked. 'We're just going to see if they know anything about him. It'll be okay.'

'But those people,' Eve answered. 'They're crying. What if it's bad news? I couldn't take it if they tell me he's ...' She couldn't finish the sentence. The word was too difficult to speak. It was hard to even think it.

'Eve, we're just going to see if they know anything,' said Stuart. 'It's what we came for. Those people in the car went out of their way to bring us here.' There was a tinge of annoyance in his voice but she couldn't relent.

Instead, she turned on her heels and started walking back to the car. It was crazy. I've asked her since what she was thinking and all she could say was, 'Dad, if I didn't go in there, they couldn't tell me that he wasn't coming home.' It was denial, pure and simple.

So they got back into the car and lied. Well, Eve lied. Stuart just sat there, his face like thunder and rage.

'He's not there. They don't know anything about him,' she said, dropping her lie on Colin and Margaret without batting an eyelid.

'Let's go to the hospital, then. It's not far from here,' said Colin, who had temporarily taken control of the map.

Eve agreed, but she wasn't even sure if she would go in there either. She had come for answers, and to find the love of her life. However, hope remained alive in uncertainty. Answers meant the end of the search and the possibility of loss. It was too much to bear.

The car turned back on to Leppings Lane. Margaret was studying the road map now and directed Colin to head towards Herries Road. To their left, and out of Eve's window, the gate leading to the turnstiles and the pens could be seen. It was silent now and empty; just hours earlier it had been a scene of panic and chaos.

Street lamps and car lights lit the night as they cruised along the lane. In the road ahead lay an obstruction. Colin brought them to a stop. A red Ford Cortina was parked in the middle of the lane, several yards in front of them. It looked abandoned. Both the driver and passenger-side doors were wide open. Its main beams flooded the tarmac.

Eve immediately recognised her dad's car. Her heart leapt and she fumbled with the door mechanism, flinging it open and jumping out. Stuart shouted, 'Eve!' She ignored him and started walking slowly towards three men, gathered under a bus shelter. One of them was on the floor looking up at the other two who were trying to pick him up.

Slowly she began to comprehend and her heart pounded hard in her chest. 'Dad!' she shouted, recognising Jimmy's form and clothing in the dark. She was crying now, but they were tears of hope and happiness.

Her father spun round and, as he did, he afforded her a clearer view of the man on the floor. It was Joe and she almost collapsed.

She didn't of course, and instead ran to him, followed closely by Stuart who had also recognised his dad. Relief filled his heart and recharged his batteries. The aching in his legs had gone and he felt like screaming his delight. He thought of home. At the end of this long terrible day, finally, he was going home.

Eve fell on Joe, who had finally made it on to his feet. He was like a baby foal, but she held on to him, transferring her strength to him and warming him with her body, holding him upright.

After the pain and misery of this, the worst day of her life, they were going home together, at last. 'I love you, Joe,' she said. 'I love you so much.'

I remember Jimmy looking at me and his expression said everything. His eyes filled with tears and he threw his arms around me. 'We found him, kid, we found him. Now let's get him home to his mother.'

Physically Joe was in one piece, and that was a blessing. But he was broken inside. In the months and years that followed, his family and friends would do all they could to mend him. He'd work hard at that himself.

Despite that, he would carry the scars of that day for the rest of his life. As a family, though, we were lucky. We would see our son find happiness, marry his childhood sweetheart and bring a child into the world. Too many people were robbed of that future, on 15 April 1989. The tragedy would also add another verse to a great Kop anthem,

'On April 15th '89
What should have been a joyous time
Ninety-six Friends, we all shall miss
And all the Kopites want justice (JUSTICE!)

A Liverbird upon my chest
We are the men, of Shankly's best
A team that plays the Liverpool way
And wins the championship in May

Walk on.'

Chapter Sixteen

Tales from a Scouse Wedding

Part Two

Something Old, Something New,
Someone's Fighting and the City is Blue

1

Jimmy and Eve arrived at the church 20 minutes late. The game was already 30 minutes old, and not knowing the score was killing them both. Suddenly, in the distance, they heard a great roar. Someone had just scored. Judging by the noise, it had to be Everton. The relatively small number of Reds allowed into the stadium wouldn't have been able to muster such a sound.

Eve looked at her dad and beamed. Jimmy curled his fingers into a fist, gritted his teeth and said, 'Come on!' Their instincts had been correct, because Andy Johnson had just scored his first of the day for the Blues. What neither of them realised was that it was Everton's second.

Inside the church, Joe was growing increasingly anxious. Not because Eve was late. He knew enough of Eve to know that she'd be there. Instead, it was the news coming from the back of the room that made him nervous.

Stuart was now 32 years of age and his devotion to the Blues had not diminished one iota in all the years that had elapsed since

1989. Throughout the relatively bleak 1990s that yielded a single FA Cup, secured by Joe Royle's 'Dogs of War', his love had only grown stronger. Liverpool had suffered through a similar barren spell, but support had also remained strong.

The contrast between the 1980s and the 1990s couldn't have been starker. The austere conditions of the old First Division were replaced by the glitz of the Premier League. Football wasn't invented in 1992, as some broadcasters and supporters would have you believe, but it was transformed.

The Taylor report brought the magical era of the standing Kop to an end. It also introduced a period of rapid ticket price rises.

On the field, Liverpool lost a hero and club icon, Kenny Dalglish. Everton had also seen the departure of their most successful manager, Howard Kendall. Both were great players in their day, enjoyed tremendous success as managers, and would return later for one final hoorah in the dugout.

More of that later.

Reds would start the decade with their last league title and would end it with just an FA and League Cup. They had fallen off their perch. Worst of all they'd been replaced by Manchester United.

The year 1990 also saw the end of the Thatcher era. The Tory Party's slow demise would eventually culminate in 1997 with the election of Tony Blair's Labour Party. The air of invincibility that had surrounded the so-called 'Iron Lady' had demoralised some, but it just spurred Liverpool on.

When, driven by a belief in her own hype, she introduced the poll tax, Merseyside threw itself enthusiastically into a campaign of civil disobedience. Levels of non-payment were so high in Liverpool that courts became backed up and anti-poll tax unions were formed on housing estates, to defend non-payers from bailiffs. The controversial policy eventually collapsed, and along with it went its architect, Thatcher. Liverpool rejoiced.

Hillsborough wasn't the only reason we hated her. It merely confirmed what we already knew.

The 90s also saw the relationship between the two teams deteriorate. Maybe it was driven by a lack of success. It was certainly a frustrating period for all of us. However, for Everton, it was hard not to reflect on Heysel and the ban that set them back in their development.

Picking up on the mood among Blues, Reds began to refer to their neighbours as 'Bitters'. I'm not sure this would have taken hold in the way that it did were it not for the segregation associated with all-seater stadia.

Those issues would have been taken care of in the moment, and on the terraces, rather than being allowed to fester for years in isolation. Instead, Reds and Blues, who had once seen themselves as the same beneath the colour of their shirts, now thought in terms of them and us.

For me, one moment summed up that shift perfectly. It happened after the 1996 FA Cup Final against Manchester United. The Reds lost the game 1-0, thanks to a strike by Eric Cantona.

It wasn't the white suits worn by Liverpool players in the pre-match walkabout that convinced me things had changed, and not for the better, but the homecoming the next day. Despite Liverpool returning empty-handed, the council invited them to embark on a parade of the city.

Some scoffed. After all, as Shankly said, 'First is first, second is nowhere.' Well, that's true, but he also spoke with passion from the steps of St George's Hall in 1971, in front of tens of thousands of Liverpool fans, after Liverpool had lost the FA Cup to Arsenal.

There's nothing wrong with welcoming home your defeated heroes, as far as I'm concerned. To me, it's about sportsmanship and support. It once marked us out as different to all the rest. That died in the 1990s, when only success and winning mattered.

I had gone to Queens Drive, after returning home from Wembley late the night before. I applauded enthusiastically as Roy Evans's Liverpool team sailed by, looking slightly embarrassed and waving half-heartedly. A decent crowd had turned out.

Then we all trudged back home, hoping for a better summer in the transfer market and a championship in 1997. Memories of winning the league hadn't quite faded yet, and I still felt we could get there again. All it would take was a decent signing or two, I thought. It was the same for Everton, who less than a decade earlier had been one of the best teams in the country.

As the throng weaved its way through the traffic, engrossed in conversations about what might have been, a car sped past, its driver side window wound down. The occupant shouted to us, his voice full of derision,

'Fucking embarrassing!' he yelled. 'Battered by United and you're having a parade.'

Then he was gone, sent on his way with a series of angry expletives and two-fingered salutes. Someone behind me shouted, 'Bitter bastards.' That moment encapsulates for me how everything had changed. Everton fans used to turn up to our parades, and vice versa. We once valued the journey as much as the destination. That was over and as we entered a new century of rivalry we took that bitterness and hostility with us.

The new millennium saw the boot-room traditions of Roy Evans supplanted by the continental science of Houllier, and with it came a return of trophies. The 2001 season was something of an epic in terms of Liverpool winning the League Cup, FA Cup and the UEFA Cup. The latter was especially pleasing as it meant the club was back on the European stage.

However, the Reds' ability to dine out on cup competition couldn't hide the fact that they were still a long way from winning the 'bread and butter', as Shankly called it. The derby was also as keenly fought as ever.

One particularly fractious encounter took place on 16 April 2001, just one day after the 12th anniversary of Hillsborough. During a silent, pre-match tribute to the 96 who had died, a tiny minority of Blues let themselves and their club down. A smattering of boos and jeers broke the silence. It wasn't representative, but it was upsetting.

Everton fans had always respected the anniversary, and their solidarity in the aftermath of the tragedy had sustained Reds throughout the darkest days of the campaign for truth and justice.

Who could forget the tremendous show of unity epitomised by the tying of red and blue scarves in a continuous chain from the Shankly gates at Anfield across Stanley Park to Goodison. As a club and a fan base, Everton did Liverpool – the club and the city – proud. What followed that show of disrespect by a few in the stands was a game of blood and thunder on the pitch. Liverpool, chasing European qualification, needed the win. A draw simply wasn't enough and defeat was unthinkable.

Emile Heskey put Liverpool a goal up in the fifth minute but Duncan Ferguson, a hero to the Blues who wore an Everton tattoo on his bicep, levelled three minutes before half-time. The game swung one way then the other.

The leveller was a blow and we sensed there was more drama to follow. However, as we waited for the second period to get underway, none of us had any idea that we were about to witness an absolute classic.

Markus Babbel grabbed the Reds' second just shy of the hour mark, and hopes were high that Liverpool could see it out. And with just seven minutes of the game remaining, we felt our confidence was justified. David Unsworth had other ideas.

Everton won a penalty after Sami Hyypia was adjudged to have committed a foul inside the box. The defender Unsworth stepped up and slotted the ball past Sander Westerweld to make it 2-2. Blues supporters were beside themselves with joy. The Reds were despondent. For all our ability in cup competition, we were still hopelessly fragile in the league. Our inability to see out a game, which had plagued us in the 90s, continued to haunt us in the noughties.

From Everton's point of view this was an example of never say die football. They had twice fought back from behind to level the game, and there seemed little time on the clock for the Reds to snatch a victory, or so we all thought.

With virtually no time left, Liverpool won a free kick. A young Frenchman called Gregory Vignal had chased a lost cause, only to be brought down some 40 yards from goal. The referee awarded the free kick, but the distance and angle seemed impossible.

Gary McAllister stood over the ball. He had floated one in to the far post from a similar position, earlier in the game. His hand gestures seemed to suggest he was about to do the same again. In the away end, I was chewing nervously on my fingernails. This was bound to be the last kick of the game.

Never in my wildest dreams did I imagine he could score directly from so far out. As he swung his boot, we all held our breath. We watched in utter disbelief as the ball flew past the helpless Paul Gerrard and into the bottom corner at the near post.

It was our turn to celebrate. Our team had refused to accept their fate, and yes, a part of me felt it was just desserts for the handful of idiots who had disrespected the pre-match show of respect for the 96.

Eventually, though, Houllier's revolution ran out of steam. He'd enjoyed a great record against Everton. His successor, as much as we loved him, had a more varied experience of the Merseyside derby.

Rafa Benítez's first taste of our rivalry would end in disappointment. Everton won 1-0 at Goodison Park, thanks to a Lee Carsley goal. Benítez made amends by winning his next three derbies, 2-1, 3-1 and 3-1. He would also go on to infuriate the Blues by referring to Everton as a small team.

I remember receiving a furious text message from Jimmy afterwards, which declared that 'Rafa the Jaffa has done it now! Small team! There'll be murder after that one.' I laughed and replied that the boss was right and they were.

He wasn't, of course, and they aren't. They may have fallen far short of the standards they once set, but they are still a historic club with nine league titles to their name. Nevertheless, I loved the fact that Rafa had entered the derby fray and could give as good as he got.

Despite Rafa's mixed fortunes, Joe was far from worried about the outcome of the game in 2006. As he waited for his bride to arrive, on 9 September 2006, he was in confident mood. The worst that could happen, he thought, would be a draw.

He should have been very concerned, though, because the Blues' new king, Andy Johnson, was about to write his name into derby folklore. The first of three hammer blows came at around 1.10pm. Eve was already ten minutes late when Stuart let out a muffled cry from the back of the church.

Some of the congregation laughed, while others looked on nervously. Joe glanced at Steve, who was clearly fearing the worse. Keith was less subtle and shouted, 'Stu! Score, mate?'

Stuart showed him a clenched fist, and replied, '1-0 Timmy Cahill.' An audible 'YES!' rang out from half the congregation and hisses of disappointment came from the rest. The minister, stood at the front, was grinning too. He quickly erased the happy expression, though, after a chilling glare from Steve.

Just before Eve walked through the door, on the arm of a beaming and immensely proud Jimmy, the Blues had made it two with a goal from Andy Johnson. Stuart again alerted the congregation with a spontaneous shout of, 'Come on! Get in there!'

This time the noises of appreciation were far less restrained and as Eve took her first steps, to the sound of the flutes and pipes of the 'Johnny Todd', or *Z Cars*, a huge cheer went up. Steve rolled his eyes to the heavens. It felt as if God was flipping him the bird.

Joe was transfixed, though, and all he could do was stare at Eve. Liverpool were 2-0 down but, in that moment, he couldn't care less. He would, later, but not now. She looked beautiful. He didn't think he had ever seen a more stunning woman in his whole life.

There was still plenty of time anyway, he reasoned. Liverpool under Benítez fought till the last. A score of 2-0 at half-time was no problem. Impossible was nothing, after Istanbul.

After the ceremony was over we all transferred to a reception in the city centre. Joe sat contented at the top table, waiting for the speeches to start. He'd left the church to the strains of Gerry

Marsden, and the growls and scowls of the Everton half of the congregation had given him some comfort.

In front of him now, sat his family and his best friends. Reds and Blues together, as it should be. He'd been so immersed in the joy of the occasion, he'd briefly forgotten about the game.

Instead he was reflecting on his own journey through life. He'd dealt with so much just to get here, and he felt truly happy. Then Jimmy ruined it all.

The toastmaster dragged Joe from his reverie, as he tapped a glass and declared, 'Ladies and gentlemen, please be upstanding for the father of the bride.'

There was a smattering of applause and one or two whistles. Jimmy took to his feet, a grin as wide as the Mersey on his face, and, somewhat poetically, he declared,

'I'm bursting with pride to be here today. The bride sure looks lovely, wouldn't you say? My speech won't take long, so you can sit back and chill, because Everton got three and Liverpool got nil!'

Laughter rang out and there was another huge cheer. Even some of the Reds saw the funny side. Not our Joe, though. He was trying his best, God love him, but, as he sat there and took his medicine, he looked like a bulldog chewing a wasp.

2

As the wedding guests were getting their second wind, and the evening ones were starting to arrive, Jimmy and I had taken up residence at a table in the bar. Joe and some of his mates were in the opposite corner and seemed to be embroiled in some sort of debate. We ignored them and began reminiscing about the old days and catching up on what we missed in the 1970s.

Obviously, I remember that period more fondly than Jimmy does. That's when Liverpool finally lived Shankly's dream of conquering Europe. The great man had secured the UEFA Cup in 1973, but he had stunned us all when he left in 1974. There was a genuine sense of bewilderment and sadness when the announcement was made.

I'm sure some Blues were glad to see the back of him, but the ones I knew held him in high regard. It was hard not to respect his achievements.

When Bob Paisley took over, a lot of us were worried. He was a respected member of the backroom staff, but some Reds would refer to him as the 'bucket and sponge man'. How wrong they were. Paisley had a rough first season, but in his second, he would come into his own.

Liverpool won another UEFA Cup and a league championship in 1976, and any lingering doubts were blown away. The rest is history of course. The man with an often-impenetrable accent would sign some of the greatest players in the club's history, including Kenny Dalglish. His six league titles and three European cups in just nine years remains unsurpassed. It probably always will be.

Somehow, we got on to the subject of Emlyn Hughes, and Jimmy's face darkened. He hated Crazy Horse, apparently.

'Never liked him after what he said at that homecoming parade; can't remember if it was '77, or '78,' Jimmy was saying.

'You mean, Liverpool are magic, Everton are tragic?' I said.

'Yes, there was no need for that. There were thousands of Blues who turned up to welcome Liverpool home that day. '77, it was '77,' he remembered. 'I know it was because it was your first win.'

'Yeah, I remember,' I said. 'He was out of order, but didn't he apologise, Jim?'

He had. Hughes issued an apology to Everton supporters after his spontaneous outburst at St George's Hall, when the Reds were being treated to a civic reception from the whole city. A lot of Liverpool fans, me included, were annoyed with him, too. He would later say he 'could have bitten off his tongue, for making such stupid remarks.'

Fair enough. When you do something daft all you can do is apologise. To my mind, though, he was guilty of an even greater sin, and that was cosying up to Thatcher. That didn't sit well with many of us.

The 70s was a tough time for Evertonians, as they would have to watch jealously as we cleaned up at home and abroad. Still, I always remembered the derby being a dull affair throughout the decade. I remember a run of ten games, in which six of them were draws, and five of those ended goalless.

There was joy at Maine Road in 1977, though. Liverpool would overcome the Blues in the semi-final of the FA Cup, after a replay, on their way to a disappointing defeat to United that robbed them of a treble.

The game saw what I believed at the time to be the greatest goal I'd ever seen. Terry McDermott's delightful chip over Everton keeper Dave Lawson in the tenth minute was utterly sublime. He would outdo himself in 1978, with a breathtaking header against Spurs at Anfield, from a Heighway cross.

Goals from Jimmy Case, Duncan McKenzie and Bruce Rioch meant that both sides would be back in Manchester four days later. It proved a bitter blow for Everton, because if truth be known they'd outplayed Liverpool for most of the game. In addition, Clive Thomas, the referee from Wales, carved his name into derby folklore by disallowing a late Everton goal.

With the tie deadlocked and heading for a replay, the ball had gone in off Bryan Hamilton's hip. He'd only just come on as a substitute and looked to have taken his team to Wembley. The referee disallowed it for offside and Blues of a certain generation remain disgruntled about the decision.

To make matters worse, Phil Neal would score a controversial penalty after only half an hour of the replay. It had been awarded by the same referee, Clive Thomas. He would make himself a pariah on one side of the city and be lauded by the other from that day on.

The final scoreline of 3-0 sound emphatic, but for a long spell Everton threw everything at Liverpool in search of an equaliser. However, two goals in the last three minutes, from Case and Ray Kennedy, sealed a place in the final for Liverpool. For Jimmy there was one game that lit up the decade and that took place at Goodison in 1978. It would also be payback for the bitter disappointment at Maine Road in 1977.

The match took place on 28 October 1978. It would be Everton's first win over Liverpool in seven years. It was greeted with sheer joy by the Blue half and disbelief on the part of the Reds. I didn't go to that one. I can't remember where I had been but I have this clear memory of walking down our road at about 5 o'clock on the Saturday afternoon.

I clearly didn't know the score, because I asked a couple of kids who were playing football against a neighbour's fence what the score was. One of them grinned and declared, jubilantly, 1-0 to Everton, mate. Andy King got the goal.

'No chance!' I said. I just didn't believe him.

I would get the shock of my life when Marie confirmed the terrible news when I got home. I would refuse to watch *Match of the Day* that night, and to this day have never seen that goal.

Jimmy had been there and had witnessed the win firsthand. He would describe that game, in the same way he did the 3-0 on the day of Eve and Joe's wedding, as a rare treat. It was back then. Liverpool had become the dominant team on the Mersey. In fact, they were probably the best team in Europe.

'That day was a sickener, Jim,' I said as I sipped my beer. The kids on the other side of the bar were getting louder and the conversation seemed more heated.

'Not for me it wasn't,' laughed Jimmy.

The era has become synonymous with hooliganism, but for me, supporting the Reds in the 70s was a joy. Going to the game was a good laugh. Standing on the Kop, I was just as likely to hear the chant of 'Kopites are gobshites' from our own supporters in the Anfield Road end, during a league game, as I was from Everton fans.

The 'road end' was also a standing terrace and had a reputation for humour and song every bit as much as the stand at the opposite end of the pitch. Many lads who graduated from the boy's pen on the Kop, would find their way into the Anfield Road Stand, and they would not want to be outsung or outdone.

One song they sung was an ode to their toughness and the Kops' alleged cowardice. Imagine it to the tune of 'Oh Susanna'.

> 'I went to Man United with a shotgun on my knee
> We went to take the score board end, the boys from LFC
> We are the road end, the pride of Merseyside
> We do all the fighting while the Kopites run and hide
> Kopites are gobshites.'

Situated next to the away fans, denizens of that terrace would take it upon themselves to defend the honour of Liverpool against all-comers. One song from the period, which is enjoying a bit of renaissance today, speaks to the reputation of these supporters, who called themselves the 'Annie Road Aggro'.

> 'Bertie Mee said to Bill Shankly
> Have you heard of the North Bank Highbury?
> Shanks said no I don't think so
> But I've heard of the Annie Road Agg-ro.'

Another ditty spoke to the violence that sadly accompanied football of that era. Rival supporters would often attempt to 'take' their rival's territory, which meant piling into the home end. The behaviour spawned many tales of anarchy and they would be immortalised in verse.

> 'They must be mad, around the bend
> They tried to take the Annie Road End
> United tried, and 30 died
> Cos we're the pride of Merseyside.'

For its part the Kop's songs were often complicated and involved supporters having to remember whole stanzas. One such example is 'Poor Scouser Tommy'. It was a hybrid of two songs, with the words adapted by the Kop.

The first was apparently sung regularly in Glaswegian pubs in the 60s and 70s, and the other is an Orange Lodge song called 'The Sash'. It goes like this,

'Let me tell you the story of a poor boy
Who was sent far away from his home
To fight for his king and his country
And also the old folks back home

So they put him in a Highland division
Sent him off to a far foreign land
Where the flies swarm around in their thousands
And there's nothing to see but the sand

In a battle that started next morning
Under a Libyan sun
I remember that poor Scouser Tommy
Who was shot by an old Nazi gun

As he lay on the battlefield dying
With the blood rushing out of his head (of his head)
As he lay on the battlefield dying (dying dying)
These were the last words he said ...

Oh ... I am a Liverpudlian
I come from the Spion Kop
I like to sing, I like to shout
I get thrown out quite a lot (every week)

We support the team that plays in red
A team that we all know
A team that we call Liverpool
And to glory we will go.'

The song first began in the mid-seventies and any Kopite worth his salt had to know the words off by heart; although there were stories of song sheets existing with the words on, I never saw one. The line about the 'Libyan sun' was a controversial one, too. I always remembered it as 'Arabian sun', and I still sing that now.

After Ian Rush's personal demolition of Everton in the 5-0 win in 1982, when the Welsh wizard got four, Kopites would honour his achievements by adding another verse to the end of 'Scouser Tommy'. It's still sung today.

> 'We've won the league, we've won the cup
> We've been to Europe, too
> We played the Toffees for a laugh
> And we left them feeling blue: five-nil!
>
> One two
> One two three
> One two three four
> Five-nil!
> Rush scored one
> Rush scored two
> Rush scored three
> And Rush scored four!'

In remembering those days, I suddenly recalled a derby match from 1979 that I hadn't thought about for years. It had everything: an own goal, tackles that would have looked more at home in wrestling, a punch up and a sending off, a streaker and four goals. The only thing missing from my point of view was a Liverpool win. The game would finish 2-2.

'Jim,' I said, 'do you remember that game at Anfield, I think it was '79. It ended 2-2, there was a barney on the pitch, and that woman ran on the pitch naked.'

He laughed. 'Remember it mate, I was there!' he said. 'I was in the Kemlyn Road believe it or not.' He pronounced it Kremlin Road, and I laughed, not knowing if he was being ironic or if it was an accident.

'Really,' I said, 'I was in the Kop.'

He ignored that. He was already drifting back through the years. The game had been an absolute cracker. Liverpool had gone a goal up in the eighth minute when Mick Lyons put through his own net. Then the Blues levelled through Brian Kidd. The game swung one way then the other, and there was hilarity when some woman, stark naked, ran across the pitch, much to the delight of the men in the crowd.

Liverpool went back in front when Ray Kennedy scored ten minutes into the second half. But Andy King levelled with roughly 20 minutes to go. Then the game exploded.

Gary Stanley went in hard on David Johnson and Terry McDermott saw red for chinning him. Stanley went off, too. This was a proper derby, and although it finished with both sides level, we'd all been entertained. Nobody could doubt the players had given everything to the cause.

Jimmy piped up again. 'You know why I remember that game so well,' he said. I didn't, obviously.

'I saw our Eve with your Joe, walking by The Arkles after the game.'

'Really?' I said. 'I didn't know they were together back then.'

'I didn't either until I copped the two of them. Soft lad had his arm around our Eve and I was going nuts,' he said with a chuckle.

'Did you speak to them?' I asked.

'Nah. They didn't see me and I was on the other side of the road at the time, by the entrance to the park. Besides, I was scared of her back then,' he laughed.

'What do you mean?' My curiosity was peaked.

'Jesus, you wouldn't have seen her in them days, would you. She had green spikey hair then and bleeding safety pins everywhere. Moody cow, too.'

I didn't remember seeing Eve in them days, but I did remember our Joe behaving the same way.

'Sounds like our Joe,' I said. 'He had orange hair; looked a right divvy. Lived in this club called Eric's and was always telling me the Beatles were a load of rubbish. I wanted to give him a clip around the earhole on more than one occasion,' I said.

We both went quiet for a moment, and then Jimmy said, 'I can't blame them for not telling us, though.'

He was right, and it saddened me. We'd behaved like a couple of idiots and we'd prevented our kids from being able to share important moments in their lives with us. As a result, we'd missed so much. I was enjoying reminiscing with Jimmy when a commotion from across the bar interrupted us. It was our Joe's table and it looked like a fight was on the cards.

3

Joe was sitting with Stuart, Steve and Keith and a few other lads I didn't recognise. Jimmy later told me one of them was Anthony Keegan, the youngest son of a mate of his. It was a potent mix of Reds, Blues and several hours of drinking.

As you'd imagine, the subject of the derby and Andy Johnson came up. There was a fair bit of piss-taking going on, which is fine. That's all part of the spoils of victory. Problem was they were already full of ale, and the more they drank the louder and more aggressive they got.

None of them can remember how the subject of Heysel got brought up, but it did. The events of May 29 1985 and the resultant ban on English teams had now been tossed like a grenade into a conversation about a derby match in 2006, by a kid who wasn't even born in 1985.

The Blues had won the league in 1985 and had a great side. While there are never any guarantees in football, a European Cup win would have moved them to the next level.

The five-year ban, Liverpool got six, set English football back years. It also robbed Everton of their chance to play on a bigger stage. The frustration of Everton fans, and players, from that era is entirely justifiable.

Joe and I had gone to that game. Our hopes were high after Joe Fagan had won the club's fourth European Cup in Rome in 1984. We had also cruised to the final, disposing of Lech Poznan, Benfica, Austria Vienna and Panathinaikos. A year earlier, we had beaten Roma on their own turf, a monumental feat. So I thought winning 'Old Big Ears' for the fifth time was nailed on.

I'd surprised Joe with a ticket and we hired a minibus and travelled over land and sea to get there. He brought a group of his mates with him, too. We planned to drive to Dover on the 27th and camp there overnight, before taking the ferry over to France and arriving in Belgium on the day of the match.

However, once we arrived at the English port, we opted to go straight to Calais. I remember there was a pub called the Liverpool and we spent a fair bit of time in there, filling up on the cheap French beer. Joe was never a great drinker and he paid for it in spades the next day, throwing up on the grass next to the van. The stick he took for that was merciless.

Then we were off to Belgium and a town called Tournai. To me this was the cleanest place I had ever seen. In the 1980s Liverpool was a city in decline and bore no resemblance to this gleaming European town.

We had a great time there and even posed for photographs with some Juventus supporters. There was a good feeling in the air and I never imagined for a second the trip would end the way it did. I went into a small shop to get some water, and the old lady behind the counter looked at me warily.

'No trouble, no trouble,' she said, realising I was here for the football.

I told her there was nothing to worry about, saying Liverpool supporters behaved themselves. That was true. Prior to Heysel the only trouble we'd encountered in Europe was from rival fans. Our treatment at the hands of Roma supporters in '77 and '84 had been terrifying.

In fact, it was widely accepted that the Reds were non-violent. They did have a reputation for industrial-scale shoplifting, mind, but there was no history of trouble on our part, before '85. I left the shop with the woman smiling and waving me off.

Then it was on to Heysel for the final. Our tickets weren't in the area where the tragedy happened. There was another section between us and the mayhem, but we could see there were problems when we got in there.

The atmosphere around the stadium was carnival-like at first. There was loads of singing and a few Italian supporters were mixing in with us, swapping scarves, etc. It was a standard European away day.

One of the lads Joe had brought with him, I think his name was Ian, suggested that we go around to the Juventus end and see what was going on there. I didn't think anything of it. So far, I'd been given no reason to believe there would be any problems.

That's when the atmosphere changed. Coming towards us, and running fast, was a large group of Liverpool supporters. Someone shouted 'Run', and I could see people in Juventus colours and masks over their faces, chasing the Reds, waving what looked like sticks. They turned out to be plastic flagpoles.

Scuffles broke out all around us and I felt frozen in time. At that point Joe and I got separated. I learned later that he had hid, with some other fella, behind one of the many kiosks that were dotted around the place. He still took a few digs from Juventus fans and the police before he finally got away and re-joined me and the others at our end of the stadium.

It was getting near kick-off by now and we decided to go inside to avoid any other problems. The ground was a crumbling mess. It felt more like an English Third Division stadium than an elite UEFA venue. There were big holes in the concrete structure and no turnstiles to speak of, as far as I remember.

A few Liverpool fans were trying to climb over the wall and were being beaten back by policemen wielding truncheons. This all added to the sense of chaos and disorganisation.

Inside we could make out the fighting on the terracing. It was obvious that segregation had broken down or maybe was non-existent. We had no idea anyone had been seriously hurt, let alone killed. We wouldn't find that out until later.

Down on the running track there was absolute bedlam. The police seemed to be handing out indiscriminate beatings, and I could see supporters from both sides with blood streaming down their faces and on to their shirts. Then a group of Juventus fans started hurling objects into our section from the track below. That was the first time I thought the game might not go ahead.

Eventually, it seemed like order had been restored and the game went ahead. When I remember that game, I rarely think of the score. Football seems irrelevant when weighed against the terrible loss of life that night. At the time, though, not knowing the scale of the disaster, I was just furious about the minutiae.

It was never a penalty, I was arguing with someone, and why didn't we get a penalty. I was even annoyed with some of our lads, who stayed behind to applaud the Juventus lap of honour. None of us had a clue that people had died.

How surreal that, almost two hours after the bodies of 39 people were carried from the rubble of a collapsed wall, people inside the same ground were oblivious to what had happened. Worst still, some, who did seem to know, appeared to be in denial.

As we walked away from the ground, some lad wearing a West Ham shirt came over to us and told us there'd been deaths. We didn't believe him and I told him to behave himself. The atmosphere around the stadium had turned nasty, though, and we decided to get out of town as quickly as possible.

We were stopped at the border by an angry-looking guard who ordered us out of the van and demanded to see our passports. Another climbed inside and started rifling through our stuff. Of course, he found all our beer and told us to hand it over.

I said I would, if he gave me a receipt. That act of defiance saw me end up in the security booth. I was given an ultimatum: either go back into Belgium and drink it or surrender it there and then. None of us wanted to stay there any longer than we had to, so we gave it up. I'm sure the border guards had a fine old night, on us.

We still had no idea of the enormity of the tragedy that was unfolding behind us. We just drove on to the port, moaning about our confiscated beer.

At the ferry terminal, there were crowds of supporters and tourists waiting to take the trip over to England. Next to us was an American couple and, on hearing our accents, one of them, a woman, asked us if we'd been to the game. It was her who convinced us that people had died. It hit us like a tonne of bricks.

Suddenly I remembered the looks we were getting from the people we passed on the way through Belgium, and it was starting to make sense. We knew there and then that things would never be the same again. Nothing on this magnitude had ever happened before.

I've discussed that night many times down the years. I continue to feel shame that our club was involved in such a horrific tragedy. There were many contributory factors: stadium not fit for purpose, poor crowd-safety protocols, no segregation. But there is no denying that the Reds who charged into a crowd of Juventus supporters were also one of those factors.

Thinking about the pain and anguish suffered by the families of those who perished makes me sick, even now. I've no idea what they must be feeling, but I can certainly imagine.

So, to hear it dredged up, often in song, by people who weren't even born when the disaster happened, sickens me. When I hear older heads doing it, I despair. The death of innocent people should never be used to taunt rival fans, by anyone.

That was the point being made around the table, as Jimmy and I wandered over to see what the row was about. Apparently, Anthony Keegan, a Blue, had used the word 'murderers' in retaliation to a comment by our Joe.

A few of the lads were now on their feet and looked ready to exchange blows with each other. The insult had been interpreted as a reference to Hillsborough. The lad's defence was that he was referring to Heysel.

'Why is that any better?' said Joe. 'You're using the death of innocent people to score points. You're out of order.'

Anthony started laughing. 'Yeah, like your lot have never come out with stuff like that. Where's your famous Munich song, eh?'

That comment struck a chord with me. I remember being at a game with Joe in the early eighties. We were in the Kop. A chant of 'are you watching Manchester?' went up and we all joined in. It was stupid, really, and it's the type of thing I frown upon now. You shouldn't be singing about a rival unless you're playing them, I say.

When that song died down, it was replaced by sickening chants about the 1958 Munich air disaster in which members of Matt Busby's Manchester United team were killed. I'm old enough to remember that, of course. It had shocked football.

Matt Busby once captained Liverpool and there was a great deal of solidarity between the clubs after the crash. Liverpool even loaned United players to help them out.

So to hear our fans singing such sickening songs on the Kop made me ashamed. Worse still, our Joe had joined in. He was probably no older than the young Blue causing bother at the wedding, at the time.

Nevertheless, I remember giving him the biggest bollocking of his life and the look on his face told me he had no idea why I was so upset. That's the problem with emotional distance. To him Munich was just a word, with no human attachment. It was a chant, a bit of banter, something you could use to wind up your opponent.

You don't hear that song on the Kop now. I guess experiencing a tragedy of our own, made us realise how sickening stuff like that is. It hasn't died away completely, though, and you'll occasionally hear it in a pub or on a coach going to an away game.

Joe and I heard it on one, travelling down to Wembley for the 2012 FA Cup Final against Chelsea. A group of young lads were sat on the back seat, drinking heavily. They were going through the whole repertoire of songs and at first it was a good laugh.

I thought it was great that these kids were leading the singing. Then they started on the Munich stuff and the atmosphere turned nasty. A couple of older fellas got up and walked to the back of the bus to have a go at them.

'What the fucking hell are you doing?' said one of them. He was twice the age and size of the biggest among the kids.

Still, full of ale and bravado, perhaps, one of the boys called his bluff. 'What's it got to do with you?' he said.

The older guy grabbed this kid by his T-shirt and lifted him off the seat. 'I'll tell you what, lad. Why don't you sing it again and I'll show you what it's got to do with me.'

The lad's mates piped up at this point. 'Alright mate. It's just a laugh, isn't it. They give it to us, so we give it back. That's all.'

He was referring to United fans' chants of 'murderers', etc. The older guy was having none of it.

'No, we don't lad. Let them sing their stuff. We should be better than that. It's a shithouse's song anyway. Sing it again and I'll throw you all off the fucking bus myself.'

I looked at Joe and he smiled nervously at me, perhaps recalling the foolishness of his youth. We all do daft things when we're growing up. The important thing is that we leave them behind as we get older. Hopefully these kids would too.

They continued to annoy us for the rest of the journey. They didn't sing that song, though.

We need more of that, on all sides of the football divide. The older heads should take their younger counterparts to task every time they spout their bile. Problem is there are plenty of people who are old enough to know better but choose to say nothing.

The argument around the table was becoming increasingly heated. Joe's mate Keith was trying to calm things down, but he was getting nowhere. Instead, Anthony was getting angrier and swearing loudly. He then blurted out something that took the row to a new level. He shouted,

'Justice for the 96 my arse. What about justice for the 39.' His words landed like high explosive.

I thought our Joe would have got up and punched him in the mouth, but he didn't. Instead it was Stuart, an Everton supporter, who stepped forward. He was shaking with rage and was nose-to-nose with Anthony.

'What does that mean, mate?' he said.

'What are you on about?' slurred Anthony.

'You know what I'm saying. You just said justice for the 39. What does that even mean?'

'It's fucking obvious isn't it. They go on about the 96 all the time. What about the 39?' He was smirking and looked really pleased with himself.

'You think a lot about the 39 do you mate?' retorted Stuart.

'You what?'

'You go to the memorial services in Turin every year, do you?'

'Oh, fuck off!' Anthony was getting exasperated now, sensing the argument was getting away from him.

'So, you want justice for them, right? Because you know all about their cause, right? So, tell me then, what does justice for the 39 even look like?'

Stuart was pushing hard now and everyone around the table had gone quiet. 'Would it mean Liverpool fans in jail? Police officers in jail? Belgian officials in jail?' he asked.

'Yeah. Too fucking right,' said Anthony. 'Justice for the 39.' He swayed a little but managed to stay on his feet.

'Okay, smart arse, well guess what. All of that fucking happened. There was a legal process, and those found guilty were punished,' said Stuart. 'It may or may not be justice. Who knows what justice is, when you've lost someone you love. Only they have a right to pass judgement on that anyway. Not you or me. It's more than anyone at Hillsborough ever got though, isn't it?'

The lad had no answer. Stuart went on, this time lowering his voice.

'Listen, mate, be angry if you want. Be angry with UEFA for banning English teams. I'm a Blue; it infuriates me too. It was nothing to do with us, but our future was stolen, through no fault of our own.

'Be angry with them for sending 50,000 football fans into a death-trap and not organising any decent segregation. Be angry with the Liverpool supporters who charged; I am too. So is he for that matter.' Stuart pointed at our Joe.

'I'll tell you what, though. You can be as angry as you like about all those things and I'm right fucking behind you. But don't you fucking dare steal Justice for the 96 and turn it into a weapon against people like this fella, by chanting justice for the 39. You know nothing about them, and you know nothing about him either.'

Stuart was crying now. They were tears of rage, but I think he had dredged up some old memories too, memories of chasing across the country looking for his sister's boyfriend, and not knowing if he was alive or dead.

Joe tried to get him to sit down, telling him it wasn't worth the aggro, but Stuart was having none of it. He went on.

'Because when you chant that, you're saying he has no right to ask for justice for him and his own. I'm not having that. Because, you know what, Justice for the 96 belongs to all of us. It's Everton's chant too. We could have been at Hillsborough. It was a fluke we weren't. They smeared us too, told lies about all of us. So, it's my song and his song. Don't you fucking dare belittle that.'

Anthony threw his arms in the air and left. The rest of them settled down, with several lads patting Stuart on the back.

Jimmy and I returned to our table. We'd gone over to help, but the kids had sorted it for themselves.

'I'm proud of your Stu there, Jim.' I said. 'You should be too.'

'I am,' he replied. 'Thing is, Tom, what he said there, at the end, I've thought about that stuff a lot over the years.' His tone was serious. 'There's something I've wanted to say to you for a while. I probably should have said it years ago.'

'Jesus, Jimmy. You've got me worried here.' I was half joking, but a part of me feared what he was about to say. I needn't have worried.

'No nothing like that, you divvy. Shut up and let me speak. This is profound stuff.' He winked, and I laughed.

'Okay. Go on then,' I said, rolling my eyes comically.

'After Hillsborough, mate ...' He paused, sniffed and I noticed a tear in the corner of his eye. He coughed and pressed on.

'After Hillsborough, I realised something. It wasn't just the disaster, it was everything that came with it. The lies and the smears. That front page, and the fight that should never have taken so long. All of that made me think about the strike, Tommy, and how I was wrong for scabbing.'

I reached out and patted him on the shoulder. 'Jimmy that's gone now mate.'

'No, I know it is,' he said. 'I'm not saying it for that reason. It's just that I can see now that if we hadn't stuck together after '89 they'd have walked all over us.

'It would have been easy for Everton supporters to say it's not our problem, like most of the country did. That would have been wrong, though. Your fight was ours, too.

'Back in the 70s, I saw your strike as your problem because it didn't affect me, but that was wrong, mate. It was my fight, too, and even if it wasn't I should have supported you.' He coughed again and took a swig of his beer.

'Really, Jim?' I asked. 'Thought I was just playing at revolution then.'

'You were,' he said. 'That was detail, though. The bigger picture was you were fighting to make things better. My quarrel with you was detail, not big picture. I can see now that when we argue with each other over the small stuff we're not defending each other. We make it easy for others to take the piss and keep us in our place.'

I was stunned to hear my old mate talking like this. 'Listen to you, Trotsky,' I said.

We both laughed at that. Then Jimmy said,

'Yeah, mate. I'm a proper lefty now, eh? Look, all I'm saying is this. In the end we only have each other. If you can't have your mate's back, then you can't expect him to have yours. Solidarity is all there is, mate. I see that now.'

'Your lad and his sister see it too,' I said. 'You raised them well, mate.'

So as the night ended, we drank a toast to our kids, and to solidarity.

Chapter Seventeen

Three Reds and a Blue Meet the Three Amigos

and

Scouser United Will Never be Defeated

After Hillsborough, solidarity had been our watchword. To be fair, it had also been in the decade that preceded it. It had needed to be.

In the 60s all we needed was love, the 70s brought us riches we could barely have imagined but in the 1980s the city of Liverpool wanted revolution. Margaret Thatcher had been elected in 1979 and had set about dismantling industry and places like Merseyside were decimated.

One after the other, factories and businesses would close. The city was haemorrhaging its population, as workers sought work across the country, and abroad on building sites in Germany. Unemployment spiralled and the place started to feel like an enclave cut off from the rest of the country, a troublesome region out of step with the new order.

The Toxteth riots erupted in 1981 and the south end of the city burned. This uprising by the mainly black population of the area has been largely portrayed in the context of race. It's true that in the grip of Thatcherite austerity the black community in Liverpool suffered some of the worst privations and social injustices. Their grievances were also shared by many of the city's white population, however. Some white youths took part in the rioting, too, and there was a general rise in militancy and anti-establishment feeling across the city.

This would find expression in local government, with the election of a left-wing council that had stood on the platform of fighting the government and resisting cuts to public services. Many of the councillors elected were revolutionary socialists, sympathetic to a group called Militant. They had broad support and won landslide elections.

On the Kop and among Blues, too, that sense of otherness that had characterised us in the 60s and 70s hardened. It became rare to see the Union Jack among supporters, as Liverpudlians of all persuasions shifted further to the left.

I can remember this once finding expression in a chant aimed at Nottingham Forest supporters during the miners' strike. The Democratic Union of Miners was a breakaway union, which split from Arthur Scargill's National Union of Miners. It had its base in Nottingham. When its members broke the strike, supporters on the Kop chanted 'Scab, scab, scab', at Forest supporters in the away end.

Merseyside would be at the forefront of the battle against Thatcherism throughout the 1980s and the Prime Minister would place us on a list of people she referred to as 'the enemy within'.

We simply didn't care. While the city fell to rack and ruin and its citizens and politicians were in open revolt, our football teams ruled the land. Football in the early eighties continued to be a blessed relief from the constant struggle of daily life.

Culturally, Liverpool was struggling to rid itself of the legacy of the Beatles. Bands like Echo and the Bunnymen are often credited with being among the first to break the mould and not try to sound like John, Paul, George and Ringo.

The decade would see the emergence of a new Mersey beat, with China Crisis, Orchestral Manoeuvres in the Dark, A Flock of

Seagulls and Elvis Costello finding fame. Later, Frankie Goes to Hollywood would camp almost permanently in the top ten, with 'Relax', 'Two Tribes' and 'The Power of Love'.

Thatcher threw everything at Liverpool in the 80s and many of us felt she set out to wreck the place. Cabinet papers released 30 years later would show we were right. Her agenda had been managed decline, and local politicians who got in her way were surcharged and removed from office.

While it's true that not everybody in the city shared that spirit of defiance and that some found the tactics of the left counterproductive, many of us felt we had no choice but to fight. In the Fazakerley area of the city, a banner strung across a local Labour club would read, 'Better to Break the Law than Break the Poor.'

This was a reference to the council's decision not to set a legal rate for services. Doing so would have meant massive cuts to services, jobs and an increase in rents. They managed to force concessions initially, but their cards were marked from that moment on.

By 1984 the whole city seemed to be putting two fingers up to the rest of the country. Despite everything we had endured, we had the most left-wing council ever, our music continued to sell across the world and our two football teams won the lot.

Liverpool won the league, the League Cup and the European Cup. Everton won the FA Cup and the Charity Shield. Every domestic trophy on offer finished up on Merseyside. Our two managers, Joe Fagan and Howard Kendall, sat atop a gleaming pile of silver and there wasn't a thing anyone could do about it.

The sense of solidarity at Wembley that year, when Liverpool and Everton met in the final of the League Cup was palpable. Chants of Merseyside on Wembley Way and in the stadium itself were as much about civic pride as a celebration of our footballing prowess.

Of course, as previously discussed, Heysel in 1985 would sow the seeds of future fractures. However, the two clubs would be back in the capital in 1986 for an FA Cup final to remember. It would be a show of Scouse power and a message to the rest of the world highlighting what a fantastic city we were.

Liverpool had eventually won the League Cup Final in 1984 after a replay and a shot from distance from Graeme Souness. Everton, the reigning league champions, were looking for revenge two years later.

They had signed Gary Lineker from Leicester City for a paltry (by today's standards) £800,000 in the summer of 1985. It was a masterstroke, and, in his brief spell at Goodison before he left for Barcelona, the striker would net 40 times in 58 appearances.

Liverpool faced a great Everton side in 1986. Their defence, marshalled by the likes of Gary Steven and Derek Mountfield, sat behind their midfield genera, Peter Reid, with Graeme Sharp and Lineker providing the goals. They were a formidable outfit.

The Reds were no slouches, either. Lawrenson and Hansen were one of the best centre-back pairings I had ever seen. In the middle we had Jan Molby and Kevin MacDonald, who had replaced Souness. We were also lethal in attack, with Ian Rush our goal machine.

Rushy was the greatest goalscorer I had ever seen, and that was saying something. I had, of course, seen Roger Hunt, Kevin Keegan and our player-manager in 1986, Kenny Dalglish. They were all great players, but Rush was phenomenal.

In that magical 1984 season, he would net 47 times, setting a club record. Liverpool had also never lost a game, in which Rush had scored. We wouldn't keep that record forever, but in 1986, with him in the side we felt invincible.

I remember that day for so many reasons. The journey down there was special. Three Reds and a Blue together in the same minibus, the jokes and the songs. I had gone with our Joe and his mates Steve and Keith and they had me laughing all the way there.

Keith was the only Everton supporter among us, but he more than held his own. Of course, the Reds won the game, eventually, 3-1. They'd gone a goal behind in the 27th minute, thanks to

Lineker. Jim Beglin and Bruce Grobbelaar had almost come to blows and by half-time Keith was in his element.

The Reds hadn't even got started, though, and in the second half Liverpool went up a gear. Rush levelled on 56 minutes, before Craig Johnston, the boy from Australia who referred to himself as the worst player in the best team in the world, grabbed the second six minutes later. His celebrations revealed just how much it meant.

A 2-1 lead against Everton in an FA Cup Final was a fragile one. With Sharp and Lineker lurking, the threat of an equaliser was ever present. As the game entered the last ten minutes, I remember my stomach being in knots. I looked at the three lads and their faces were a picture.

Steve and Joe looked like they were both about to burst. Steve's face was as red as his mop of hair and Keith was hopping up and down every time Everton advanced over the halfway line. Then the ball fell to Rush. I couldn't see who laid it on from where I was, but I remember that hard, low, diagonal blast to this day.

I've seen the ball hit the camera in the back of the net a hundred times or more on video and DVD since then, but the sheer joy we felt at Wembley when Rush scored in the 82nd minute to clinch the league and cup double is hard to beat.

Dalglish had become the first player-manager to win a double and it was an achievement even Keith was quick to acknowledge. It's a mark of how different things were between us back then, that Everton fans stayed for the lap of honour; I will also remember our Joe's mate clapping the Reds as they walked around the pitch.

The game was a sideshow, though, compared to what happened in Mayfair that evening. We'd booked into a hotel room in London. It wasn't exactly the Ritz but it was somewhere to lay down our heads after we had drunk the capital dry.

Keith had a mate who owned a Pub in London's Mayfair district. It was called the King's Arms and it was in the Shepherd Market area. Quite a posh part of the city. As soon as the game was over we headed straight there and were at the bar all night.

The prices were astronomical compared to Liverpool, and we must have blown through a month's wages that weekend, easy. At around eight o'clock I was starting to feel a bit queasy. The bar was rammed at this point and stuffy. You could smoke inside pubs then and I could hardly breath.

The lads agreed to escort the old man outside. I was 45, and to them I was ancient. We sat at one of the tables in front of the pub, soaking up the last of the evening sun. I took in some fresh air and began looking for my second wind. There was no way I was going to be outdone by my son and his mates.

Next to the pub was a short piece of road leading to a dead end. In it was parked a huge black limousine with the driver still in it. I'd only ever seen one of these on the television.

'Tell you what, lads,' said Keith. 'How great would it be to have somebody waiting in a car like that just to drive you around.'

'Must be fucking loaded. Probably a business man or a politician,' said Joe.

'Could be one of the players,' Steve mused.

'No way a player can afford a motor and chauffeur, mate. I know they earn a lot, but not that much,' said Keith.

I agreed. 'Besides,' I said, 'we'd have recognised them when we were in there, wouldn't we?' They all agreed.

Steve got out this camera. It was an old thing that ran on about four batteries and you had to wind the film on after every shot. He took it to every game.

'Here we go,' said Joe, laughing.

Steve ignored him and started taking pictures of the car and the driver. The driver just read his newspaper and ignored this Scouse paparazzi. Then Steve turned to a fella sat at one of the tables next to us and asked him to do a group shot of the four of us.

Back then you couldn't view your pictures on the little screen on the back of the camera. You had to wait to see if the shots had turned out okay, after having them developed at a chemist's.

We were having a fantastic time, but Steve suggested we sample a few other local establishments. We agreed and off we all went.

We did the rounds and then made our way back to the King's Arms about 10.30pm and sat outside for a few more beers.

From behind us, we could hear the most terrible singing you could ever imagine. It was coming from further down the road, but gradually getting closer. Then from around the corner, unbelievably, appeared Oliver Reed, Michael Caine and George Best. The trio had their arms around each other and were singing their heads off. They breezed right past our open mouths and fell into the limousine, which had been parked there all night waiting for them. Keith ran inside to tell his mate, only to be told that the place was a regular haunt for the three stars.

We stayed there a few hours more, until Steve fell asleep in the pub. That was our cue to head back to the hotel and I asked Keith's mate to call us a taxi. We'd drank so much that I couldn't remember the journey or getting into the room at all.

I woke up the next day and my head was pounding. I was so thirsty I could have drunk the Thames dry, but too pig-sick to lift my head off the pillow. When I eventually dragged my arse out of that bed, I headed straight to the bathroom and drank from the tap over the sink.

It was a relief but did nothing for my headache. Regretting the fact that we'd brought no paracetamol with us, I decided to confront my reflection in the mirror. That's when I noticed one of my eyebrows was missing.

I had murder with the three of them but not one of them would own up. I was fuming, and dreading having to go into work with only one eyebrow. They tried their best to look contrite but I'd catch them sniggering several times.

The journey home was in silence until we stopped at the services for a toilet break and a cup of coffee for me. My head was still giving me grief and I badly needed some sleep. As we sat there recharging our batteries, I could eventually see the funny side and we all started laughing.

A few days later we all decided to meet up in the local to have a look at the photos. It was really just an excuse to have a few more beers and relive a memorable weekend in the capital. Steve had picked the photographs up from the chemist beforehand and hadn't opened them until he got there. They were still sealed in the plastic outer wrapping when he arrived.

We went through them one by one, excitedly recalling the events of the day, when Keith noticed something in one of the pictures. It was the one of the four of us together, taken by a stranger outside the King's Arms.

'Jesus Bloody Christ!' said Keith. 'Look at that!'

We all got closer as he laid the photograph in front of us on the table and sat back with a huge grin on his face. What he had spotted, sitting a couple of tables back from us outside that bar, was none other than Oliver Reed, Michael Caine and George Best. The three drunken amigos had seen us having our picture taken and had done the 1980s equivalent of 'photobombing' by raising their glasses in the air and grinning for the camera.

It had blown us away. A priceless memento of a fantastic weekend watching our teams do battle. However, that wasn't the end of it. As Steve continued to thumb through the photos he came across the real money shot.

There, in glorious technicolour, was a picture of me, collapsed on the bed, mouth open and catching flies. On my forehead was a big blob of shaving foam and standing over me, grinning like a madman and holding a razor in his hand, was Keith.

He went bright red. He was caught bang to rights and we all burst out laughing.

We were back there at Wembley again in 1989, but the atmosphere was different. This time the journey had been long and the hill steeper and more treacherous than it had ever been before. We climbed it anyway, and when we found ourselves at the summit, we could have found no better opposition.

As Gerry Marsden sang 'You'll Never Walk Alone' from a platform in the centre circle, the Blues joined in, scarves held aloft, flags and banners held high. The city could never be divided, simply because there were Reds and Blues in the same family.

They'd created a mile of scarves from Goodison to Anfield in a symbolic show of unity. Ian Snodin tied the first scarf to the gates of Goodison Park. It would have stretched across Walton Road and across Stanley Park until it reached the Shankly gates.

At Wembley, on 20 May a giant banner displayed at the end of the stadium read, 'LIVERPOOL FC THANKS YOU ALL'. Similar displays went on in the derby matches that followed the tragedy and whatever bitterness exists today about Heysel and European bans, it was non-existent in the aftermath of Hillsborough.

The game was a spectacle. Liverpool would eventually win, capturing their second double of the decade, but Everton didn't lie down. They fought valiantly, twice coming from behind to level the score. In the end an extra-time goal by Ian Rush separated the two.

In the stands nothing separated us. It was Merseyside United, a lesson to the world about how to do football rivalry. I celebrated the win; any fan would. It felt like catharsis after the horror of April, but I was also proud of my city and of the Blues stood all around me at full time. They applauded their own and ours, despite their disappointment at the result.

I look back on those days and they feel like a land lost in time. I wish we could find our way there again.

For all the trauma of the 1980s, I will hold on to the many magical and hilarious moments that football gave us. This was just one of them, but we would revisit it many times over in the years that lay ahead.

Chapter Eighteen

Truth and Justice and Jimmy's Last Stand

'Passengers, please be aware that due to the service of remembrance for the 96, delays are likely due to the increased volume of people travelling.'

The driver's announcement barely caused a flicker among the people in our compartment. 'The 96' was a phrase burned into our consciousness over 27 years.

The platform had been packed with people, some wearing Liverpool tops, others Everton colours. The Blues had been there throughout the whole journey. On the night of the disaster, I had leaned heavily on Jimmy, a staunch Evertonian with blue blood flowing through his veins, as I searched for my boy.

Everton supporters had turned up in their droves at the Shankly gates within hours of the tragedy, tying scarves to the railings. I would see them at every memorial for more than a quarter of a century, too.

Now we were all headed into town together for 'Truth and Justice Day', as we had dubbed it. It was 26 April 2016, 27 years after the Hillsborough disaster and four years since we had lost Jimmy at the FA Cup semi-final against Everton in 2012.

He'd made it. We got him there in the end.

I remember the day we found out he was finally going to be released in time for the game. The doctors and nurses on the ward had been sceptical that things could be sorted in time. He was very ill, and Elaine would have struggled to care for him at home without help. He also needed equipment, like a portable toilet and oxygen.

Sorting all of that takes time. Elaine had bought a single bed, and Joe, Stu and I had gone around there to assemble it the night before he came out of hospital. He never did get to sleep in it.

We hadn't realised it, but a specialist nurse had come to see Jimmy on the ward the week before they let him out. She had brought this big document with her. It was called 'Preferred Priorities of Care' and it was all about where he wanted to spend his final days, what his last wishes were and stuff like that.

He'd gone through the whole thing with her and written down everything he wanted. He'd planned it all out in detail. So, when the consultant had suggested that getting Jimmy home in time for the game on Saturday was impossible, he had pulled out this document as his trump card.

It listed a series of questions, and under each one Jimmy had written his answers in black ink. His handwriting looked like a child's, a product of the medicines he was taking and the fact that he was so terribly weak at that point.

Under the first question, 'What has been happening to you?' he had written,

> I've got cancer because I smoked and drank too much, but I've had a cracking life. So, I regret nothing, apart from the fact that I won't get to see my grandson grow up, kiss my wife goodnight every night and have a pint with my best mate ever again. At least I got to see my little girl get married though. If you let me out, I'll at least get to see Everton beat Liverpool at Wembley and that will top it all off.

Then came the next one: 'What are your preferences and priorities for your future care?' Jimmy wrote,

Take me straight from here and load me in the back of a van, with my family and my mates. Drive me to Wembley. If I survive that, I want you to perform heroic measures so that I can get back there for the final. If we win it, who cares. After that, you can do what you like with me.

'Where would you like to be cared for in the future?'

I've lived my whole adult life with one woman, my Elaine. She has looked after me, kept me on the straight and narrow and put up with my moods and daft behaviour down the years. When I go, whenever that is, I want to be by her side, wherever that is. She'll know what to do. She always has. If my mate Tommy and the rest of our families are there, too, then that would be perfect.

Finally, the form asked for any 'Further information'. Jimmy had simply listed what looked like a set of final demands.

1. The Blues to knock Liverpool out of the FA Cup
2. Win the FA Cup
3. My mate Tommy to wear an Everton shirt at my funeral
4. Bury me within earshot of Goodison Park. I want to listen to the match for all eternity.
5. Justice for the 96

His replies to the questions made us laugh and cry. I can imagine they'd had the same effect on the nurse who'd helped him complete it. To be fair to the ward staff, they pulled out all the stops to grant Jimmy his final wishes.

We eventually got him out of the hospital on the Friday evening and the whole family drove straight down to London in a minibus we'd hired. Jimmy slept on the back seat, propped up on a pillow and with a thin plastic tube blasting oxygen into his nostrils from a cylinder that sat next to him.

Elaine had a great big bag full of meds with her. We joked that she was like a walking pharmacy. There were all kinds of prescription drugs in there and she would keep him topped up the whole way there. I often wonder what would have happened if the police had pulled us over, with all that 'happy juice', as Jimmy called it, on board.

Back on that Merseyrail service to Liverpool Central, I gazed at his family and mine and reflected on how his final wish, Justice for the 96, now seemed to be within our grasp.

The inquests in Warrington had delivered the news we had all been waiting for. It was a great victory for the families of those we had lost, as well as those campaigning for the survivors. Hillsborough was no accident, the jury had declared. Instead, our brothers and our sisters had been unlawfully killed.

Liverpool fans had played no part in the disaster, the inquest concluded. Kelvin MacKenzie's headline in that infamous rag, that has since become a pariah on Merseyside, was a lie. It was total vindication for a people and a city. We had truth, we had justice. Now we wanted accountability.

The whole family was together on that train. Joe, Eve and little Robbie, who was now 12, sat across the aisle from us. In front of me was Marie and Elaine, and Keith was sat next to me. Behind us was Stuart, his wife Sophie and their two little girls, Lucy and Mollie.

There was of course a gaping hole left by Jimmy and Joe's mate Steve, who had also passed away years earlier, after a short illness. They hadn't made it to see those accidental death verdicts quashed, but they were doubtless there in spirit.

As the train pulled out of Fazakerley station and headed into town, I cast my mind back to the night of Joe's wedding. I remembered Jimmy and how he had talked of the importance of sticking together. I recalled how Stuart had argued so passionately for unity and solidarity. Above all, I remembered how proud we had all been of Eve and Joe, and their Red and Blue union.

The vigil wasn't due to start for another hour and a half, but we wanted to make sure we were there in plenty of time. It may have only been Wednesday, but already it had been a momentous week and I was weary with emotion.

It had been a troubling build-up to the verdicts. After coming so far, we'd all feared another slap in the face. Had that happened, it may have broken us. When it didn't the sense of relief was incredible, but as the adrenaline had worn off the exhaustion had kicked in.

Back in 2012 we had woken up early on the morning of the game. We'd all booked into the Hilton, near the stadium and were occupying the same floor. Marie and I went to Elaine and Jimmy's room to see if she needed any help. Eve had slept in there too, on a pull-out bed, just in case her mum needed any help.

He'd had a difficult night, but when Eve opened the door he greeted us both with a smile and a wave. His wife and daughter had given him a wash and a shave, and he was ready for battle.

'Are you feeling confident, lad?' I said.

Jimmy took a few deep breaths before he blew hard and then said, 'I'm always confident, kid. You?'

I was the opposite usually, but on that day, I just thought we'd have too much for them. With Luis Suarez in the team we could always score, and I just didn't see them outgunning us. Not in a million years. Since Kenny had returned to the hot seat, after the botched attempt at management by Roy Hodgson, it had been a case of played three, won two and drawn one.

The draw had come in Dalglish's first derby on 16 January 2011, after the new owners had brought him back to replace Roy Hodgson, who was sacked on 8 January. The omens weren't good. To start with, we were missing Steven Gerrard and Jamie Carragher.

I had been in the Main Stand for that one. I remember Liverpool's Raul Mireles had opened the scoring, on his debut, smashing one in from inside the box. The Kop immediately started chanting 'Dalglish!' presaged by that rhythmic clap.

It was probably too soon to attribute the goal to the new boss, but his appointment had given us all such a lift. We were also desperate to make amends for a 2-0 reverse at Goodison earlier in the season, and we fancied that Kenny could do it.

That defeat, back in October 2010, had been embarrassing. Goals by Tim Cahill and Mikel Arteta had clinched all three points. It had all taken place in front of John Henry and Tom Werner, who were attending their first derby match as owners. The Gwladys Street had sung,

'Oh, John Henry, you've bought the wrong club.'

This was Anfield, though, and we owed Everton one, but early in the second half the game got away from us. In what was a crazy six minutes, starting within 30 seconds of the restart, Sylvan Distin and Jermaine Beckford put the Blues 2-1 in front. The game had been turned on its head.

I was fuming and thoroughly embarrassed. The phone in my pocket vibrated and I knew who it was before I even looked. It was a text message from Jimmy, who at that point was still well enough to go to the game. In full caps it simply said,

'IT AINT OVER TIL ITS OVER!'

I looked over towards the Everton end in the Anfield Road Stand imagining I could see him. I couldn't, but I felt like he was looking over at me and grinning to himself. I felt like smashing my phone.

Then I remember Martin Skrtel scuffing a shot at Tim Howard in the Everton goal. Maxi Rodriguez went for it at the same time as the keeper. Howard looked to have brought him down at the Kop end. The celebrations were wild and I worried they may be a bit premature.

Luckily, we had Dirk Kuyt, a man from the Netherlands with ice running through his veins. He was brought to the club after David Moores had personally loaned Liverpool the £10 million it had taken to buy him. Kuyt rose to prominence under Rafa Benítez.

His reputation as a workhorse didn't do him justice. This was truly a man for the big occasion, famed for late penalties against Arsenal and one at Goodison to win the derby with virtually the last kick of the game. The pressure never seemed to get to this lad.

He didn't disappoint, and Liverpool were level. It was only a draw, and it wasn't a great performance, but the team had shown heart and we knew reinforcements would soon arrive. The January transfer window would see the departure of Fernando Torres and the arrival of Luis Suarez and Andy Carroll, two men who would play a pivotal role at Wembley, a year or so later.

As I left Anfield, I sent Jimmy a text. It simply said,

'NO MATE IT CERTAINLY ISN'T.' It was a reference to his earlier barb.

The memory of that day drifted through my mind as we headed for the vigil in 2016, along with so many others. The train stopped at Central, jolting me from my reverie and we all made our way off the platform, standing in single file on the escalator. The station was packed. Clearly there was going to be a big crowd at the vigil on the Plateau. We made the short walk to St George's Hall from the station. The city centre or 'Town', as we call it, had changed so much since 1989, though some things have endured. We passed the city's 'statue exceedingly bare,' which had hung over the Lewis's building for so many years. I gazed over towards the Adelphi Hotel, much maligned but still a defiant symbol of another era. Then we turned left on to Lime Street.

There was a buzz in the air. It was like a victory parade of sorts – you could say the greatest of them all. I spotted the shirts of other teams' supporters among the crowd making their way to the service. Liverpool is a student city these days, so maybe some had left their halls of residences to pay their respects. I like to think some of them travelled from outside, too.

There were also plenty of Everton shirts on show. Football's brotherhood and sisterhood all together in one place, to celebrate a great victory, a win for the people.

Back in April 2012, I had been a little worried about the atmosphere before the game. Coming just one day before the 23rd anniversary of the Hillsborough disaster, a minute's silence had been planned before kick-off. I remember hoping that no idiots would attempt to hijack it.

That day, we had piled into the minibus after breakfast and made our way to Wembley. We had a wheel chair, courtesy of the community nursing team, and we were able to push Jimmy around the stadium, before making our way inside.

The place had changed so much since the days when Merseysiders had made it their own in the 1980s. What a decade that was. The Reds and the Blues would win eight league titles, three FA cups, two European cups, a cup winners' cup and five league cups between them. Nineteen trophies in ten years. Incredible.

Now, the scene of so many of our conquests had been replaced with the sort of generic bowl-like affair that epitomises modern stadium design. Gone were the twin towers, replaced with a giant steel arch.

Images of Dalglish and Moyes adorned its façade along with a huge representation of the FA Cup. The area around it was uninspiring, though: little more than a giant concrete car park with a few businesses dotted here and there. It would improve in the coming years, but it had a long way to go back then.

'I like it,' said Jimmy.

We made our way to the Bobby Moore statue to pose for family pictures. Elaine had been keen to take some shots of us in our respective colours, standing together. She wanted to put them on Facebook.

Then we went inside.

Marie, Elaine, Jimmy and I were all sat together. The kids were in another part of the ground. With Jim being in a wheelchair, we were located near pitch level, which was a bonus.

As the teams stood around the centre circle, players' heads bowed, the referee blew his whistle to signal there would be a minute of silence. I held my breath, but to my delight you could hear a pin drop.

To my left Marie squeezed my hand, remembering that terrible few hours 23 years ago when we literally didn't know if our son was alive or dead. To my right, decked out in blue and white, Jimmy and Elaine looked at us, smiling but with tears in their eyes.

Fast forward to 2016 when the crowds at St George's Hall were huge. We stood in front of the steps, with the monument to the unknown soldier at our backs.

This place had been the scene of so many huge gatherings down the years, hosting great protests in the name of social justice, women's suffrage and workers striking for fairer pay and conditions. It had also seen tremendous celebrations, as our city's victorious sportsmen returned time and again, their arms laden with silverware.

This time we were there to do both. The people gathered in their tens of thousands, maybe more, were honouring a great protest movement and a huge victory for truth and justice. To our left the faces of 96 men, women and children stared down on us from a huge screen. I'd like to think they were smiling on us, as proud of our efforts on their behalf as we are of them.

It was a spectacle of colour and sound. The red of Liverpool scarves and shirts were everywhere, but there was plenty of blue on show, too. Everton flags hung from lampposts and were draped across the stone lions which had borne witness to so much.

Hanging in front of the huge pillars were banners spelling out the words TRUTH and JUSTICE, backlit with red light. Music wafted through the air. It was John Lennon. He was singing 'Gimme some truth'.

We hadn't asked for it, as he did. Instead we'd fought for it, demanded it. The establishment had resisted through the decades, but they were no match for the long arm of the people.

Four years earlier, Liverpool and Everton were going toe-to-toe on the football pitch. In the stands, the fans were once again segregated as they have been ever since the Taylor report called time on standing and replaced it with oceans of plastic seating.

We were near the halfway line, where the vast swathes of red shirts met with the army of blue ones. I felt a tinge of sadness. We should be standing next to each other, I thought. I knew it was a pipe dream. Those days are long gone.

Both teams went at it. Jay Spearing flashed one over the bar, after a cut back from Andy Carroll and then Leighton Baines drove the ball high over Brad Jones's bar from a free kick 20 yards from goal. I felt nervous, for the game and for Jimmy.

I kept wondering if he was comfortable. When I'd ask, he'd just give me the thumbs up, nodding enthusiastically. He looked frail and the oxygen tubing connected to his nose was jarring. I just kept reminding myself that we'd finally given him his wish. He was here, and it hadn't seemed possible just a few days earlier.

People around me jumped up as Skrtel hit a tame effort at Tim Howard. A little later, Elaine had to restrain Jimmy as he tried to leave his wheelchair after Nikica Jelavić attempted a spectacular but ultimately unsuccessful overhead kick.

It was end-to-end stuff, just like a derby match should be. Then, from my point of view, disaster struck. I've no idea what Jamie Carragher and Daniel Agger were thinking, but as the ball bounced between them both hesitated and gifted an easy one-on-one between Jelavić and Jones. There could only be one winner and the Croatian made no mistake.

He'd scored six goals in eight games but there could have been none more satisfying for him or his supporters in that moment. The Everton end of the stadium went ballistic. I remember looking across and seeing scenes of mad, jubilant chaos, with arms flailing in the air as Blues jumped for joy, hugged each other and bounced around.

I was gutted, and I looked to my right at Jimmy. The years had been rolled back, that grin lit up his face again and his eyes sparkled once more. In my head I was at Anfield in the 60s again, I journeyed across the Park to Goodison and then stood at Lime Street to greet our teams. My whole life and my connection with this fixture flashed before my eyes, and the collective emotions overwhelmed me. I was crying.

Jimmy turned to me, his fists punching the air, his smile of elation lighting up his face. He'd lived for this moment. All week, he had dreamed of it. As he looked into my eyes, the smile faded a little and he said,

'What's up with you, soft lad?' His voice was weak and he took a few breaths before continuing. I leaned in to hear him better. 'Plenty of time left, lad,' another pause, and then, 'You'll lose like, but plenty of time.' I laughed. Whatever life had thrown at him, nothing could change the man.

The celebrations died down and the ball was back in motion once more. Gerrard and Carroll both saw efforts go begging and Jelavić blasted a free kick wide of Liverpool's upright. Then the referee blew his whistle, signalling the break.

Back at St George's Hall, as we waited for the speeches to start, we were reflecting on that day at Wembley. It had been a deeply emotional time and all of us felt some comfort in the fact that we had been able to deliver on one of Jimmy's final wishes.

Stu turned to me and with a hint of sadness in his eyes, said, 'I know you won't think so, Tommy, but I'm just sorry we couldn't give him the result he wanted back in 2012.

Of course, two goals in the second half from Luis Suarez and Andy Carroll had won the tie for Liverpool. It had been a bitter blow for the Blues, but for Reds it was another example of that never say die attitude that has epitomised the history of our club, indeed the DNA of our city, too.

I turned to Stu and said, 'Well, I like to think we did.'

'He looked confused and said, 'What do you mean? You lot won the game. He'd have been fuming.'

'Yeah, he would if he had seen the second half,' I said. Stu realised what I meant and smiled.

As the players had left the field at half-time we had stood to applaud them off. I was annoyed as hell with them, but there was still 45 minutes to go. Anything could happen I thought.

I became aware of a problem out of the corner of my eye. Elaine was leaning over Jimmy and he was slumped a little in his chair, his left arm had slipped off the rest and was hanging over the side of it.

All I can recall now is the frantic look on his wife's face, Marie with her mouth agape and her hand placed over it trying to shut out the screams of grief. Then I remember the flash of high-vis jackets and medical boxes, us explaining that Jimmy had not wanted to be resuscitated, and then he was gone.

The rest of that game is gone for me, too, lost in the grief and the pain of losing a best mate. One thing had helped me through the days ahead and as I looked into Stuart's eyes, in front of St George's Hall, I said,

'I always prefer to think of it this way: when your dad left us, the last thing he had known was that Everton were 1-0 up. For him, they are 1-0 up for all of eternity.'

The days that followed were not about football. They were about family and friendship, until I carried him into the church on the day of his funeral, that is. Just as he had requested, I was wearing an Everton shirt. It was too small for me and barely covered my expanding gut.

I had worn it gladly, though and I carried him proudly, along with Stu and our Joe. We were two families who followed different teams, bonded by one love. That's how it should always be.

As the inquest delivered its verdicts years later, Everton Football Club would play the Hollies' song 'He Ain't Heavy, He's My Brother' at Goodison Park. In the centre circle stood two children in football kits, a girl and a boy. The girl wore a number nine on her back, the boy a six.

We all understood and appreciated the symbolism of that song and the gesture. When the road was long, the Red half of the city had leaned on the Blue half. It helped us get by in some of the darkest times in our history.

So as the speeches came to an end, and the vigil wound up, we sang another stirring rendition of 'You'll Never Walk Alone'. We certainly hadn't. Then we made our way back to Central Station.

The crowds on the platform were so large, the station had put in place a queuing system. A guard, too young to remember Hillsborough, was chatting to the waiting people. 'I wasn't even born in '89,' he was telling them, while reassuring all who'd listen, 'don't worry, I know all about it. My kids will, too.'

Next to me a girl with an out-of-town accent was talking to someone back home on her mobile phone. 'Yeah, it's loud here,' she said. 'I'm in Liverpool, what do you expect?' she laughed, adding, 'I've got a headache, they're so noisy.' Then she noticed me and realised I was listening. I just smiled and looked away. After all, she was right, we do have big mouths. It's just that history has taught us that people only listen when we're loud, and when we shout with one voice.

Eventually I boarded the train back to Fazakerley. As I sat watching my family, I felt content. They looked happy and their laughter filled the carriage. We'd seen some dark days, I thought; the very worst kind. We had almost fallen apart completely at one point but we were together now, stronger than ever.

Inevitably, thoughts of my absent friend drifted into my mind, as they so often do. We laid him to rest in Everton cemetery but he's never really left us. His final resting place is just a mile or two from Goodison Park. On a matchday, with a favourable wind, you can hear the roar of the crowd.

I go there sometimes, and I listen with him. I miss him a lot. He was my brother.

Afterword

In 2018 Liverpool supporters carried a banner across the continent to Kiev in the Ukraine. It proclaimed,

> 'IF I HADN'T SEEN SUCH RICHES I COULD LIVE WITH BEING POOR'

It's a song lyric that could apply equally to Reds and Blues. Both of Merseyside's teams have witnessed riches beyond the wildest dreams of most other supporters. We've also lived through barren spells. Between us, though, we have won 61 major honours. Ours is the most successful region in English football history.

When I look back over the decades, I am struck by how the greatest periods in the history of our rivalry have been those in which both our teams were competing as equals. The 70s were a time of unbridled joy for all Liverpool supporters, but who can forget the sixties, when Liverpool and Everton won six trophies in ten years, and had two of the best managers in the land. Or, what about the 80s when we won 19 between us. Our managers then were both ex-players who went on to lead us to unparalleled success.

As I write, we are both standing on the cusp of bold new eras. Liverpool and Anfield is in a continual phase of renewal and redevelopment. Our manager is cut from the same cloth as those who delivered so much glory down the years. We have players who excite us and promise so much.

For Everton supporters, there is hope that a difficult period is coming to an end. The promise of a new stadium, on the banks of the Mersey, is exciting for them and the city. There's a new manager in the hot seat and the prospect of renewal lies tantalisingly close.

So, here's to an exciting new phase of our rivalry. May the best team prevail.

In this book, we've looked back over more than 50 years of the Merseyside derby. It is my sincere hope that in the next 50, a new generation will write another instalment that is as glorious as the previous one but with none of the pain and anguish.

You'll Never Walk Alone

Nil Satis Nisi Optimum